HIS EYES FLASHED
LIKE A TIGER'S

"Shall I tell you how beautiful you are in that sari?" Jai asked, his glance devouring her. "Shall I tell you how your lips invite me? How I would make a banquet of your mouth, your luscious breasts, the tender whiteness of your thighs? How I would like to make love to you here, this moment, if we were alone, if such a thing was possible?"

A soundless moan filled Julie's throat. Without thinking she thrust her hips against his body. Jai's response was so powerfully immediate that a violent trembling possessed her.

She forgot the grand ballroom, the dignitaries, the dancing couples whirling all around them. All else vanished except the dark man holding her and the distant sound of music, far away....

WELCOME TO...

SUPERROMANCES

A sensational series of modern love stories
from Worldwide Library.

Written by masters of the genre, these longer,
sensual and dramatic novels are truly in keeping
with today's changing life-styles. Full of intriguing
conflicts, the heartaches and delights of true love,
SUPERROMANCES are absorbing stories—
satisfying and sophisticated reading that lovers
of romance fiction have long been waiting for.

SUPERROMANCES
Contemporary love stories for the woman of today!

CYNTHIA PARKER
TIGER EYES

A SUPERROMANCE FROM
WORLDWIDE

TORONTO · NEW YORK · LONDON · PARIS
AMSTERDAM · STOCKHOLM · HAMBURG
ATHENS · MILAN · TOKYO · SYDNEY

To
Eve Measner

Published February 1984

First printing December 1983

ISBN 0-373-70100-4

Printed in Canada

CHAPTER ONE

A BLAST OF DRY HEAT rocked Julie Connell back on her heels as she stepped out of the huge Air India jet. Swaying, she grasped the stairway railing. She took a deep breath and scanned the distant crowd gathering behind the glass of the terminal.

Joining the mass of passengers, she descended to the asphalt runway. This was one of her favorite parts of any reporting assignment—the arrival in a new country. Even in a city as cosmopolitan as New Delhi, the sense of entering a foreign culture was instantly apparent by the dome-shaped temples glimpsed in the distance and the background murmur of unfamiliar languages. It was a moment to savor.

Despite the hurry and confusion of debarkation, several men from the flight paused to watch her as she worked her way through the crush of rumpled tourists. Her shoulder-length, golden blond hair—richly thick, and rippled with natural waves—always attracted attention in countries where black hair predominated. The Halston Ultrasuede suit she had chosen for the flight was becoming in its chic severity. This, combined with vibrant dark blue eyes and a trim yet shapely figure, completed the all-American, golden-girl look that caused so much good-natured envy among her female co-workers in the newsroom. Men had a way of seeing her once and wanting her forever.

Julie crossed the wide expanse of pavement, her carryon bag slung over her shoulder. Nothing in the way she carried herself or the composed expression on her face hinted at the tension building up inside her. She wanted to look what she was—a competent professional, here to uncover an important, complicated and potentially dangerous story.

When her boss, Wes Harding, had first broached the idea of an in-depth report and analysis on terrorism, Julie had not been surprised. Some years ago the *Courier*, in an effort to distinguish itself from its opposition, had adopted the policy that the best papers cover news from a global perspective. Since that time the paper had begun to specialize in overlook copy, reporting on trends involving many countries that affected Americans. Because of this approach, it was fast developing a reputation for foreign news, much like the *Wall Street Journal* had for financial news.

A series of articles on terrorism fit in perfectly with the *Courier*'s news policy. Julie could still recall the tingle of excitement that coursed up her spine at receiving the assignment. This was her greatest professional challenge to date.

"Harding!" she had exclaimed, "you don't mean it!"

"I mean it," he had responded, his eyes not leaving the copy he was scanning.

"Me?"

"You did a good job on the global-food-supply item. This is much the same thing."

"This involves action," Julie reflected, sitting down on the corner of his desk. "The other was statistics."

"It was a broad topic. You tied it together well, without overgeneralizing. Now get your delectable backside off my desk and get to work."

In the months that followed, Julie spent hours researching the underworld of terrorism. She had her other duties, as well, mostly writing up copy from the wire services, and occasionally covering a few other stories. But every item about terrorism was her special prerogative. That grim topic had taken her to cover an assassination in Paris, a kidnapping in England and last, and worst, the bombing of a train station in Rome.

Slowly a terrible picture was forming before her eyes. "The purpose of terrorism is to terrorize," Lenin had once said. The hollow feeling in her stomach every time she covered

another attack attested to her own growing
fear.

And now India.... The stringer in Bombay
had called yesterday. He had heard a rumor
that a secret gathering of international terrorists was to take place soon somewhere in
Asia, possibly northern India. A summit
meeting, so to speak. Julie wanted to be
there. She wanted to be there so badly it hurt.

She shook her head. She must not lose her
objectivity. A reporter should walk a delicate
line—emotionally close enough to a story to
report it, without becoming biased. But what
she had seen in Rome—hundreds of innocent
bystanders killed or maimed—had been
enough to convince her that the terrorists had
slipped from killing for a cause to killing in-
discriminately.

The gaping doorway of the terminal loomed
before her, overflowing with greeting parties,
well-wishers and porters. Julie hoped the man
she was coming to see, Prince Jaiapradesh
Mishra, had sent someone to meet her. Otherwise she would have to struggle through that
crowd alone.

Too much depended on Prince Mishra, Julie reflected. Having few contacts of her own
in New Delhi, she was going to need his help
to get her investigation off the ground. She
would have to work quickly to build up her
own sources of information, something that
correspondents who were part of a permanent

bureau here would have. She needed introductions, government contacts, acquaintances, friends. Yet from all accounts she had been able to gather in the few hours she'd had to prepare, Mishra was shrewd and unpredictable. Whether he would be of much use to her remained to be seen, although Harding had sent her to him. And Wes Harding was seldom wrong when it came to news.

Entering the terminal, she hesitated, taking in the amazing scene before her. An exotic, colorful theater of life surged around her, ballooning to fill every corner of the packed room. People of all races, dressed in costumes of all description, milled, talked, smiled, chatted, shouted, argued, greeted, cried, hugged, bid farewell. All the varied phases and emotions of human existence seemed concentrated right here.

But even the excitement of the moment was overshadowed by the familiar twisting pain in her heart. Julie realized she had unconsciously been searching the sea of faces before her, seeking out one in particular. Memory, like a searing hurt, rushed through her as she thought of the boyish grin Eddie had always flashed whenever he first saw her. She had loved the way the sight of her had invariably made him light up with anticipatory pleasure.

His career as the acknowledged top stunt man in the movie industry had taken him all over the United States for filming. During

their four-year relationship Julie had flown
to see him on location whenever she could get
away from work. He had always been there
to meet her at the airport. Somehow those
warm moments of greeting had left such an
impression on her that whenever she got off a
plane even now, two and a half years later,
she found herself searching for him.

Which was ridiculous, for he would never
be there to greet her again. Ever. Because two
weeks after she had agreed to marry him, he
had died in a horrifying car crash on a set. He
had been doing what he loved to do, living
life to the hilt in a wild, daring, adventurous,
wonderful way, tempting fate with his chal-
lenges right to the very end. But this had not
made it any easier to accept his death.

Sometimes Julie even blamed herself,
though logically she knew it could not be her
fault. If only she had gone along with the
marriage idea sooner—he had always said he
would give up stunt work when they had children. Yet when she had accepted his extra-
vagant diamond ring one romantic evening in
the penthouse apartment that had been their
weekend lovers' nest for two years, she had
wondered why she did not feel the radiant
happiness so often described by her engaged
friends. At the time, however, getting engaged seemed the right thing to do.

There did not seem to be any reason to put
off marriage, not when he had wanted it for

so long and had agreed that she would continue with her career. Julie had always hoped
to find a man who would touch the rich
womanliness she sensed hidden within herself. Instead, Eddie was her favorite, most
comfortable friend.

And then two weeks later he was dead.
Julie had done her best to accept it. But situations reminiscent of times she had spent with
him still had a way of sneaking up on her un-
awares. Even if he had not been the man of
her dreams, he had been her constant companion. She still missed him.

A pair of dark burning eyes watching her
intently brought Julie abruptly back to reality. A tall man lounged against the wall,
somewhat apart from the crowd around the
departure gate. Beside him a small man in a
brown suit was speaking rapidly, accompanying his words with sweeping arm gestures.

The taller man nodded once at something
the other said, then turned his eyes again in
Julie's direction. As she met his gaze, Julie
noted that despite his relaxed posture his entire body conveyed the impression of strength
and athletic grace. His broad shoulders, narrow hips and muscular limbs set him instantly
apart from other men. The straight aristocratic features of his lean face would almost have
seemed harsh if it was not for the unmistakable intelligence that marked his countenance.
He seemed to be warding off boredom by ex-

amining Julie, evaluating her coolly, critically.

His initial inspection became gradually more detailed. Julie felt the color rising to her cheeks as his eyes traveled over her face, her body, her clothing. As used as she was to the close scrutiny of men, never had she encountered anyone quite as self-possessed as this. Or as handsome. She felt as if in some way he was seeing her, every part of her, thoroughly. Her skin began to tingle as though a fierce blaze emanating from those piercing eyes was actually burning her flesh.

A flame flared in the depths of his dark pupils as he watched her. A flame of pleasure, of desire. Strange, sudden yearnings stabbed at Julie's heart. To bring pleasure to such a man. . . . Her body quivered in response to the thought. Something about him was different: he possessed a subtle magnetism that fascinated her. A tremor of excitement raced through her. She took an unconscious half step toward him.

The man straightened. A faint appreciative look flashed across his face.

Julie caught herself in midstride. What had she been going to do? Walk right into his arms? Those eyes had mesmerized her—had stirred a sensuality in her that she had not known existed. For an instant she had felt beautiful, and sensuous, and as exotic as India itself. She looked up at the man who had done this to her and was angry to find both understanding and humor in his glance.

Julie tilted her chin and regarded him coldly for a moment, irritated that he could unsettle her so easily. Unabashed, he held her gaze until Julie was forced to drop her eyes. In this culture he might misinterpret her look as a bold invitation. She was about to turn away when the man in the brown suit broke off his monologue to glance over his shoulder at her.

The moment she glimpsed the small man's features, Julie knew she had seen him before. She had a good memory for faces and in another instant she had him placed. He was Joe Wolfe, an advisor to the U.S. State Department. She had met him briefly about a year ago at an embassy reception in Washington, D.C.

She did not know Wolfe's official title, but she did know one thing for certain: he was an expert on international violence. Finding him here in New Delhi sent a rush of excitement through her. More than anything preliminary research had unearthed, this chance encounter convinced Julie she was on the right track. She stepped forward, hand outstretched, a dazzling smile on her face.

"Mr. Wolfe, how nice to see you again! I'm Julie Connell," she added. "We met in Washington last year."

"Ms. Connell, yes, of course." He took her hand and shook it.

Julie was quite sure he did not remember her, but the glint of admiration that flashed in his eyes indicated his willingness to renew the acquaintance. Julie pursued her advantage. "I'm not surprised to see you here. How serious do you think the terrorist threat is in India now?"

"Do you always interrupt private conversations?"

The abrupt question made Julie flush. She glanced up to meet the stranger's eyes, repressing a sharp retort to his harsh query. Even in her determination to interview Joe Wolfe, she had not been able to erase her awareness of his companion. The dark-haired man's rudeness took her by surprise. In general people responded more positively toward her.

"I guess I don't consider a discussion in the middle of an airport to be of an exclusively private nature," Julie replied, trying to keep her irritation from showing in her voice. If Wolfe was leaving on a flight today, she needed to speak with him now.

"Mr. Wolfe is in a hurry. He has a flight to catch," the tall man confirmed. An English accent tinged his deep voice. Yet he did not look English to Julie. And he had an intriguing cosmopolitan air.

"Come, Jai," Wolfe intervened diplomatically. "We can spare a few minutes to shoot the breeze with one of my fellow Americans, can't we?"

"I would appreciate a few minutes of your time," Julie pressed with a warm smile.

An announcement boomed out over the loudspeaker. By the time it had been repeated in three different languages, the dark-haired man had turned his back on Julie and was ushering Wolfe toward the security area. The American turned and waved at Julie.

"Sorry! My flight!" he called.

She stepped forward to follow him. Even if she could get in a question or two it might help her know where to start her investigation in India. She found her path blocked by the broad back of the stranger, who had paused to let a woman pushing a baby stroller in line ahead of him. Before she could step around him, someone behind Julie shoved her forward hard against him.

She drew back at once, aware of an electric sensation where her body had pressed against his, almost like a low-voltage shock pulsating through her breasts and torso. Surprise flashed in his eyes as he turned toward her—surprise and something else, some unidentifiable emotion. But when he saw who had jostled him, his eyes narrowed.

"Are all American women as pushy as you are?" he asked.

"I can't possibly be as pushy as you are rude!" she retorted. "Excuse me! I need to speak with Mr. Wolfe."

She brushed past him, her face crimson, unable to remember when she had disliked someone as much. She made a strong mental effort to formulate the questions she needed to ask Wolfe. But after a minute or two of struggling through the throng of departing passengers, she knew it was useless to persist. Wolfe could not be seen anywhere nearby.

Disappointed, Julie turned and walked quickly back through the thinning crowd. She wanted to avoid another encounter with the tall stranger. She noted with relief that he seemed to have disappeared. Yet somehow the impression of the man's brute power and animallike vitality stayed in her mind—an intense feeling disproportionate to the briefness of their encounter. She did not like the way that man had made her feel for a moment—oddly helpless.

A white-turbaned man with a graying beard approached her as she moved toward the luggage area. He seemed to hesitate.

"Madam Connell?" he inquired politely. At Julie's nod, he said, "I am Gunam Singh, Prince Mishra's chauffeur. The maharani asks me to greet you on her behalf and to bring you to the palace."

As she gratefully handed her bag to the man, Julie felt a twinge of disappointment at the realization that the prince had left it to his aged wife to attend to her arrival. But then he was one of India's most powerful men and she was, after all, only a journalist, even if she did represent one of the most important papers in the Western world.

She was eager to meet the prince in person. Although he did not hold an official position in the government, he was a close friend of the prime minister and the president. There was little that went on inside India that Mishra did not know about. Due to his family connections and shrewdness, he had considerable political clout. Besides that, he was said to be fabulously wealthy. He employed huge numbers of workers in his steel and textile factories in southern India.

His title, still worthy of great respect and social position, was retained from the era of separate princely states before those provinces were incorporated into a nation at the end of British rule. For several centuries his family had ruled a small but resource-rich state in northern India. His grandfather, with a treasure in gold and jewels, had been considered one of the richest men in Asia. Unlike many other rulers, Mishra's family had always been unusually popular with the lower classes. According to a clipping in the *Courier*'s library, the current prince was admired as a bold sportsman and big-game hunter. Of course, Julie thought, by now he is probably too old for that.

"I met him when I was a reporter in England a few years ago," Harding had told her. "A remarkable man, even though he doesn't get along with people particularly well. He's not a man you can push.

"I've arranged for you to stay in his household, Julie. The maharani is a special friend of mine and when I cabled her, she immediately sent an invitation. That way you can be safe as well as comfortable. Being in that environment will also expose you to the right contacts to get the information you need. Anybody who is anybody in the government comes to the prince's house sooner or later. And, he is said to have a remarkable intelligence network of his own, though whether you can get access to it is another matter.

"Stick to the terrorist story. If you want to do a few feature articles on cultural values, we can always use them in the Sunday edition. But leave the daily news coverage to the wire services and the local stringers. I don't need a bureau in New Delhi.

"Try not to antagonize the prince," her boss had added with a wry smile. "He's difficult, but I think you can handle him. That's why I'm sending you—you might be the only one who could get along with him. He respects guts." With that enigmatic praise, Wes had dismissed her from the office.

The chauffeur whisked Julie through a special VIP channel at the immigration desk, saying, "Guest of Prince Mishra." The officials seemed to recognize him, for they only nodded to him in an overburdened manner as they hurried to stamp the passports of the long line of passengers who had gotten off the New York flight along with Julie.

"Come this way, please, madam," said the driver in his heavily accented English. Julie liked his merry eyes and gentle manner. She deduced from his turban and full beard that he must be a follower of Sikhism—a religion of the Punjab region of northwestern India. Indian religion and philosophy had always intrigued Julie. To be able to observe the cultural variety of India firsthand was a dream come true.

"Do you have your claim tickets?" asked her escort. "I will send a servant for your baggage. It takes a long time for it to be unloaded. He will bring it later."

Outside the building, Julie again was taken aback by the burning heat. Gunam Singh hurried her to a luxurious Mercedes limousine and held open the rear door for her. The air-conditioned interior felt heavenly. Julie leaned wearily back against the cushions. She realized with a start that she had been traveling for more than twenty-four hours. Maybe that was the reason for the tension headache she felt coming on. She brushed her hand across her brow, wishing she had packed some aspirin in her purse.

She closed her eyes, enjoying the smell of wood and leather from inside the car. There

was another smell, too. Julie wrinkled her
nose, absently trying to place it. She liked it,
whatever it was. A faint muskiness. Very
masculine.

Opening her eyes she saw that Gunam
Singh had paused before getting into the
front seat of the limousine and was now
walking rapidly away from the car, an eager
bounce in his formerly sedate step. Looking
back at the terminal building, Julie saw a tall
dark-haired man in a white suit walking
toward the driver. He somehow managed to
appear cool and unwrinkled despite the temperature. He seemed, even at this distance,
almost too masculine, too overpowering.
Recognition dawned. It was the man who had
been with Joe Wolfe! The same antagonism
she had felt for him in the airport welled up in
her again.

Julie watched as the chauffeur conferred
with him. Julie wondered how long he had
been standing there. Somehow the thought of
being unknowingly observed by this man was
unsettling. He nodded once in the direction of
the limousine and then crossed over to a low
red sports car. The chauffeur returned to the
Mercedes. When they pulled out of the park-
ing lot into the congested airport traffic, the
red convertible was already out of sight.

The newness of the scenery soon captured
Julie's full attention. Fragments of Indian
life flicked past her, like still shots in an old-

time movie, as the big car sped down the boulevard. The ragged farmer walking behind his ox-drawn plow, the old woman leading a gaunt cow to milking. . .each scene so different from any in the industrialized European countries she had visited on other assignments. Julie felt a deep desire stirring in her, a desire to understand the richness of this culture, of this land. "Mother India" her children called her.

She noted the relative poverty of the people along the roadside. Actually it was not as bad as she had expected, although she had been told it was much worse in the southern states. Still fertile enough ground for insurgents, she supposed, especially when one compared the people on the side of the road to someone such as her host who could afford the limousine she was riding in.

But she was not here to report on the inequalities in the distribution of wealth. For one thing, it had nothing to do with her story. Terrorists were just as prone to attack in a democratic country with a large middle class as in a country such as this one with clearly segregated economic classes. Secondly, it was misleading to apply one's own standards to a different culture. Julie knew that a strong caste system had existed for countless centuries in India as an integral part of the Hindu religion. The people believed that they were born into the level of society most advantageous for their spiritual evolution. Rich or poor did not matter as much as the potential for spiritual growth within the social strata most suited to their needs.

In a few minutes the fields dropped away, to be replaced by the outskirts of the city. Soon the Mercedes was threading its way through a remarkable assortment of vehicles. Julie watched, fascinated, as she counted ox-carts, horse-drawn wagons with wheels taller than a man, bicycles, even camels loaded with ungainly bundles of straw, all massed in the heavy flow of traffic along with lumbering trucks, rickety taxis, buses, scooters, motor-cycles and occasionally an automobile.

Her headache grew worse. Julie brushed her thick hair back from her forehead in irritation. She thought she had gotten over those headaches. It had been a long time since she had had one as bad as this, not since the first months following Eddie's death. Julie closed her eyes hoping to ease the pain.

She opened them again as the car swung smoothly off the main road. Julie found herself in a world far different from the noisy streets of a few minutes before. Here there was very little traffic. The houses sat far apart, with carefully tended lawns and gardens. Waist-high walls encircled the grounds. They seemed much more like country estates than homes in the bustling, thriving capital city of the country with the second largest population in the world.

"This is near the embassy section," Gunam Singh informed her, sliding back the glass partition behind his seat. "All the countries have their representatives in this same area. The street to our left, Panchsheel Marg, goes right past your American Embassy."

Moments later a parkway came into view. The road curved into a large cul-de-sac here, feeding the traffic back in the direction it came from.

A wall, higher than the ones she had seen previously, followed the curve of the road. Beyond it Julie glimpsed a landscape more gorgeous than any she could have imagined. The limousine turned into a long driveway. A riot of exotic colors exploded everywhere—blossoms of enormous size clung to the stone wall, lined the well-cared-for, intricate paths and clustered in the air above on the branches of widespread trees.

Pushing a button on the leather armrest beside her, Julie lowered a side window. She took a huge breath, drinking in the mixture of fragrances in the air.

"It's lovely...." She looked around. "All the flowers...everything looks so green and cool...is this Prince Mishra's home?"

"Yes. You will see the house when we go over that hill."

The car paused, engine humming softly, while a turbaned gatekeeper ran to open the huge wrought-iron gates. Julie noted that two guards armed with rifles and bayonets were posted beside the gate, as well. Both the guards and gatekeeper waved to the chauffeur and stared curiously at her.

"What magnificent tigers!" Julie pointed to the top of the two tall gateposts. On top of each post lay a large bronze tiger. The inanimate images conveyed a wild and predatory fierceness that belied the languid grace of their reclining pose. The strange contrast of qualities moved Julie. She was reminded that India was a land of bitter ethnic rivalries while at the same time the birthplace of the philosophy of nonviolent resistance, called *ahimsa*.

"Those tigers are the mascots of the Mishra lineage," Gunam Singh told her. "There's another pair at the house. They were cast at the time of the dynasty's conception. It is said they embody the essence of the Mishra princes," he added, as the big car glided over the smooth curve of the hill and the mansion came into view.

CHAPTER TWO

THE PALACE GLEAMED WHITE in the bright Indian sun. Gigantic marble columns ran the
length of the building, and a dome of carved
marble decorated what must be the entrance
hall, with smaller domes marking the end of
the two forward-curving wings of the building. The structure was saved from severity by
the gorgeous floral displays placed along the
wide veranda and twining up the pillars. Julie
studied the grace, refinement and elegance of
the building with an appreciative eye. It was
beyond doubt an architectural feat—a moving composition of flowers and marble,
nature and stone.

The Mercedes slid to a quiet halt at the foot
of the wide marble stairs. A footman, dressed
in white cotton shirt and trousers girded at
the waist by a gold-embroidered red sash
from which hung a heavy sword, came forward to open the car door. Julie stepped out
of the limousine, feeling as though she had
been transported into another world. The
wide expanse of lawn stretching before her
with the forms of gardeners moving among

the abundant flowers; the ornately carved columns of marble towering above her, much bigger now that she was beside them than they had appeared from the distance; the dignity of the huge doorman next to her: all these things seemed to belong to a different age, another era.

She ran her hand along the back of the bronze tiger lying at her feet, one of the pair that flanked the marble steps to the veranda. They were replicas of those she had seen atop the gateposts, only larger. They seemed so lifelike that she would not have been surprised to see the tip of the long, thick tail twitch, or the lips curl back to expose cruel flesh-tearing teeth. The workmanship impressed her as being of museum quality.

"If you will come with me, madam, the maharani is waiting to greet you."

Her heels clicking on the marble stairs, Julie followed the doorman up onto the veranda and through the large bronze doors that gave entrance into the mansion. She had the impression of thick, richly colored carpets spongy beneath her feet, softening the footfalls of her high-heeled sandals; of dark mahogany walls, doorways and staircases, all polished to a magnificent gleam; of a white marble dome suspended above her head. Then she was being led into a large room with book-lined walls, and a pleasant-looking older woman rose to greet her.

"You must be Miss Connell. I'm Bharati Mishra. Welcome to New Delhi!"

"Thank you," Julie replied. A thread of apprehension in the back of her mind dissolved. She felt an immediate liking for the woman before her. Plump and gray haired with late middle age, traces of what must have at one time been remarkable beauty still remained in the maharani's refined features. Julie liked the older woman's soft voice and comfortable manners.

"How nice that you could come visit," the maharani was saying. "Wes Harding is an old friend of my husband's and mine, and I am happy to be able to do him the favor of watching out for you. I know I will enjoy having you here so much!" The Indian woman's sincerity was unmistakable.

"You make me feel very much at home already," responded Julie, smiling and taking the armchair offered her.

"Bring some *lassi* please, Ram," said the older woman to a manservant who had materialized beside them. After he left, she continued. "I did not realize until this morning when I got the cable confirming your arrival time that Wes was sending a female reporter. Even when the cable said *Miss* Connell, I had no idea it would be someone as young as yourself." She smiled at Julie.

"I'm twenty-eight."

"It's difficult for an Indian woman like

myself to get used to the idea of women traveling by themselves and having careers, although of course even here sometimes women have taken roles of great leadership in national affairs, as you know. And my own daughter was sent to school in Switzerland for two years.''

"You have a daughter?'' asked Julie, eager to know more about her hostess.

"Yes, a lovely girl. You'll like her, I'm sure. She lives here, since she isn't married yet. I hope you two can become friends.''

"Do just you and your husband and daughter live here?'' asked Julie, her eyes traveling over the tastefully furnished room.

"Oh, dear, my husband has been dead for several years, Julie—I may call you that, mayn't I? I'm surprised Wes Harding didn't mention that to you.''

Julie's head snapped back to face the plump woman beside her. If the maharani's husband was dead, with whom was she supposed to work? Leaving New York in a hurry as she had, she must have confused her instructions, though she could not understand how she could have done so.

"I'm terribly sorry, maharani. I had no idea,'' she said in confusion. "I can't imagine what Mr. Harding was thinking of!''

Privately she was cursing whichever librarian it was who had missed the clipping about the prince's death. Like any large newspaper, the *Courier* kept its own library of world events, recording news items of every conceivable sort and cross-indexing them for future recall. The first thing a reporter would do after receiving a new assignment would be to go to the "morgue," as old-time newspaper people called it, and have the librarians pull out everything on file about the project. Any mention of the death of a man of Prince Mishra's importance should have been included in the files, even though he was not actually a government official and tended to use his immense influence behind the scenes.

"Think nothing of it," the maharani was saying in her unperturbed manner. "It happened quite long ago and I have ceased to sorrow. We Hindus believe in reincarnation, you know. We feel that the physical body is only a temporary home for the spirit of a person. When one body is worn out and dies, then the soul drops it and relocates in a new body. Each new birth gives the soul another chance to evolve toward spiritual perfection, which is the goal of all Hindus. Of course we miss those who have died, but we try not to grieve overlong. We believe that to do so would be to selfishly hold back our loved one from going on to the next step of evolution."

"Thank you for being so nice about it," responded Julie. She took the cold glass filled with frothy white liquid that the returning manservant held out to her on an ornate silver tray. Sipping the beverage, she found it to be as sweet and refreshing as it looked—a tangy yogurt taste with the subtle undertone of rose water. "But I can't imagine why Mr. Harding made a point of telling me to interview the prince. I understood that to be my primary reason for coming to New Delhi first."

"Why, he means my son, of course," replied the maharani. "He is Prince Mishra now." Julie was surprised to see an anxious look flit across the older woman's face. "He, ah—that is, I have not had a chance to mention to my son that you would be staying with us," her hostess continued. "He is on a business trip to Bombay at the moment, though I expect him back this evening." Julie wondered why the mention of her son should discompose the maharani. "But Priya and I will so much enjoy your company," the Indian woman added with a sudden smile. "Certainly Jai will be glad about that."

"Glad about what, mother?"

The quiet male voice startled both women. Julie set down the sweet *lassi* drink on the table beside her chair, trying to get a grip on the feelings of dismay and anger that flooded through her. Then she turned to inspect the man whose presence here was the last thing in the world she wanted. Like everything else about him, his voice was unforgettable.

He was standing in the doorway, the warm sunlight from the windowed hallway outlining him effectively against the darkened interior where Julie and the maharani had been sitting away from the heat of the day. She would recognize that powerful form anywhere. He was the rude stranger from the airport!

The thought came, unbidden, of the bronze tigers lying at their leisure, guarding the entrance to the palace. He had about him the same indolent, languid grace that nevertheless projected a distinct feeling of predatory, barely restrained fierceness and uncivilized strength. Julie suddenly wondered how she could not have recognized him for what he was: a prince, a man of tremendous importance.

He stood a moment longer, regarding the women, neither of whom seemed capable of speaking. Then he crossed the room toward them with the smooth stride of a born athlete. Julie had the impression of a tall man, broad shouldered, narrow hipped, powerfully built. Even the way he moved reminded Julie of the bronze tigers. Only this man was alive, flesh and blood, and somehow much more threatening than any tiger could possibly be. She noticed he had changed into riding clothes and was holding a polo helmet and crop under his arm.

He came nearer, perfectly at ease in the luxurious surroundings. Julie recalled that the prince came from a lineage of rulers so old that they were no doubt enjoying all the culture and refinements of life when her own ancestors were probably still illiterate serfs. He seemed so sure of himself, so much the master of the entire situation. . . .

Julie felt ruffled by his presence. The feeling irritated her and she reacted by immediately squaring her shoulders and sitting straighter in the chair. She forced a look of cool composure onto her face and a half smile of greeting onto her lips. She refused to be unnerved by his stern countenance. She knew from her past dealings with men that if she wanted to be taken seriously as a journalist, she must stand up to them from the beginning—prove her own strength and refuse to be intimidated or stopped by whatever rank, wealth or power they chose to hide behind. Otherwise they might flirt with her, even patronize her. But they would never level with her, never answer her questions truthfully. In short, never accord her the respect she needed to do her job as well as possible.

"Why, Jai," said the maharani, regaining her composure. "I am so glad you have returned. I really did not expect you until tonight. I would like to introduce you to a new acquaintance of mine. Miss Julie Connell, this is my son, Prince Mishra."

He stopped some paces away from them, nodding slightly in Julie's direction. He glanced at his mother and then back to Julie, regarding the latter with polite disinterest. Julie tilted back her head and met his eyes squarely.

"A friend of Priya's, perhaps?" He turned toward his mother as he spoke.

"No, no, not exactly," replied the maharani. "Though, of course, I hope they do become friends soon. Julie is going to be staying with us for some time, Jai. I have asked her here as my guest." The maharani rose as she spoke and Julie stood up, also.

"To what or whom do we owe this pleasure?" asked the prince, not looking at Julie. Even though his quiet voice was still polite, somehow his tone was not pleasant. He made the words seem probing, even demanding.

"Why, to my dear friend, Wes Harding," replied the maharani. "He was kind enough to send Julie to stay with me for a while." Julie caught an evasive note in the older woman's voice and sensed she was edging away from telling her son the reason behind Julie's visit. Her hostess seemed to want to avoid a confrontation with the prince, though why there should be one Julie had no idea.

The maharani put a soft hand on the American woman's arm. "Julie, you explain everything to Jai, all about your interesting work and so forth. I have a few things I must attend to just now." With that, the older woman left the room, leaving Julie staring after her.

A long silence filled the library after the door clicked shut behind the maharani. Julie discovered the prince had moved away from her, footsteps muffled by the thick carpet, and had gone over to a table by the mantel on which sat several cut-glass decanters. The clink of ice informed her he was mixing a drink.

"Would you like a drink?" he asked.

"No, thank you." The antagonism in her own voice surprised her. This was not the first time she had been left alone with a man who did not know her and, she had a strong suspicion, did not want to. She should be handling it better. Only her head ached. Painfully.

He continued to fix his own drink, his back to her. Standing behind him, Julie felt annoyed. The prince seemed in no hurry to complete his task and return to the entertainment of his guest. But then, she was not a guest. She was here to get a story. Julie realized now that he had not even known of her arrival. Why was she feeling so on edge then, so oversensitive? What did it matter if he was not bending over backward trying to make her feel welcome? She must be getting spoiled. Men were usually so attentive. Well, she did not need to be fussed over; she just needed information.

As the silence continued, Julie found her eyes straying to the man before her. He would be in his middle thirties, she guessed. She could not help but notice the powerfulness of his legs, encased in glove-soft riding boots that seemed to mold the calves closely enough to almost reveal the muscles beneath. His total masculinity excited a response in her that was new and, under the circumstances, unwelcome. She turned her back on him and made a pretext of examining the contents of a nearby bookcase. An unaccustomed feeling of weakness swept over her, forcing her to reach out to the shelves for support. She leaned her head against her arm, fighting against a wave of dizziness.

"Are you ill?" The impersonal tone of his voice close behind her robbed the words of any appearance of concern.

Julie straightened with a jerk, pushing herself away from the bookcase. She did feel strange. But she had no intention of admitting weakness of any kind to this man. Strong himself, she doubted he would have any sympathy for human frailty. She turned to face him.

"I'm all right. Just fine." She tried to organize her thoughts.

He was watching her intently, as though debating something in his mind. His dark eyes flicked over Julie, then returned to her face. He seemed on the verge of reaching out to her, but changed his mind. He took a sip of his drink instead.

"What were you doing at the airport when I saw you? Did you think I had forgotten?" he added, noting the sudden color in her cheeks. "You must know you are rather unforgettable."

"My plane—I had just gotten in. From the States." Her voice seemed to echo in the room. As though from a distance, Julie became aware that her heart was beating too fast, pounding and pumping in her chest. Her face felt heated. She was finding it unusually difficult to deal with this man.

"You—you were coming in from Bombay, I guess," she said. "The maharani mentioned it. Did Joe Wolfe go to Bombay, also?"

He continued to stand, legs apart and drink in hand, watching her. He did not answer.

Julie looked around for her purse. She needed her notebook. Questions to ask. Her head ached abominably. She found it hard to keep her perspective, to remember that this man was a dignitary, an important contact. He seemed too intensely alive, too masculine, too overwhelmingly real—not a cardboard political figure who was all smiles, handshakes and pleasant words.

He was speaking to her again. Something about the airport, why she had come. Difficult to concentrate. Stern, harsh words. He seemed angry. She shivered. The coolness of the room was now uncomfortably chill. A wave of confusion passed over her. She staggered against the bookcase, feeling sick. She had the vague thought that if only those un-smiling eyes would soften when they looked at her, she would be safe. Then she slid forward into a deep pit of blackness....

Strong arms broke her fall, wrapping around her, encasing her like bands of steel. They held her still and secure, until slowly the dizziness and darkness began to recede. A faint muskiness filled Julie's nostrils—a rough masculine scent, yet pleasant. Quick thudding, strong and regular, drummed next to her ear.

"Do you feel cold?"

Julie nodded, surprised to realize she did feel chilled. That seemed strange; it was so hot outside.

"Heat exhaustion. You are probably more vulnerable today because of the fatigue from your long trip. Your resistance is low."

She nodded again. He was holding her close against his broad chest. A delectable warmth crept into her body. She felt weak, but relaxed.

"You'll feel better in a few minutes. Stay in the house where it is cool for the rest of the day. But right now you need to be kept warm because of the subnormal body tempera-ture," he informed her. "You are delectable like this!" he said softly, as though amused.

She pushed back away from his chest a few inches. "I never faint," she assured him, a smile in her own eyes. "This is an illusion. Objective, impersonal, professional women never faint. But thank you for catching me anyway. Did I really faint?"

"Dead away," he replied. "Unless it was a ruse to get me to hold you. Women aren't above such things, heaven knows. And I can't determine any other reason for you to be here. My mother seemed strangely reluctant to broach the subject herself."

The smile died in Julie's eyes. She leaned back farther in his arms to see his face better. "I'll forget you said that," she said in a conversational tone. She slipped out of his grasp and stood up, straightening her suit. He rose, too, in one smooth, swift motion, picking up his unspilled drink from the floor as he did so.

"I'm sorry. I asked for that," he said evenly.

"I do prefer the heat-exhaustion explanation," she replied, her eyes cold. "It's so much more tasteful between strangers, don't you think?"

The maharani chose that moment to re-enter the library, closing the door behind herself with a soft click. She looked from one to the other of them, smiling. "I just told Priya about Julie coming to stay with us. My daughter welcomes you as much as I do, Julie." To Jai she said, "Has Julie been telling you all about her exciting work as a newspaper reporter?"

"A reporter?" His gaze swung back to Julie. Any lingering warmth those fierce eyes might have held vanished abruptly, to be replaced by suspicion and distaste. "No, she hasn't. Is she one?"

"Why, yes, of course, Jai. That's why she is here," replied the maharani, puzzled. "She is employed by my friend, Wes Harding, on his newspaper in the United States. You remember Wes, don't you? I recall he wrote me that he met you once or twice while you were at university in England."

"Ah, yes. I remember him now." The prince continued to regard Julie for an instant longer, then turned toward his mother. "I've heard that some reporters will do anything to get a story," he remarked idly. "I'd never really credited it . . . before now!"

Julie looked up at him, her blue eyes flashing with anger. She itched to slap his face. Could he really think for an instant that she had purposely pretended to faint in his arms in order to help get a story for the paper? She couldn't accept such a ridiculous explanation. He must have some other reason for wanting to get under her skin. Or maybe he was just one of those men with a basic disrespect for women. . . .

"Well, yes, I suppose so. But Julie isn't actually reporting in the usual sense," the maharani was saying. "Wes explained it briefly in the cable he sent me. She is here as part of a project she has already been working on. I assumed Julie would have told you all this while I was out," she added a little anxiously.

"No, she didn't say anything," her son answered. He walked over and picked up his riding crop, which lay on the side table. "She just got right to work."

"Oh, of course," said the maharani, relieved. "I am sure she is very efficient," she added, glancing at Julie sweetly.

"Oh, yes. Very efficient." He stepped over and kissed his mother's cheek. "Will you excuse me, *mataji*? I have a polo game this morning."

"Come, Julie," the maharani requested after her son had left the room. "I have your room all prepared for you. I think you will like it." Julie repressed the series of pithy, faintly obscene comments she would have liked to address to the prince's absent back, and followed her hostess from the room.

"I'm glad Jai is reacting this way," the maharani told her as they entered the hallway. "Frankly, I was a little afraid to tell him myself, about your work that is. He has very strong feelings about the press." She laughed. "He is so strict with Priya and me, never letting us say anything to the reporters who are always calling. You can't imagine. Really, I do not see why he makes such a fuss! The reporters are always so friendly. They want to know all about us, for the society pages, you know. Except we do not go out very often now, so I would not have much to tell them anyway.''

Julie could find no answer to these uninvited revelations. She was incensed. *So on top of everything else,* she was thinking, *the provoking Prince Jaiapradesh Mishra hates the press.*

CHAPTER THREE

JULIE FOLLOWED THE MAHARANI in a daze. The hallways, with their vaulted ceilings and arched windows, seemed endless. Julie's legs were shaking with illness and fatigue by the time her hostess stopped in front of a beautiful carved-teak door.

"These will be your rooms while you are here with us."

"Thank you."

"I know you must be very tired. Just make yourself at home. A bath has already been drawn for you. I think maybe you should take a long nap."

"It was a long trip."

"Yes, I'm sure. And all by yourself! Well, sleep as long as you like. Don't worry about mealtimes. Whenever you wake up, just ring the bell beside your bed and food will be brought to you."

"Thank you."

"You know, Julie," the maharani added, "I admire you very much for what you are trying to do. Wes told me about your stories on terrorism. If there is anything I can do to help you, please tell me. I was much influenced by Gandhi when I was younger—by his teachings of nonviolence. That's certainly a better solution to political change than the methods these terrorist groups use. Gandhi wasn't able to succeed with his ideas at that turbulent time in history, but I still believe nonviolence holds the key to the future."

"I appreciate your support," Julie replied, touched.

"Thank *you* for coming to us," replied the gracious older woman.

Alone in her suite Julie tried to replay the events of morning in her mind. She knew she had not handled the first meeting with the prince well. It would have been better to have explained her work before any misunderstanding could arise.... Despite her best efforts to think things through in a rational manner, however, Julie found her thoughts kept drifting back to the moment when the prince had held her. She recalled in the minutest detail the feel of his strong arms around her.

"I'm too tired to think," she groaned wearily. "The whole thing is so absurd!" Julie fought her self-directed anger—how could she have let this important contact get off to such a bad start! Somehow she had allowed Jai Mishra to control the encounter from start to finish. That was no way to get a story. She shook her head. This defeatist thinking wasn't going to get her anywhere. Remembering the hot bath awaiting her, she headed for what looked like the door to the bathroom.

The bedroom was a study in elegance. The pink-and-blue wool carpet, hand knotted in the mountain province of Kashmir, felt thick and luxurious beneath her bare feet. The walls of the large room were covered in the palest of rose silk, with matching drapes of a darker shade. The windows opened, French style, onto a wide balcony decorated with large clay pots overflowing with flowering plants. A big tree just beside the balcony drooped its flower-laden branches almost into Julie's room, as though offering its fragrant cream-colored blossoms specifically for her pleasure. The furnishings of the room were as well chosen as everything else Julie had seen in the palace.

"Not a wonder I can't think straight," she murmured to herself with a sigh, as she pushed open the bathroom door. "This room is right out of a fairy tale." Only the prince is ill-tempered and sardonic, she thought angrily. Stripping off her wrinkled clothing, she stepped into the waiting bath.

Her first impulse after the scene in the library with the prince had been to leave the palace immediately and take up residence in one of the main hotels in Delhi. But now, as Julie lay luxuriating in the shell-shaped marble bathtub idly stirring the scented, steaming

water to and fro, she realized she would have
to stay here as planned, despite the prince's
animosity toward the press. This was the best
base for her investigation. Harding had already decided so, and Julie knew he was
right. Even if Prince Mishra himself was not
helpful, just the status she would gain in the
eyes of the Indian diplomatic community
from being his houseguest would ensure a
warmer reception to all her inquiries.

Newspapers maintaining a permanent bureau in India considered the country one of
the toughest assignments foreign correspondents could draw. Most foreign correspondents were overseas for three-year periods.
But India was one of the few areas designated
as a hardship tour, and appointments only
lasted two years. One of the main reasons for
that was the extreme difficulty reporters had
in getting any accurate news reports from the
Indian government. In this news-repressive
atmosphere, Julie knew she could not afford
to throw away any edge that she could get,
even if it meant temporarily putting aside her
personal feelings.

She splashed her feet, watching the mounds
of bubbles go skidding across the surface of
the water. Jai Mishra's attitude was not
unique, naturally. Just inconvenient. It was
not unusual to encounter people in the upper
echelons of the social or political strata with a
poor opinion of the press. Julie had always

felt that people with a lot of money or prestige got in the habit of having things pretty much their own way. Then along would come some journalist out for a story, not caring whose toes he stepped on—in fact, the bigger the toes, the better the story.

Often the reporter was in the right, uncovering something readers had a right to know. Occasionally a journalist was blatantly irresponsible, however, causing an endless amount of damage by slanting a story to fit preconceived prejudices, quoting out of context or even misstating facts. Press coverage of public figures could sometimes result in harassment, an invasion of privacy by flashbulbs and tape recorders. Everyone had an aspect of his life he preferred to keep confidential; for people in the public eye secrecy was often impossible.

As an aristocrat and an heir to wealth, Jai Mishra had probably been hounded by reporters since childhood. Nevertheless, Julie thought she could win him over. As a business leader he would certainly understand the value of a well-researched series of articles detailing the potentially destructive operations of the secret network of international terrorists. As a human being, he must desire to see such merciless killers exposed and captured.

Too tired to even look through her suitcases for her nightgown, Julie slipped naked between the cool sheets of the huge canopied bed that dominated the bedroom decor. She stretched out her long legs, pointing her toes to flex the high arch of her delicately shaped feet. The crisp cotton sheet brushed her bare breasts, rubbing against sensitive nipples. She relaxed into the comfort of the bed, aware of a warm yearning in the depths of her abdomen. Sighing, she plumped her pillow and buried her cheek. Even though the sun shone brilliantly behind the drawn curtains she fell asleep almost instantly. Not only had her journey been long and exhausting, but also she had not yet adjusted to the twelve-hour time change that made it the middle of the night now in New York City.

She awoke many hours later. Rubbing her eyes and rolling over in bed, she saw that a young woman was watching her timidly from the partially opened door.

"Good morning, madam. My name is Sukundala," explained the girl with a smile. Julie saw she was small and dark skinned, with the typically soft features of the southern Indian. "Would you like your breakfast now?"

The maid started the tub water running before leaving the room. When she left, Julie arose. She bathed quickly and then dug out of her suitcase a loose-fitting sundress with tiered ruffles of white eyelet and slipped it on. As she bent over to close her luggage, a crumpled newspaper stuck in one corner caught her eye. She pulled it out. Crossing over to the bed, she laid the paper out flat on the sheet, smoothing the wrinkles with her hands.

The *Courier* crowned the front page in bold script. Beneath that in smaller letters was the paper's motto: "Bringing The News To The People." The date was three weeks ago.

A picture in the upper right-hand corner above the fold—the key spot for the big news story of the day—showed the remains of a large stone building. Two walls were still standing, surrounded by piles of rubble. Smoke streamed from smoldering ashes. Uniformed police scurried in and out of the ruins. In the foreground of the picture innumerable sheet-covered bodies lay side by side, awaiting identification. The by-line on the story beneath was Julie's.

She stared at the photo now, but in her mind's eye she was seeing the real scene all over again. The place was Rome. The building was the train station that had been bombed during the busiest part of the day. Again she smelled the burning rubble; she tasted the dry fear in her mouth. How long would the reality behind that picture continue to haunt her? Until the terrorists responsible were captured? Until the end of her days?

Absently Julie reread the words she had dictated over static-filled telephone lines to

the New York office from her dingy Italian
hotel room:

> Shocking even the most hardened radi-
> cals, terrorists today exploded four
> bombs simultaneously in one of Rome's
> largest train stations. The explosions,
> which occurred during the busiest hour
> of commuter traffic, killed at least 75
> persons and wounded 110 others. Italy's
> most active terrorist organization, the
> Communist-backed Red Brigades,
> claimed credit for the attack.

It was her first front-page story, but that
fact was not able to bring Julie any pleasure.
She could only remember the stricken faces of
the survivors, the miserable cries of the
wounded. The cold bodies of the unknown
dead.

Her glance flicked to the newspaper again.
Were the same men and women who perpetrated this act in Rome three weeks before in
India right now? She knew national terrorist
organizations often traded their best "hit"
squads back and forth across the globe. It
was possible the same team had been "invited" to Asia next. Certainly they would be
planning something else if they were meeting
now.

Could it be stopped? Only if the terrorists
were tracked down and exposed first. Of

course, that was not her job. Every country in the world had special intelligence personnel. And yet, how many times had a clever investigative reporter exploded a story that destroyed the facade of a hypocritical person or organization of them more effectively? Julie smiled to herself. Why did all correspondents feel that they must be watchdogs for the public?

She knew her co-workers felt she got too involved in her work. "Julie," Fred Grason, home on leave from the Middle East, had told her, "you can report a story without either loving or hating the participants in it. Look at me. I've seen it all. But I don't bring it home with me. I couldn't you know, or I'd never be able to live with myself."

But Julie could not divide her life in two sections—career and personal. The two were one. Wasn't her work really her life now? Especially since Eddie's death.

Restless, she left the bed and walked over to the open door leading to the balcony. As she stepped outside a soft breeze swirled her dress against her bare legs. The tree-shaded marble felt cool under her feet. Julie breathed deeply. Her eyes strayed across the green expanse of close-clipped grass, smooth and dense as a carpet. In the distance, beyond a well-placed grove of trees, she caught a gleam of gold. The tigers on the gateposts. . . .

Had her personal life really ended when

Eddie died? She plucked a white bloom off the bough that hung across her balcony. She had hesitated a long time before agreeing to marry him. Yet he had loved her, she who had no family of her own, and that meant more than words could say.

When Julie was twelve, her mother had died from cancer. She never knew her father. A mining engineer, he had lost his life a year after her birth in a small-plane crash over Alaska's barren snowfields. Julie's earliest memory was of her mother crying over his faded photograph. A helpless witness to her mother's grief, even as a child she had known the desolate sense of abandonment death brings.

When her mother had died, Julie moved in with Aunt Agnes, her mother's sister. Agnes Craufield knew her duty, so she opened her home to her orphaned niece. A reserved and practical woman who did not believe in displaying emotion, she never took time to open her heart. Not that Aunt Agnes did not care. But she had her own family—one Julie was never part of, even though she lived with them for five years.

Julie always tried to avoid thinking back to those teenage years, so full of anguish. Sensitive and warm by nature herself, she had never been able to understand her aunt's apparent coldness. Only after Julie had grown up did she recognize that Aunt Agnes had merely treated her as she treated everyone else. At the time, lonely and lost after her mother's death, Julie had interpreted her lack of emotion as rejection.

In high school Julie learned to channel her need for praise and approval into her schoolwork, winning the recognition and affection of her teachers. The college scholarship she won enabled her to leave her aunt's home. And even if a dorm room was not much, at least it was hers. She felt less an outsider in an impersonal campus dormitory than she had in her relative's home.

In the last half of her senior year at Colorado State she met Eddie Bryce. He had been performing a stunt—jumping off a cliff into a nylon air bag in the foothills out past the campus, where a movie company was filming a chase scene. Lots of the kids from the college had gone out to watch. After the stunt was over, Julie had interviewed him for the college newspaper. He asked her out.

That was the beginning of her life, as far as Julie had been concerned. In the four years they were together, Eddie was mother, father, big brother and lover all rolled into one. He had filled that aching void left by her parents' early deaths. Then, his own violent death had reinforced the now-familiar theme of abandonment woven like a crimson thread through the tapestry of Julie's life. She had withdrawn into herself, determined never to be hurt again.

In the nightmare following Eddie's accident, Julie left California and moved to New York. She had been working hard at the *Courier* ever since, pouring all her energy and emotion into journalism. Her work was something she could count on.

My demanding boss likes my work, Julie reflected, raising the blossom in her hand and sniffing. "You find your story with your heart, then write it with your head. It's a good combination," he had said. High praise, indeed, from the reticent Wes Harding.

An engine roared somewhere down the driveway. Julie glimpsed bright metallic red flashing past behind the trees as the prince's sports car rolled into view. It pulled up at the front doors of the palace. The driver cut the engine and jumped out. Julie recognized the tall, lean figure of Jai Mishra. As though he felt her eyes on him, Jai paused on his way up the wide stairs. Turning, he looked directly at her balcony. No hand was raised in greeting. Julie had not forgotten his accusations in the library. He obviously had not, either. In a moment he turned away and entered the palace.

Looking down, Julie saw she had crushed the fragile flower in her hand. That man was impossible. After all, she did not write for the gossip columns. She had a legitimate reason to be here—an important reason. As for fainting in his arms on purpose, *he* had been the one to diagnose her weakness as heat exhaustion. Even if he was handsome, surely women did not just throw themselves at his feet on first sight. Although when she had first seen him in the airport, the feelings he aroused had been somewhat along those lines....

That was before I met him, Julie thought, with a short laugh. *I know better now.* She tossed the broken flower over the railing and went inside.

Julie was breakfasting in her sitting room when a gentle knocking on her bedroom door interrupted her thoughts. A slender black-haired girl entered at the sound of Julie's greeting. She crossed the bedroom toward Julie, every motion infused with perfect grace. She paused in the doorway of the sitting room, her eyes cast down in shyness.

"Good morning, Miss Connell. I am Priya, the maharani's daughter. I thought you might like company while you have breakfast."

"How thoughtful of you! Please sit down."

The girl settled herself on the opposite side of the table, her large eyes reflecting both warmth and intelligence. Classically beautiful, she had the light skin and aristocratic features characteristic of Indo-Aryan ancestry.

"What a lovely sari you are wearing,"

Julie commented, admiring the shimmering blend of pink-and-gold silk with an embroidered border of metallic gold threads.

"Do you like it?" Priya's melodious voice reminded Julie of the maharani. "We call this shot silk when the fabric is woven of two different colors of threads. It looks one color one minute and another the next." She smoothed the silk with a ring-bedecked hand. "I will get you one if you like them."

"I could never keep it on," Julie protested.

"I will show you how. Mother says you will be staying here with us for some time. We can go shopping together. Then I will help you put one on."

She flicked her heavy braid out of her way and relaxed gracefully back in her chair, chatting about her plans for Julie's entertainment. Watching her, Julie found it hard to believe this warm young woman could be the prince's sister. Except they were both extremely good-looking, the one so completely feminine, the other so domineering and masculine. The maharani must have had Priya quite late in life, Julie mused. The princess was many years younger than her brother.

As though reading her thoughts, Priya asked, "You have already met my older brother, Jai, haven't you?"

"Yes, I have," Julie answered, trying not to let any of the various emotions evoked by the thought of the prince show on her face. No doubt Priya adored her big brother.

"I'm so mad at him!" she exclaimed with sudden feeling. "I used to think he was the most wonderful brother in the world... but not anymore!"

"What happened?" Julie asked, touched by the distressed look on the Indian girl's face.

"Marriage," Priya replied, her voice tight with suppressed emotion.

"He's married?" Julie asked. She had not realized....

"No, not him—me. My marriage."

"Oh." Julie wondered why she should feel so relieved. It was nothing to her if Jai Mishra was married. He could have a dozen wives for all she cared. "Somehow I got the impression from your mother that you were not married," she said.

"I'm not married. I'm... I'm betrothed."

"I guess I don't understand, Priya," Julie said, putting down her piece of toast. She liked this girl, even though to Julie, who had been making her own way in the world for a long time, Priya seemed young for her age. The fact the princess had probably led a very sheltered life would account for that. Furthermore, the anguished note in her voice touched the American woman's heart. Julie could remember too well what it was like to grow up needing someone to talk to and not having anyone who really seemed to want to listen. "Don't you want to get married?"

"Oh, I would love to be married!" exclaimed Priya, her face suffused with a sudden glow. "All women want to be married. At least here in India," she added. "I know when I was at school in Switzerland, some of the girls felt differently about it. But here there is only marriage."

"Well, if you want to be married and if you have gotten engaged to someone...." Julie paused, not knowing exactly what to make of Priya's obvious distress.

"If *I* had gotten engaged to...to someone that would be fine. That would be supreme!" the princess added, clapping her hands together for emphasis. She reminded Julie of a beautiful doll. "But *I* didn't do it! Jai did it, without even consulting me!"

"You don't mean an arranged marriage, do you?"

"Yes, that's exactly it! He arranged the whole thing and just told me about it a few days ago."

"I had no idea that custom was still being adhered to," Julie replied. It was hard to imagine something so different from Western culture, where dating, singles' clubs and the faithful office water cooler were a way of life for unmarried people.

"Oh, yes," replied Priya. "Arranged marriages are still prevalent in India today, especially among the more traditional families. Usually the marriage is arranged by some friend of the family, who knows two families, one with a boy and one with a girl of an age to be married. Sometimes children are even betrothed at birth, although not so much anymore."

"But how do they know if the couple will like each other?"

"Marriage here is not so much a joining of individuals as a joining of families." She turned the rings on her fingers. "The wife goes to live with the husband's family, so it is important that the two families like each other and have similar backgrounds. Often the bride and groom never even meet until the wedding day."

"But don't they have any choice in the matter at all?"

"*That* is the point I have against Jai!" exclaimed the girl, her large eyes flashing in renewed wrath. "Usually the groom has much to say about it, especially when he comes from a good family and if he has a big salary. Often the bride has no choice—she is given by her parents to the man they feel can best provide for her.

"But in *my* case—of course I will have a large dowry. Actually, dowries are outlawed now, but that does not stop people from following the old tradition. Jai will see I have one. So it stands to reason I don't have to take just anyone for a husband. Normally in these circumstances he would have consulted me to see if I had any...preference.'' Julie could see that Priya was puzzled as well as angry at her brother's actions.

"Well, why not speak to your mother, the maharani, about this, Priya?'' Julie suggested. "Certainly, being a woman, she would sympathize with you. After all, she is your parent, *not* the prince.''

The Indian girl toyed unhappily with a silver teaspoon. Julie's heart went out to her. What good would all that beauty and intelligence and wealth do her if she was unhappy in a marriage not of her choosing?

"In India,'' replied Priya after a moment, "the oldest male in the household makes all the decisions. Since my father's death, Jai is the head of our house. It is for him to see me properly settled in my husband's home—it would be considered his duty. A woman is taught to obey first her father, then her husband and then her son. My mother would not try to go against anything Jai decided, no matter how unhappy it makes me!

"But I have a mind of my own. I won't marry him—whomever Jai has picked! Jai will meet his match in me. I, too, am a Mishra! Please excuse me!'' The distraught girl rose quickly and ran from the room.

Feeling she should let Priya recover her composure before seeking her out, Julie finished her breakfast in silence. The more she thought about it, the more she could not understand the young woman's conflicting emotions. Priya seemed to accept the idea of arranged marriages as a natural part of life— certainly she had been raised to comply with that concept. And yet when applied to herself she was opposed to it.

Was it possible that Priya had some particular young man in mind for herself? It did not seem likely. How could she have met him, as secluded as her life seemed to be? Besides, if she liked someone already, all she had to do was to tell Prince Mishra about the young man. Unless, perhaps, it was someone her brother would not approve of.... If that was the case, poor Priya! Personally, Julie could not think of anyone whom she would rather not cross than Jai Mishra.

CHAPTER FOUR

AFTER BREAKFAST Julie investigated the contents of her largest suitcase. With so much to do, she was not in the mood to unpack. She pulled out a businesslike sleeveless navy dress with white piping and gave it a shake.

"Wrinkle free, just like the tag promised," she observed with satisfaction.

She dressed in haste, buckling on a wide red belt for accent color. Remembering the heat outside, she dispensed with nylons. Her legs were still tanned enough from the trip to Rome to look good bare. Low-heeled navy sandals completed the outfit. A quick check in the dressing room three-way mirror increased her self-confidence. She grabbed her notebook and stepped out into the hallway.

Just when she was wondering where to find the maharani at this time of the morning, Julie saw Sukundala approaching.

"I have a message for you, madam. Prince Mishra requests your presence in his office now, if you have no other engagements."

"All right." She might as well start with him as anyone. At least he was willing to see her—she had wondered if she would even get a chance to talk with him, considering his attitude toward the press.

"Please follow me, then. Prince Mishra's offices are in this direction."

Five minutes later Julie placed her hand on an ornate brass doorknob and pulled open a heavy oak door. The room before her was large. Floor-to-ceiling arched windows overlooking a rose garden formed one wall. A glittering chandelier hung from the center of the ceiling. Hand-carved hardwood molding outlined the ceiling and doorways. Another fabulous rug—this one in hues of maroon with flashes of plum and turquoise—covered most of the parquet floor.

Despite every luxury, the room was very much an office. Filing cabinets lined one corner. Several maps and an equal number of building blueprints covered an enormous bulletin board. A male secretary labored over a typewriter in an adjoining alcove. Julie recognized the impatient clatter of a telex machine coming from behind a partly closed door.

In the center of the room behind a desk sat the prince. He glanced up as Julie entered.

"That will be all, Hari." The secretary rose and left the room.

"Come in, Miss Connell." Jai indicated a chair facing his desk. She crossed to it, aware of his eyes on her, and sat down.

"Explain your work."

"I am a foreign correspondent for the *Courier* of New York. I specialize in in-depth coverage and analysis of global news. I deal with problem situations that transcend the boundaries of any one country, occurring simultaneously in several nations and apparently interconnected. I was sent here as part of my latest assignment."

"What assignment?" The abrupt question was intended to be neither helpful nor interested. Julie was all too aware of the man's critical scrutiny. She wondered whether he had had a run-in with a journalist in the past, or whether his dislike just reflected the general attitude of the upper class for newshounds.

"International terrorism," she replied, trying to gauge his reaction. His expression did not change, but she thought she detected a sharpened intentness in his alert eyes.

"You came here to report about terrorists? How did you know about them? Their movements here have been extremely cautious so far."

"We have what are called 'stringers' for our paper," Julie explained, relieved to have stirred his interest. "Stringers don't work full-time for our paper. They are stationary, living in their native country and often holding other jobs. If something newsworthy happens in their area, they send us a story, and if it's good enough, we print it. Many of them have had contact with our paper for years."

"And?"

"Well, we have a stringer in Bombay. We don't keep a foreign correspondent in India. The cost is prohibitive. We rely on stringers and the wire services for daily news of India."

"And this man in Bombay told you about the terrorists?"

"Yes. He cabled us that he had heard a rumor of a major international summit meeting for terrorists to be held in northern India, possibly New Delhi, in the near future. This man has developed many sources for tips and leads over the years. We've learned to trust him. He is more accurate than most local stringers. But since this report was outside his district, he couldn't follow up on it. Besides, it could be a very complicated story. The foreign desk editor thought it was important enough to send someone over here right away."

"Your editor may be right." Jai continued to regard her in silence, but with less obvious cynicism. His interest was apparent. "Why were you sent?"

"I was the logical choice for this assignment since I've covered every terrorist incident for the last several months."

"Where?"

"England. France. Three weeks ago, Rome."

The lids flickered once over his dark eyes. "Ah, yes. The train station."

"That's right." Julie tried to keep her voice detached. It was impossible to think of that day without.... She closed her eyes a moment.

"Not a pleasant assignment, I take it." Jai's voice had lost its coldness. It was almost comforting.

"No," she replied, opening her eyes and meeting his. "Not pleasant at all."

The prince got up from behind his desk and walked over to the windows. Julie watched him as he stood with his back to her, apparently contemplating the rose garden. His changing moods fascinated her—so cold one minute, so capable of compassion the next. Not a simple man to understand.... *Too bad I cannot write an article about him,* she thought with a smile.

He turned toward her. "Would you care for something to drink—ice tea, perhaps, or lemonade? Lemonade is a good antidote to this heat."

"Thank you." She could have used some yesterday in the library. Julie remembered the feel of his arms holding her, his broad chest against her cheek. The memory carried a rush of heightened awareness throughout her body.

Jai might almost have read her thoughts, the way his eyes met hers across the room.

"Why don't we continue our discussion over here by the windows?"

Seated in a comfortable chair with a frosty glass of lemonade in hand, Julie admired the scenery outside. "Roses must do very well here," she commented. "I've never seen so many varieties."

Jai leaned back in his chair. "They like sunlight, of which we have an abundance."

"Yes, you certainly do!" Heat waves shimmered in the distance beyond the trees. The lawns around the palace, however, looked lush and cool. Julie set her glass aside. "I understand you have a large intelligence organization of your own, Prince Mishra. Is that where you got your information about the terrorist activities you mentioned?"

"Do you realize the danger involved in your assignment here?" asked the prince after a moment, ignoring her question.

Julie smiled at him. "Journalism is a high-risk profession these days, hadn't you heard? There is potential danger in almost every overseas assignment now. Even in routine news coverage, one never knows when one might be stepping on the toes of organized crime, the Communist Party, or a 'special interest' group not opposed to intimidation or actual violence in order to try to suppress certain information from reaching the public."

"Nevertheless, any attempt to get close to

terrorist activities deliberately provokes danger.''

"I guess it does," Julie replied. "And yet the media is crucial to their plans. The experts I have interviewed in our State Department felt media coverage is the terrorists' main objective. The hit squads choose their victims according to what effect the organization wishes to make upon the public.

"For instance, the kidnapping I covered in England. I think the terrorists wanted to further demoralize the British, who are already overburdened with economic problems. So they kidnapped and murdered a well-loved elderly statesman. I really think *which* statesman they killed made little difference—they got the effect they wanted. It made everyone feel so helpless...." She forced herself to take a deep breath, to relax the fingers gripping her gold-plated pen. That wonderful old man.... It had made *her* feel so useless, so angry....

"If you think that because they need the media to gain their objectives, terrorists would overlook it if you got in their way, you are very naive, Miss Connell."

"I have seen the terrorists' work," Julie replied coldly. He had touched her professional pride. "I don't think I could underestimate their lack of—humanity—ever again after that."

A spark flashed in his eyes. A proud man

himself, Jai could respect pride in others. "Nevertheless," he replied, "you are my mother's houseguest. I cannot allow you to expose yourself to danger while you live under my roof."

Julie had met with this attitude before from men. Why did some males think that excitement and adventure were their own exclusive domain? "I'm good at looking after myself," she stated. "I don't take chances. Besides, most of my job is tedious, careful research—although reporting can have its dramatic moments, I admit."

"There are others concerned besides yourself," he interrupted sharply. "Do you think those organizations stop with just one crime? What if they decide to retaliate against you while you happen to be out shopping with my mother, or perhaps my sister? Do you think they would resist an opportunity like that?"

Silence stretched out between them as Julie considered his words. Jai Mishra leaned back in his chair watching her. It was hard to think with his eyes raking over her. He saw too much—aroused too much. Somehow she could never quite forget the spontaneous attraction she had felt for him, both in the airport and later in the library. The memory of that sudden exhilaration was always present in the back of her mind. It was totally inappropriate for the business relationship she hoped to establish with him. . . .

"Aren't you going a bit too fast?" she asked, turning away from him and gazing in the direction of the hundreds of blooming rose plants. "In the first place, at this point I have no information whatsoever about the terrorists, other than that they *may* be meeting somewhere near here. I had hoped—" Julie paused, glancing at Jai "—you might be able to help me with that.

"Secondly, I admit the terrorists may be aware that I'm here on their trail, because I know they keep tabs on the journalists who are covering them. But I don't think I'm close enough to uncovering their plans to be a threat to them yet. I arranged with my editor to let it out that I'm here to do a feature on India's improved relations with Russia. That would involve a lot of the same type of research—talking to people, going to embassies and so forth. For now at least there shouldn't be much danger. If at some point you feel I may be endangering your family, I'll move at once to a hotel."

His face relaxed somewhat. "You must know, Julie, that your presence here could not endanger my family more than they already are."

She glanced at him, surprised he had used her first name and at the warmer tone of his voice. Julie never knew from one minute to the next if what she said would please Jai or anger him. What had Harding said? "He respects guts." She wondered if the prince thought her brave to face the terrorists. Or to face him. She would have trouble deciding which took the most courage! But he had just given her her first item of information and she wanted to follow it up.

"Is your family in danger from the terrorists, Prince Mishra?" she asked.

"Call me Jai." Julie liked his smile. It was warmer than she would have thought possible for a man who seemed habitually reserved.

"My family," he continued after a pause, "is a prime target for a terrorist attack. Consider the advantages I offer. First, I'm a member of the aristocracy. The revolutionary plan is always to remove the old to make way for the new. No matter that my title is only a courtesy now, that I have no kingdom to rule. Getting rid of me and my kind can only be a good thing for the spread of world communism or global revolution.

"Secondly, I have power in the government. I use that power to oppose greater Russian domination of Indian affairs. I oppose unnecessary dependency on any other country for that matter. India, with proper development, will stand on her own feet. She has the natural resources. She has the people. She also has the wisdom, buried in her ancient traditions, to contribute culturally and spiritually to the well-being of the world. Rather than see India dependent on either the

Soviets or the Americans, I would like to see this country use its influence to balance the two superpowers and thereby help preserve global harmony.''

His words surprised Julie. She had assumed Jai would be concerned first and foremost, as most people were, with his own affairs. Beneath his cynical exterior was a streak of optimism, even idealism.

''So that is another reason then that left-wing groups might concern themselves with me,'' he continued. ''I block their progress in the government. There are those who think India would make an ideal Soviet satellite. It goes without saying that the international network of terrorist organizations is Soviet backed.

''Next, my business concerns. I am, as you must be aware, a major industrialist. To destroy me or my companies would be to strike a blow against capitalism. And the loss of jobs for all my employees would help destabilize the nation. People out of work, with no prospects, will turn to anyone—even revolutionaries—for help.''

''What then,'' asked Julie, ignoring her growing physical awareness of the man next to her, ''is your exact relationship to—your specific interest in—the terrorists?''

''I am their enemy.''

Julie drew back. The soft menace of the prince's voice startled her. She could only be glad the words were not meant for her: he would be an implacable adversary.

He looked at her. "How much of what I say to you goes into your newspaper?"

"Well, I'm covering terrorist activities. When they act or the government acts against them, I'll report. If any of the information you give me would supply useful background for understanding the terrorist problem, I'll use it when the time comes."

"Spoken like a true professional." He did not seem to care much one way or the other.

"You have not given me any sensitive information about terrorist activity here in India, if such information is available to you," she pointed out.

"No. Nor do I intend to." The mask of reserve reappeared on Jai's face, as tangible as though a steel wall had clanged down between them. He rose and returned to his desk. It was clear that although he might be willing to humor Julie's journalistic efforts out of respect for his mother, he had no intention of making any serious attempt to aid her investigation. Julie stood up, realizing the interview was over.

Just then the door to the office opened. Priya entered. She stopped when she saw Jai standing behind his desk.

"Good morning," he said. "To what do I owe this honor?" His voice was affectionate and playful.

A brief look—of hope, followed by pain—crossed the girl's face. Then she turned deliberately toward Julie, ignoring her brother's greeting.

"Mother and I are going sari shopping in a little while, Julie," she said. "We hoped you would join us. I can show you the shop I told you about where they sell the shot silk. And then we can go to lunch at the Ashoka Hotel, if you like."

"That sounds marvelous, Priya," answered Julie. An hour or so of shopping would give her a feel for the city. "It was nice of you to include me."

"Mother is in the yellow salon. You might wish to join her there, when you are finished here." She tossed a quick glance in her brother's direction. "I will be ready in a few minutes and then we can leave."

"All right. Thank you."

The young princess left the room without speaking to her brother. After she was gone, Julie turned to Jai. His face reflected neither anger nor irritation at Priya's behavior. He watched the door closing behind his sister, a speculative look in his eyes. Julie felt the awkwardness of the moment more than he seemed to. As though reading her mind he said, "Save your sympathies. The emotional swings of an adolescent girl affect me not at all."

"Maybe they should, then," retorted Julie, stung by his callous tone.

His swift movement took Julie off guard. He was around the desk and beside her before she could react. He grasped her arm above the elbow; she could smell the musky scent of his powerful body. His fingers dug into her flesh. She jerked her arm in an attempt to dislodge his hold. His grip was viselike. Worse than the pain in her arm was the quivering weakness of her knees. A rush of sensation spiraled through her body. His nearness overwhelmed her.

"Don't presume to advise me on my family affairs, Julie." Jai's voice was quiet, but his eyes flashed with anger. "I brook no interference. You have been here less than two days. You know nothing about us."

"I'm learning fast," she hissed.

To her surprise, the prince laughed. His eyes locked with hers. Deep within the dark pupils she saw the mysterious green flame. He let go of her arm.

"I begin to think there are some things I would like to teach you," he said.

Julie left the office without speaking. The only answer to such a leading statement from a man as handsome as Jai Mishra was a definite "no comment."

She found the yellow salon more by chance than by design. Entering, Julie saw that the room's name was apt. It was sunny, decorated in complementary shades of gold and yellow. Monotony had been avoided by con-

trasting various tones and fabrics. Fringed
velvet cushions of deep gold enhanced the
beauty of a pale yellow silk damask sofa. The
cream-colored carpets must have been custom
woven because their floral border matched
the pattern in the pink-and-yellow silk
drapes. Huge vases of fragrant yellow roses
topped the marble coffee table. A shining
grand piano stood in one corner of the room.

The maharani was sitting in a velvet chair
by the arched windows that, like in many of
the palace rooms, lined one wall. The older
woman smiled as Julie entered.

"Good morning. Did you sleep well?"

"Well and long both," she answered, seating herself across from her hostess. "Thank
you for sending my breakfast to my room.
Priya was kind enough to keep me company
while I ate. Your daughter is very beautiful,"
she added.

The maharani laughed. "Well, she should
be. Her name in our language means pretty.
Maybe being named Priya made her grow up
to be that way. In India we believe sound has
a great influence in nature. That is why our
pundits—holy men—chant the Vedic scriptures all the time. Just the sound of those ancient hymns is said to enliven the minds of all
who hear them, even if the listeners do not
understand the meaning of the words."

"What language are your scriptures written in?" Julie asked, intrigued. She remem-

bered scientific studies she had read about houseplants growing better if one played music for them. It seemed possible that certain sounds could make human beings grow in health and well-being, as well. Certainly the opposite was true. Noise pollution—discordant noises such as rush-hour traffic or shrieking alarms—caused stress.

"Our scriptures are called the Vedas," the maharani replied. "Veda means knowledge. The Vedas are written in the Sanskrit language. Are you interested in Indian culture, Julie?"

"Yes, very much so. I've always enjoyed reading about it—it is so different from my own culture. When I was young, though, I never dreamed I would come here one day to see India firsthand," she added.

The maharani smiled. "You will find that much of our culture can't be seen. Hindus do not have nearly as many monuments and temples as, say, the Muslims. Hindu culture is preserved in the traditions of daily living—in the minds and hearts of the people—and in the recitation of the Vedas from father to son."

"You seem very well versed in these traditions," Julie commented.

"Do I? Well, even the young children know the stories from the Vedas. At holidays and celebrations there are often plays acting out part of the scriptures. And the men of a family learn to recite the Vedic verses."

"Not the women?" asked Julie.

"That's the privilege of the men," replied the maharani. "The woman's responsibility is to preserve the family dharma—the path of righteousness—that allows the entire family to flourish."

"How does she do that?" Julie questioned.

"Through the purity of her own life," replied the older woman. "Through her own spiritual enlightenment. Because she is the mother, the strength of all the others grows out of her own strength.

"Priya tells me that her European school friends thought that women in India were— what did they call it—"second-class citizens." In some ways, of course, I guess we are. Yet the most important responsibility— the well-being of the entire society—is entrusted to us. But tell me, did you have a nice talk with Priya?"

Julie hesitated, remembering how the girl had rushed from the room in tears over her engagement.

"I enjoyed talking with her," she said after a pause. She wished she could discuss the young princess's engagement—maybe encourage the maharani to intervene on her daughter's behalf. But she did not feel that she knew Priya or her mother well enough to make any suggestion. However, the maharani brought up the subject herself.

"Did Priya tell you she is engaged to be

married soon?'' asked the older woman, her eyes bright with happiness. "Jai has arranged it all. The young man comes from one of India's best families. I am told he is suitable in every way."

"Is Priya happy with her brother's choice?" Journalism taught one how to ask a leading question, Julie reflected.

The maharani's face became grave. "She should be the happiest girl in the world. Prakash Das is a lucky—what is the English word...ah, yes—catch, even for a girl of Priya's standing. His ancestors are famous in Indian history. He is well educated and respected, and I understand he is handsome, also."

"Has Priya met him?"

"No, but that's not unusual. His family doesn't live in Delhi, so there is no reason the children's paths would have crossed. Jai has done well with this, and yet Priya is furious with him. Jai says she is too much influenced by Western ways. In fact, I guess I can tell you now since it has all worked out all right—" the maharani broke off smiling at Julie. "I was a bit worried when I got Wes's cable and realized you were a woman reporter. I was afraid Jai might think, well, that Priya might...."

"Be influenced by me?" Julie suggested. So that was another reason the maharani had seemed apprehensive when they first met.

"Yes, but Jai does not mind, which was what worried me," the maharani said. "Of course I knew the minute I met you that you were just right to be a friend to Priya. You are a very warm person, Julie. We are lucky to have you as part of our household."

"Thank you." Julie was touched by the older woman's sincerity. However, she thought Jai minded a lot. *Not only does he think I'm a nosy reporter but also a bad influence on his little sister,* she mused.

"Anyway, Jai could certainly not blame you for the way Priya is behaving, because her attitude changed before you even got here," the maharani finished. She picked up a silver bell from the table beside her chair and rang it. A servant appeared, the same one Julie had seen yesterday.

"Some ice tea, please, Ram."

"You say Priya's attitude has changed," Julie persisted. The young princess's problem interested her. "Then she didn't always mind this engagement?"

"Well, her engagement was only finalized a few days ago," replied the older woman. "But Priya was looking forward to being engaged for ever so long. She has been begging Jai to arrange it for her these last two years. But he wouldn't do it. He said she was still too young.

"When he told her about it a few days ago, I thought she would be overcome with joy. At last she had got what she wanted—and such a good match, too. But she turned white in the face and said she didn't want to marry now. Then she cried and said she refused...oh, well. There is no point in describing Priya's tantrum. Only, it was so unlike her—she has always loved her brother and done anything she could to win a word of praise from him. And this odd behavior has not passed, as I thought it would. She is still upset...."

"Maybe it is just that Priya does not like her brother's choice, then," Julie commented. Her sympathies were with the young princess. As far as Julie was concerned, no girl should be forced to marry if she did not wish to. Jai's lack of regard for Priya's feelings in this matter did not surprise Julie. It just proved what she had already discovered for herself: that he was autocratic, unfeeling and egotistical.

"Oh, no. It can't be that," the maharani was saying in her gentle way. "I keep telling you, Julie, it is an excellent match!"

Julie hesitated. "Well, maybe Priya has... someone else she cares for, then."

The maharani looked surprised. She sat straight in her chair and cocked her head to one side as though considering Julie's words. The American woman wondered if she had breached etiquette by even suggesting such a thing. However, the older woman's voice was pleasant and sincere when she replied. "But

Priya has never shown the least bit of preference for any of the boys she knew growing up. And, of course, her school in Switzerland was not coed, so it couldn't be anyone she met there.'' She gave a little laugh. "But I daresay it will straighten itself out. Young people—especially girls—tend to be emotional and moody sometimes. Maybe she is just a little nervous at the thought of marriage. But she will realize there is no need for that—her husband will most surely be pleased with her.''

As Priya entered the yellow salon just then, the conversation ended. All smiles, the young princess seemed to have forgotten the woes of her engagement for the moment.

"Sorry I'm late,'' murmured the beautiful girl. "But now we can go. Julie liked the silk in my sari this morning, mother. I thought maybe we should go to Sari Paradise first. They always carry a large selection of shot silk.''

The shop Priya named was located on Ring Marg, the wide road that encircles the entire city of New Delhi. When Gunam Singh pulled up to the store's front door, the shop's proprietor himself came out to greet the maharani.

Inside, the shop turned out to be a large rectangular room with floor-to-ceiling shelves. Stacks of folded saris filled the shelves in colorful array. Julie soon learned that these were arranged by silk type and weight—chiffon, shot silk, silk satin, jacquard border prints, raw silk and even rare hand-painted or hand-embroidered ones.

The proprietor and several salesmen rushed back and forth pulling folded saris from the high shelves in response to the two Indian women's rapid instructions. In a few minutes the area around Julie was covered with yards and yards of bright silk. Julie began to see that even though the costume was always wrapped in the same fashion, choosing a becoming color and silk took as much skill as shopping for Western clothes. The endless variety of shades and patterns amazed her.

In the end she picked three: an orange chiffon with threads of gold running through it, a border print in peacock blue and a pale yellow Kashmiri silk. Priya made her a gift of a sari of shot silk, the spring green and soft pink threads shimmering with every step Julie took. The maharani added her own gift: one of sky blue elaborately embroidered with silver threads.

The proprietor called the shop's tailor to take Julie's measurements for the tight-fitting *choli* blouse and floor-length slip to be worn beneath the sari. Then, the women were served complimentary drinks while their purchases were packaged. Somehow Priya had managed to pick out several saris for herself, as well.

"Gunam Singh will return here tomorrow for your slips and *cholis*, Julie," the maharani told her.

"Will they be ready that quickly?"

"No problem, madam. No problem," the shopkeeper assured her in heavily accented English.

As they left the shop the sunlight seemed brighter than ever to Julie after the store's dim interior. She wondered if she would ever get used to New Delhi's dry heat—it always felt like a furnace blast in the face when she stepped outside. The three women hurried into the cool limousine. They did not notice the dark car that pulled out behind them as Gunam Singh steered the Mercedes away from the curb.

CHAPTER FIVE

THE ASHOKA HOTEL was a gigantic building made of beautiful pink stone. Named for an ancient Indian emperor, it boasted over one thousand guest rooms. A favorite haunt of foreign diplomats because it was near the embassies, the hotel provided Western tourists and businessmen with all the comforts of home as well as the finest Indian food and service.

The maître d'hôtel escorted the women to a table by the windows. As she picked up the menu, a movement across the large dining room caught Julie's attention. A tall man in a business suit pushed open the double doors to the restaurant. He radiated charisma—as he entered the room he became the center of attention. Julie heard conversations stop, then slowly resume. She felt her own interest stimulated by the man's enticing self-contained power.

The headwaiter hurried to greet him, bowing low. The man said something and the maître d', all smiles, turned and gestured at the maharani's table. As the newcomer strode toward them, lithe and self-confident, the portly headwaiter scurried in his wake. He was halfway across the wide room before Julie recognized him.

"Why, Jai," exclaimed his mother, "what a delightful surprise! I had no idea you would be free to join us in the middle of the day like this or I would have invited you."

"Well, I presumed upon your hospitality, mother," he said, smiling. He bent to kiss the maharani's cheek, then seated himself between his mother and Julie. "Actually, I overheard Priya arranging this little luncheon. I felt sure her failure to include me was a mere oversight." He smiled across the table at his sister. His voice was teasing and, Julie felt, conciliatory.

Priya, whose face had suffused with involuntary pleasure on first seeing her brother, now feigned cold disinterest. But her eyes sparkled with both anger and curiosity, leading Julie to suppose that for Jai to join his family like this was considered a rare and unusual event.

"Was your shopping trip a success?" Jai enquired. He gave no sign of resenting Priya's obvious lack of welcome. Julie was glad he did not take Priya to task for her rude behavior—the young princess looked frustrated and on the verge of tears. Julie found herself wondering if perhaps Jai were not more sympathetic to his sister's feelings than he let on.

"We had a wonderful morning," the maharani was exclaiming. "We helped Julie pick out her first saris."

Jai turned to her. "You'll be lucky if you get any work done here at all," he said, smiling. "My mother and sister will first have to be convinced that you aren't a new doll for them to dress up." His bland tone indicated that the discord of their previous encounters was forgotten for the time being. Julie felt a sudden relief at the temporary truce. Battling wits with the prince was nerve-racking—it was too easy to come out second best.

"That is not fair, Jai!" his mother protested, tapping his hand with the folded sandalwood fan she carried. "Besides, Julie looks absolutely gorgeous in everything we got her."

Again he turned to Julie. Face to face with Jai in this relaxed setting, Julie found herself magnetized by him. The prince's tan, his high cheekbones and aristocratic features, the glorious waves of black hair, his strong white teeth when he smiled—his eyes, dark and alive with intelligence and secret humor.... Julie felt her body stirring in reply to his nearness, as an unsounded chord awaits the musician's touch.

Half-smiling, he reached over and removed the menu from Julie's hands. The sleeve of his perfectly tailored suit brushed her bare forearm. A cool shiver of delight swirled at the base of her spine and floated upward.

"I agree with you, mother, that choosing something for someone as beautiful as Miss Connell must be very satisfying. I should enjoy that pleasure myself. . . . If you will allow me, Julie, I will order for you. You may not be familiar with Indian cuisine yet."

He ordered for them all, beginning with expensive, flavorful *basmati* rice. *Toor dal*, made with split lentils and turmeric powder, combined with the rice for the main protein source of vegetarian Indian cookery. Cool, refreshing cucumber *raita*—thin-sliced cucumbers in spiced yogurt—provided a tempting side dish.

The waiters returned soon carrying large, circular stainless-steel trays. Shallow silver-dollar-shaped indentations around the edge of the tray were filled with rice, *dal*, and *raita*, as well as *matar panir*—a delicious blend of peas and fresh cheese—and date chutney. The center of the tray was piled high with *puris*—deep-fried bread puffed out to form a delicate thin-skinned treat. Reaching over, Jai covered Julie's slender hand with his own.

"Here, Julie, I will show you how to eat Indian food so as not to lose any of the flavor. After you have had food without the taste of metal in your mouth, you will wonder why anyone ever bothered to invent forks."

Guiding her motions, he instructed Julie to tear off a piece of fried *puri*. That he stuck boldly into the well of *matar panir*. Scooping out a bite of food, he forced Julie's awkward fingers to fold the *puri* around the thick pea blend. Her hand seemed swallowed up by his much larger one. She felt his long fingers resting on the back of her own. She struggled to fold the *puri*, which must be done with one hand. The tingling, burning awareness of his touch increased the difficulty of her task a thousandfold.

"Now, the rewards of your labor." Jai guided the morsel to her mouth. As Julie opened her lips to receive the delicacy, her eyes met his over their hands. His dark laughing eyes belied his solicitous attitude: he knew very well the turmoil his touch inflamed in her. He bent forward in a casual gesture that allowed his free hand to brush the thick blond curls spilling over her shoulders. Julie quivered as though her hair were composed of nerve endings. She met his look with a new awareness—sensual and curious—shining in the depths of her ocean-blue eyes. He recognized it and smiled.

The maharani and even Priya were laughing.

"Really, Jai, I think Julie could eat better by herself!" his sister exclaimed.

"Better, but not as well, dear sister."

"At least you did not get her fingers

sticky," his mother pointed out. "In some parts of India, though, Julie, the people put their hands in the food, as well. The farther south one travels, the more the hand and even the arm goes into the food bowl."

"Has your family always lived in northern India?" Julie asked.

"As far as we know," Jai replied. "We think we are descended from the Aryans, the fair-skinned invaders who swept out of central Asia in about 1500 B.C. They drove the resident Indians—the dark-skinned Dravidians—down toward the southern end of India. The Aryans became the noblemen—the lords of the land."

"That was over three thousand years ago!" Julie declared.

"The Aryans were latecomers really," Jai replied with a laugh. "Have you heard of Mohenjo-daro?"

"The ruins of a very advanced civilization they found a few years ago?"

"Yes. That civilization flourished here in the Indus Valley—Pakistan now—as long ago as 2500 B.C. The ruins show that the quality of life in those cities was higher than many Indians enjoy today."

"It's such an old country! I almost can't conceive of it. We Americans were proud to celebrate our bicentennial!"

"Well, the India we know is not many years old. She has thousands of years of a long and bloody history. There were constant invasions from Asia—Alexander the Great, the Scythians, the Huns, the Arabians, Persians and Afghans. Various religious groups battled for dominion. Power fluctuated between Hindu, Muslim and Buddhists. The best rulers, of course, showed tolerance toward other religions, but many tried to impose their own beliefs on the whole population.

"Then, toward the end, the East India Company gained control until it became so corrupt that the British Parliament took over and Queen Victoria became Empress. And now, after less than forty years of independence from Britain, the Indian state watches Russia's invasion of Afghanistan with a wary eye. What a temptation it must be to the Soviets to push on through Pakistan—a very weak fence—and convert fifteen percent of the world's population to the doctrines of the Communist Party at a single stroke."

"What are the chances of that happening?" Julie asked.

"Invasion isn't such a remote possibility to us as it is to you, Julie. It's been happening here for centuries. Whether it happens again will depend partially on the effectiveness of the terrorist groups you are so eager to find. If they can succeed in destabilizing the country—interfering with industry so more people are out of work, making the government look ineffective and bungling, creating so much trouble that the national leaders are forced to adopt harsh, repressive policies and make the innocent suffer along with the guilty. . . . The terrorists' goal is to undermine order so the Russians can step in 'to lend a hand' like they did in Afghanistan. The Soviets have invaded or absorbed at least fifteen foreign countries since World War II. Their doctrine is one of aggression.''

"Julie! How could you get Jai started talking politics,'' Priya complained. "It will ruin our whole lunch.''

"Really, dear, you can't expect him to discuss things of interest to us,'' interposed her mother. "If you had been married to a diplomat like your father as long as I was, you would have learned to listen to conversations like this by the hour. In fact, Prakash will be a likely candidate for government leadership some day, so you should learn to take a polite interest in these matters. Please continue, Jai.''

"Not on your life!'' replied Jai, laughing. "I didn't realize I was putting you to sleep.''

Unlike Priya and the maharani, politics fascinated Julie. Not only did she need a broader understanding of Indian history and government to put the terrorist story into proper perspective, but she realized she had been enjoying the interchange with Jai. His grasp of the situation impressed her—a wealthy playboy need not be so well informed. She respected him for his involvement in his country's future. And, she thought, when she was admiring his fine intellect, it kept her from dwelling on the nearness of his lithe, powerful body.

At the maharani's ill-timed mention of Priya's fiancé, the princess's face had grown white with frustration and anger. To forestall an outburst, Julie asked, "But were your family really princes for all that time, Jai? How did they survive?"

He smiled at her, aware of her attempt to divert attention from Priya's glowering countenance. "Our ancestors showed a degree of adaptability bordering on fickleness," Jai replied, wrapping a piece of *puri* around a morsel of rice as he spoke. "The princely states in India have existed in one form or another time out of mind, until India became a nation in 1947," he explained. "My ancestors, though predominately Hindu, didn't hesitate to become devout converts to a wide variety of religions over the centuries, when such an action could ensure their continuation as a ruling dynasty. Also, they adopted a general policy of leniency toward those of other religions under them. By keeping their constituency well fed and unoppressed, they always had a strong well-trained army to pit against any encroaching warlords. More than once they accepted wives from conquering peoples, gaining immunity through assimilation. My great-great-grandfather, for example, wooed and won an English noblewoman for his wife.''

If he was anything like you, Julie thought, *the poor woman didn't stand a chance.* She watched his expression, touched by the hand of insight and memory of his forefathers, fluctuate with fleeting emotion.

"In fact we got on well with the English. The princes who accepted Britain's 'benevolent protection' were allowed to keep sovereignty over their lands and people. Britain controlled the foreign affairs of the princely states, as they were called, but the states were not British territory and the inhabitants were not subjects of the Crown. So things went on as before. Generally, the people in the princely states were less influenced by Western civilization than those in British India.

"What to do about the princely states when India declared independence from Britain was a major issue. In the end it seemed that only a united India would survive. Most of the princes, my father included, could see that the future of the people lay in democracy, not monarchy. So the new nation bought the states from their hereditary rulers. My father moved his family to the palace in New Delhi and became a diplomat for the new government.''

"Do you ever regret the . . . change?" Julie

asked. It was a long glorious past to leave behind.

"I never regret progress," Jai replied. He pushed his napkin aside, meeting Julie's eyes with a level gaze. The wry smile she was beginning to recognize twisted the corners of his lips. "After all, my family has survived this long by sticking with tradition when they could and moving with the times when they had to. Are you finished with your meal, mother?"

"Yes, Jai, and I'm so glad you could join us."

"What do you plan to do the rest of the day?" The prince listened with at least assumed interest as the maharani described a visit to a shawl factory she had in mind and a proposal she wanted to put to the head gardener about building a lotus pond. Over dishes of caramelized Indian ice cream Jai tried to draw his sister into the conversation. But Priya maintained an ominous silence to the end of the meal.

"Come with us to the book shop in the lobby, Jai," the maharani suggested, as they rose from the table. "I want to get your opinion of a new translation of the *Ramayana* I thought Julie might enjoy."

Jai helped Julie with her chair. She fought an urge to sway back against his chest as he stood behind her, to brush against him as if by accident. Really, he's like a magnet, she thought. How was she going to be able to work around a man who held such an unnerving attraction for her? *Keep your mind on your work, that's how,* she mentally reassured herself. She was too much a professional to lose her objectivity on a story by getting involved personally with a source. She ignored the light ripples of sensation flowing through her arm when Jai's hand rested on her elbow as he guided her from the dining room.

In the bookstore Jai and his mother conferred in Hindi about the merits of the latest English version of the Indian epic poem, while Julie and Priya browsed through the periodicals nearby.

"Have you ever been to Hollywood?" Priya asked, picking up a slick-covered movie magazine with a picture of Clint Eastwood on the front.

"I lived there for several years," Julie replied. "In Los Angeles, which is the same thing."

"Really! Were you ever in a movie?"

Julie laughed. "No. But my boyfriend— my fiancé—was in lots of them. He did the stunts that were too dangerous for the stars or that took special training." She was aware of Jai's head turning toward them.

"Your fiancé? You were engaged!" Priya exclaimed. "Why aren't you married?"

"Well, I...you see...." Julie paused.

Such hard words to say. Her face contorted with old pain.

Jai stepped over to them. "I find your manners lacking, Priya," he said, his voice cool. "Go wait in the car while mother makes her purchases."

"It's all right, Priya," Julie intervened. "He...my fiancé died before we could be married."

"I'm sorry, Julie," the girl whispered. "I didn't know."

"Of course not. How could you?" Julie smiled at Priya to reassure her. "It was quite a while ago. Please don't give it another thought." *I must learn to take my own advice,* she added silently. She looked up to find Jai watching her. In the depths of his eyes burned the tiger flame.

When they finished in the bookstore, Julie excused herself from accompanying the maharani to visit the shawl factory. She waved goodbye to Priya and her mother, then returned to the hotel lobby. Jai had already left to keep a business appointment.

Alone, Julie walked over to the concierge's desk and purchased the day's English editions of the *Indian Express*, *Hindu* and the *International Herald Tribune*. In the bookstore she had bought several local magazines plus the overseas copy of *Time*. Attracted by the clicking of a Teletype machine, she wandered down a shop-lined corridor until she found what she was seeking—a continuous news printout provided as a service by the Ashoka to its patrons.

Julie saw nothing of interest in the computer paper spilling out of the machine. She retraced her steps to the lobby, then settled into a deep armchair in a secluded alcove by the window to study the magazines and papers she carried. Her purpose was twofold. First, she needed to become familiar with the current Indian social and political climate to recognize something newsworthy when she saw it. Secondly, reading the local papers was a way to probe for any telling nuances or possible leads hidden in the daily news, the personal columns, financial sections or far down in the full text of some boring politician's speech.

An hour and a half later Julie rose, stretched and dumped her stack of papers and magazines in the nearest wastebasket. She hailed a taxi in front of the hotel. Her next step was to visit the embassies. She decided against the American Embassy today. Sometimes the smaller diplomatic missions—such as the Canadian and the Swiss embassies—had extra time on their hands and were inclined to be more helpful.

Bluish gray dusk hung on the horizon when Julie returned to the tiger-crowned gates of the Mishra mansion. She was relieved to find that the guards had apparently received orders to allow her admittance. Her spirits lifted as the taxi deposited her beside the entrance stairway. After a tedious afternoon of news gathering, the warm companionship and elegant hospitality promised by the brightly lighted arched windows was welcome. Julie realized, to her surprise, that she was looking forward to seeing the prince, as well as his mother and sister.

Jai was not at dinner that evening, however. Julie listened with half an ear and a pleasant smile to the maharani's recital of her afternoon activities and to Priya's repeatedly expressed desire to take Julie shopping again. Julie's own thoughts revolved around the almost insurmountable difficulties attached to gathering confidential information in a news-repressive society where she had no personal contacts among high-ranking insiders or responsible government sources. The embassy officials she had met today were friendly, even cooperative, but they had no information about the terrorist issue to offer her. India, they assured her, had no established terrorist organization. Why borrow trouble, they asked, by trying to find out if one was being formed. "You will know soon enough if one is organized," a senior official had told her.

The problem was that Julie was trying to get a story on something that had not happened yet. The incidents in England, France and Italy were news. What she was doing now was acting on a hunch—actually, Wes Harding's hunch. Her job was to be in the right place at the right time when a story did break, and to have all the background information needed to put the incident into perspective. A summit meeting of international terrorists would be an important story. The meeting would prove that such attacks around the world were not random but rather methodical steps in a concentrated assault against democratic rule. Understanding the true nature of the problem would help democracies deal with the terrorist threat.

Julie wished she could have seen Jai this evening. She had looked forward to discussing the problems involved in her story with him, even if he did not want to help. At least he understood the situation and was interested in it. Just unburdening herself to a knowledgeable listener would have been a relief.

"Does the prince often dine with you at night?" Julie asked, during a lull in the maharani's conversation.

"Sometimes," the older woman answered. "I think tonight he must have had his dinner brought to his office. He often works through the meal hours."

"I don't see why," Priya interjected, with a sullen pout. "We have enough money as it is."

"As you refused to speak to him at lunch," replied her mother calmly, "I cannot see what possible interest you could have in the matter, Priya."

Dinner came and went without Jai making an appearance. Afterward Julie sat in the yellow salon reading the evening papers. Each time she heard footsteps in the hall, her breath caught in her throat. It was always just a passing servant. At last she retired to her room, feeling strangely discouraged and let down.

The soothing luxury of Julie's bedroom engulfed her as she stepped across the threshold. She slipped out of her navy dress, hanging it in the wide closet along with her other clothing, which Sukundala had unpacked. In a few minutes Julie was soaking in the marble bathtub, twirling her fingers through the bubbles and luxuriating in the touch of smooth, fragrant bath oil against her skin. Stepping out, she took a thick towel from the heated rack and dried off, feeling two hundred percent better.

So what if Jai had not come to dinner when he knew she would be there. She had only wished to discuss her work anyway. Yet the thought of him—his intense seductiveness and lean powerful body—sent a heated current spiraling through her bath-warmed body. Her eye was drawn to the gold-laced mirror opposite the shell-shaped tub. The steam had fluffed her heavy hair around her face. Her slender body—curved with full ripe breasts, and long firm thighs—radiated a new, eager awareness. Her own blue eyes—deep and dark as the Mediterranean—stared back at her, bright points of light reflecting off the irises. What would Jai Mishra, international ladies' man, think if he could see her like this, she wondered. Would he think her beautiful?

Julie folded the towel over the rack, and made a face at the mirror.

"Journalism, Julie, think of journalism. A man who doesn't even join you for dinner is not overwhelmingly interested in your company, we can assume," she admonished herself, laughing at her own absurdity. She was sure Jai had not thought of her once after leaving the Ashoka, despite the teasing charm he displayed at lunch. No doubt he was just keeping in practice. While she, on the other hand, had thought of him several times since then. . . .

CHAPTER SIX

JULIE OPENED AND CLOSED three or four
drawers but could not locate where Sukundala had put her nightgown. It was a warm
night anyway, so she gave up looking for it.
Turning off the light, she paused to draw
open the heavy curtains. Starlight softened
the darkness outside; a glow over the distant
trees promised a moon later that night.
Stumbling in the dark, she made her way
back to the bed. She was asleep the moment
her head hit the scented pillow.

How long she slept she had no idea. When
she woke it was pitch-black in her bedroom,
except for where a wide splash of moonlight
stained the carpet silver over by the windows.
She wrapped her bare arms around her naked
body and lay still, enjoying the beauty of the
moment. She realized that the fact she was in
India would account for her awakening like
this, bright and fully refreshed, in the middle
of the night.

It is probably afternoon in New York, she
mused idly. Even as she was wondering how
long it would take to get used to the time

change, she realized she was not alone. She sat bolt upright in bed.

"Don't move," commanded a man's voice.

Julie sucked in her breath with a frightened gasp. A spurt of wild, pure fear shot through her veins. She shrank back against the deep pillows. Her heart felt like a heavy block of ice cracking apart inside her chest.

"Don't scream, either," added the bored, sardonic voice.

Julie gasped again, this time in anger.

"How dare you—" she began, furious at having betrayed her alarm.

"And also don't talk," the voice said with cold finality, which nonetheless contained the faint undertone of amusement.

"How dare you come into my bedroom!" Julie whispered, recognizing the voice as Jai's and trying to locate him in the darkness. "Get out of here at once!"

His tall form, a black shadow enveloped in lesser blackness, stepped away from the wall separating the bedroom from the sitting room. The one movement conveyed such a tangible threat that Julie huddled back in the center of the gigantic bed, unconsciously holding her breath. She wondered how long Jai had been standing there. He must have entered the bedroom through the sitting room, which had a door to the corridor. When he had opened the bedroom door, she must have woken.

"If you think..." she began, the words bursting out through tightly compressed lips.

"Be quiet!"

Jai glided smoothly across the large room, ignoring the area around the bed altogether. Julie realized that the prince was moving toward the French windows, avoiding the revealing patches of moonlight. He held something in one hand that looked like a walkie-talkie.

Watching him move lithely around the clusters of scattered furniture conjured up the image in Julie's mind of a tiger stalking its prey in the night jungle. Certainly the man before her appeared at home in the dark. More than ever before he seemed to her both dangerous and mysterious. All her anger suddenly forgotten, Julie was consumed by curiosity.

"What is it?" she whispered.

Instead of answering, Jai raised the box in his hand close by his lips and spoke into it in Hindi. His voice was cool and unexcited, as though he were giving precise instructions.

Her journalist's instincts fully alerted, Julie groped frantically around for a robe or covering of some kind. In an inspiration, she started to pull the sheet off the bed to wrap around herself.

"Don't do that," ordered the prince's voice from the dark. "The white can be seen from outside." He was standing at the edge of the windows. When he spoke the words were so low Julie could barely hear them.

"Damn it," she hissed, "I don't have any clothes on!"

"Your choice. But leave that sheet alone."

"But I want to see what is going on!" Julie pleaded, her voice as soft as his.

"Your choice."

Julie gave a quick glance at the deep darkness of the room. Even her sleep-accustomed eyes could make out only the faintest of outlines in the blackness surrounding the patches of bright moonlight on the floor. She slipped from beneath the protective covers and stood beside the bed, her bare feet sinking into the thick carpet.

Peering again toward Jai's shadow by the window, she was unable to distinguish whether or not he was even looking in her direction. This reassured her. She crossed the wide expanse of the room, heading toward the opposite end of the windows from where Jai stood. Imitating the prince's stealth, she set one foot in front of the other with the ancient prudence of a primitive huntress. She moved naked through the darkness, her senses now awakened to the exotic combination of fresh night air, moonlight and unbearable suspense.

"I see very well in the dark."

Jai's mocking, amused voice coming out of the night pinned Julie where she stood, poised for flight, right in the middle of the room. The fleeting image of a rabbit caught in the glare of oncoming headlights passed through her mind. She leaped for the cover of the curtains hanging beside the tall windows, damning his infuriating coolness and hunter's eyesight under her breath. She wrapped her lithe form in the heavy silk drapes, closing her ears to the prince's deep masculine chuckle.

When her breathing calmed down, she peeked around the edge of the curtain and looked out the windows. At first she could see nothing other than the fascinating beauty of broad, well-cared-for lawns bathed in sparkling moonlight. Then a movement in the shadows under one of the umbrella-shaped shade trees caught her eye. She stared at the spot, unable to distinguish any distinct form.

"What is it?" she whispered to the man across the room from her. "Under that tree...."

The prince did not answer. Instead he spoke barely audibly into the two-way radio right next to his lips. Julie shuddered as she watched, aware of the deadly, purposeful vitality radiating from this intense man. Again he reminded her of a hunting tiger, his calculating calmness contrasting so greatly with her own thudding heart. She longed to know exactly what it was she was witnessing.

Her eyes turned back to the lawn below just

as a tiny beam of light flashed up at her. She stared at it, puzzled. Then sudden illumination burst in her brain. The spark of brightness was a ray of moonlight reflecting off a metal barrel.

"Rifles! They have rifles!" her warning whisper cracked. She leaned forward to see better.

"Get back! They'll see you!"

Jai's sharp command came an instant too late. Julie saw a gun pointed directly at her. Just as a scream was forming in her dry throat, the barrel lowered again as though it had been pushed aside by some unseen hand. The next moment three dark figures were running across the wide lawn without even bothering to avoid the moonlit areas, desperately straining to reach the distant wall that enclosed the estate. The intruders must have decided nothing could be gained from shooting, now that the essential element of surprise was lost. Instead they ran to save themselves.

The prince spoke rapidly into his radio and in a moment rustling sounds of pursuit filtered up to Julie though the open windows, contrasting with the peacefulness of the soft night air. A minute later all was still below. Only the rich fragrance from the flowering tree outside wafted toward the tense figures of the two people within the bedroom.

While Jai replied to a squeaky voice coming over the walkie-talkie, Julie reached for her kimono-style bathrobe, which she had just spied lying neatly folded across the back of a nearby chair. The maid must have put it there when she had come in earlier that evening to open the windows. Julie breathed a sigh of relief as she slipped into the wide folds of the lovely aqua silk, beautifully embroidered in silver with a dragon motif. She turned back toward the prince just as he finished issuing his orders.

"I'm sorry," she stammered. "I think I scared them away."

He regarded her coldly without saying anything. Abruptly he turned away.

"I really am sorry!" Julie repeated. She took a self-conscious step toward Jai, holding out her hand. He stopped, and turned back.

"I wonder."

"What do you mean? Of course I'm sorry. Obviously you were planning to catch them and probably would have if they hadn't seen me."

"We may catch them anyway," he answered. "I'll know in a minute or two. My guards are Punjabis." Julie knew from her background reading that the large powerful men from the northern province of Punjab were considered great warriors.

"Do you have any idea who they were?" she asked.

"What does it matter?" he growled.

"Don't let a little detail like that interfere with a good story. The reporters I have come across have had more fertile imaginations. Why not improvise?"

"I think you're the one jumping to conclusions," she replied. "Who knows, perhaps those people had a valid reason for being here tonight, although I admit it is unlikely. I don't write about something until I know the facts. India has so many poor people. Maybe they only wanted food. It's possible they didn't even mean any harm."

"With rifles?" he said sarcastically.

She recalled the fear she had experienced when the rifle barrel had pointed at her, looming up out of the darkness below as though it was much closer.

"Well, in any case, it's not my story. I'm only here to report about terrorists."

"Don't be a fool! Who do you think those thugs were? Housebreakers don't go about their business armed with rifles," he answered in mounting irritation. "This was probably an attack on my family—maybe a kidnapping attempt. Or perhaps they just intended to break into my offices here to get vital information."

"Do you mean to say you think those men might have been terrorists?" She stared at his face through the darkness. "Oh, why did I let them see me!"

"Exactly my question. Why?"

Something in the way he spoke raised the hair on the back of her neck. The crackle of the radio cut across the charged air between them. The prince listened a minute, spoke and then signed off. He regarded Julie silently.

"Well," she ventured. "What happened?"

"They got away."

"Oh."

"Some homemade explosive devices and a Kalashnikov rifle were found abandoned under the trees. Naturally," he continued after another long moment of silence, "had we caught them, we might have been able to discover who they were, or what they wanted, and maybe even who sent them. If they hadn't been warned away...."

"Warned away!" she gasped. "Are you out of your mind?"

"Then tell me this. Why were their preparations taking place where they could only be observed from your room?"

"But this is a guest room, isn't it?" Julie countered. "If they knew anything about the floor plan of your home, they probably expected this room to be empty."

"I am not totally naive, Julie," he replied, leaning casually against the wall, his eyes raking over her. "It's the oldest trick in the world to send a beautiful woman to infiltrate the enemy's fortress."

"I am here as a foreign correspondent,

nothing else!'' she snapped. ''I don't like being called a spy! And furthermore, I wish you would stop thinking of me as a woman and start thinking of me as a journalist!''

''Let me tell you something, my little shrew. The only reason you are here at this moment is that you are a woman. I would have thrown any other reporter out instantly.''

Julie clenched the silk bathrobe closer around her trembling body. The increased huskiness of his voice stirred her own attraction to him. Suddenly she was aware of the two of them alone together, of the intoxicating moonlight, of his irresistible allurement, of her own nakedness beneath the robe. Somewhere, deep in her consciousness, she admitted her vulnerability. His raw masculine vitality thrilled and excited her.

''Tell me about the terrorists,'' she said, ignoring her confusing emotions. ''That is what I was sent here to report about.''

''But tonight you interfered with what happened,'' he replied pointedly, ''instead of just reporting it.''

''I made a mistake. I said I was sorry. Why must you always distrust everyone and everything!''

''Indian princes live longer when they distrust the motives of those around them.'' His voice was harsh. ''This isn't America, Julie. This is India. We play the game of life by an entirely different set of rules here.''

"I don't like your rules!"

"Then the terrorists shouldn't have sent you to do their dirty work for them," he answered. "But since they did, I intend to see that you get on with it." He walked toward her, his dark eyes gleaming out of the blackness, burning into her.

"You are wrong. I have nothing to do with the terrorists. Please get out of here." She took a step backward. "I'm here on business, Jai. This isn't the time or place for anything else."

"Do you really think there could be a better, more romantic time and place?" he murmured, drawing close to her.

Somehow his words were so true that Julie did not try to argue. She found him quite simply the most attractive man she had ever met. He reached out to her and she yielded to his touch as if it was the natural thing to do. His hands slid down her back, pulling her against his chest. A terrible, enervating pleasure invaded her traitorous body.

"Jai, please! Let me go!" she whispered.

His mouth closed off her protests, settling possessively on her soft lips, crushing them beneath his. As his lips burned into hers, all thoughts of protesting ceased. His kisses became a slow pleasure for her, intense and sweet. Julie felt a sharp pain in her chest, like the snapping of a band of restraint. Her mouth began a tentative exploration of his.

Ever so slowly, as if with a will of their own, her arms reached up to encircle his dark head, pulling him closer. Shuddering with a strange ecstasy, she pressed against him, hating the clothing that divided them.

His rough hands caressed the bare skin of her back where he had pushed aside her robe. With a sharp jerk he pulled the robe down off her shoulders to her waist. The same nakedness that had inhibited Julie a few minutes earlier was now an intense relief. She felt no shyness under his admiring gaze. Only a tremendous eagerness, a desire to give of herself to him. . . .

Jai reached up and touched her breast with a caress so gentle it seemed strangely out of character for him. He cupped the ripe fullness in his hand, one fingertip seeking out the erect nipple.

"So smooth, so soft. . ." he whispered, his breath rasping. "So white. That was what they saw from the ground," he murmured into the throbbing pulse of her neck, "the whiteness of your skin."

Even as she distinguished the muffled words, she felt him stiffen in her grasp. He held her an instant longer, but coldly, as though the fervor of a second earlier had changed to ice. Only his ragged breathing revealed the passion that had gripped him a moment before.

"I did not fully realize just what clever

enemies I have," Jai said without emotion, his harsh voice grating on the night air. "Tell them that I never make the same mistake twice."

He stepped back from her. Deprived of the strength of his body, Julie swayed unsteadily. His powerful hands gripped her shoulders; she sank beneath them, until she dropped to her knees.

"And tell them, my beautiful, experienced courtesan," he said with cool indifference, "that you are not safe here. Tell them that I will destroy you if you get in my way, just as I've always destroyed anything that threatened me or mine. Even your deceptive fragility won't deter me—your heart must be made of granite by now."

Then he was gone, disappearing into the night as silently as he had emerged from it.

JULIE WOKE THE NEXT MORNING hoping last night was all a bad dream. It did not seem possible that the terrorists had been so close to her and that she had inadvertently interfered with their capture. In the months she had been working on this story, she had developed a slow, burning revulsion for any human being who perpetrated terrorism in the world. To think that a few such people— people who laid merciless waste to human life, human potential—were still at large because of her carelessness made her sick.

Julie paced back and forth across her room, glaring at the telephone now and then in an agony of impatience. She had placed a call to the *Courier* after the prince had left her room the night before. She knew it could take anywhere from two to twelve hours to get an overseas line. She wanted to file her story of the previous night's incident with the foreign desk as soon as possible. Then she intended to talk to Jai.

The prince's accusation that she was in league with the terrorists rankled worse than anything else about the whole affair. It was vital to convince him that he was wrong. Not only would he not help her if he believed she was affiliated with the terrorists, but also she could not stand to have anyone—especially him—think such a thing of her.

At first Julie had been furious at Jai's accusation that she was an accomplice to the terrorists. But now she realized that, to a suspicious mind, her inadvertent lack of caution had warned the terrorists away. She had appeared in an incriminating light and she had to set matters right with Jai at once.

As to what happened afterward.... Julie paused in midstride. She smoothed her white linen skirt with a well-manicured hand. That man had an almost hypnotic effect on her—an attraction so great that she gravitated to his arms like a hummingbird to nectar. Yet she was not sure she even liked him....

The shrill buzz of the phone interrupted her thoughts. Picking it up, she verified her connection with the foreign desk and began to dictate. She had to shout at the top of her lungs to make sure she was heard over static.

"Terrorists attempted an attack against a well-known industrialist and conservative political leader at his home in New Delhi early this morning. Private guards of Prince Jaiapradesh Mishra, whose family ruled a princely state in northern India prior to national independence in 1947, surprised three trespassers on the vast lawns outside the prince's home. Several homemade explosives and a rifle of Soviet manufacture were found abandoned after the intruders fled from guards.

"India has no cohesive terrorist organization at this time, but the assault had all the earmarks of professional terrorist incidents seen elsewhere in the recent flare-up of terrorism worldwide...."

When Julie finished dictating the story, her boss came on the line.

"Julie!" he shouted. She could barely distinguish his words.

"Yes!"

"Contact the stringer in Bombay. I want him to know where to reach you. He has another lead."

"Will do!" she shouted back. The connection broke off before she had a chance to ask for details. She sat still for a moment, phone in hand, staring out the window with unseeing eyes. It had been great to hear Wes Harding's raspy voice for a moment—it brought back the reality of the newsroom and strengthened her own sense of responsibility. She was a professional with an important story to get. She was *not* a light-headed girl waiting to be swept off her feet by a handsome prince!

She depressed the receiver button on the phone and placed a call to Bombay. She had meant to call the stringer yesterday, but her visits to the embassies had taken longer than she had planned. When she finally got through to the paper's stringer, Anand Naoroji, he sounded almost as far away as Harding had.

Anand told her that a group of unemployed youths from Bombay had been recruited to attend a multinational terrorist-training camp in Algeria. They were going for a four-week course. He did not know whether or not they had left yet, or who recruited them. When Julie asked how he got the information, Anand laughed.

"Not from any source who would be familiar to your readers. Now, Julie, you must try to come to Bombay while you are here," he told her, before ringing off. "My wife and I want you to be our guest."

"Thank you. I'll try!" she promised.

Anand's information was not anything she could use, since she had no source to whom she could attribute it. But it lifted her spirits, giving her hope that she was indeed on the right track. Terrorists meeting in India would try to organize a local terrorist organization before they left for their own countries. It was not necessary that the different national terrorist groups have a common ideology. Their immediate purpose was to dismantle whatever society they were in. Yet in all the ideological publications by terrorist organizations Julie had read researching her story, she had never found a clear definition of the kind of society the terrorists hoped to create to replace the ones they intended to destroy.

She slipped on the white suit jacket that matched her skirt over her sheer cotton blouse, and bent down to buckle on her favorite white high-heeled sandals. She mused over Anand's news as she brushed out her thick hair and forced the glorious waves into a smooth chic knot.

She had heard about such training camps. Her research indicated that thousands of terrorists were being trained in camps in Cuba and other countries under the influence of the Soviet Union. There the recruits studied Brazilian terrorist Carlos Marighella's *Mini-manual for Urban Guerrillas*—forty-eight densely packed pages that comprised the standard terrorist textbook. KGB officers taught them all they needed to know about coded documents, fake passports, making their own explosives and so forth. Any lingering feeling of kinship and tenderness recruits might feel for the rest of the human race was permanently eliminated during those weeks of intensive preparation.

Julie shuddered. She dabbed an extra portion of L'Air du Temps on her wrists, forcing herself to think of other things. Suddenly she wanted to talk to Jai. She wanted to see him to be reassured that right still had might.

CHAPTER SEVEN

JAI'S OFFICE DOOR STOOD OPEN. Julie hesitated in the doorway. Priya was standing with her back to Julie, facing Jai across the polished surface of his desk. Julie caught the princess's last words, which were spoken in English:

"...get to choose their own husbands now."

A silence greeted this remark. The girl fidgeted.

"You can't deny that you are unfair, Jai," she said after a moment. "I think—"

"You are not thinking at all lately, Priya," interrupted her brother. "I have never seen you employ your excellent mind less than you have this past month."

"You...you can't make me give up just by belittling me!" Priya declared, her voice strained by emotion.

"I am not belittling you. I'm suggesting you show some sense. Don't let yourself be manipulated by people who don't have your interests at heart."

"Do you mean Julie? She is my friend!" the girl exclaimed.

"Maybe. But do you think it wise to make friends with people you hardly know? Your position is such that someone might wish to cultivate your friendship for a specific purpose."

"Perhaps," replied Priya with dignity, "some...person...might want to be my friend for my own sake."

"Of course. But not everyone."

Priya burst into tears. "Oh, Jai, I hate you! You make everything seem so sordid! If you were in love...."

"Are you in love, Priya?" he asked, his voice suddenly sharp.

"I...I...I am *not* going to marry Prakash Das! Not for anything in the world!" She whirled away from the desk, tears streaming down her face, and rushed out of the room, ignoring Julie, if she saw her at all.

"Eavesdropping?"

"I came to speak with you." Julie entered the office and closed the door behind her. He studied her as she walked toward him. She sat down without being asked.

"Jai...." She leaned forward and put both hands on the edge of his desk. "I want to apologize for last night."

"But why should you? You were very good." He leaned back in his chair, his eyes on her face. The open neck of the loose cotton shirt he was wearing revealed the power-

ful muscles of his chest. "I found you very
enjoyable."

"Damn you!" Julie felt her face flush hot.
Only the fact she knew she had been in the
wrong the night before made her force herself
to continue. "You know I mean about letting
the terrorists see me. I'm sorry! Believe me, I
am not one of them. I want to see them
caught as much as you do. They disgust me!
If you could have seen that train station in
Rome—those slaughtered bodies....

"I have researched membership in each of
the major terrorist groups. Truly idealistic
people don't stay with those organizations—
they realize they have been duped. The ones
who remain are the ones who like to kill and
have discovered a certain flair for it. I want to
see terrorist leaders captured, and I want my
readers to understand how the terrorist network works."

He regarded her in silence. Julie waited.

"What you say may be true," he said at
last. "I prefer to believe it isn't."

She sat back and stared at him.

"Why?"

Jai toyed with a pencil on the desk. "Maybe I feel safer that way. I can't afford—" he
glanced up at her "—to take any chances."

"You can't just go around believing what
you want about people," she said in exas-
peration. "You are condemning me on one
shaky piece of misconstrued evidence."

"My ancestors used to behead people with less evidence than that," he replied with a laugh. He stretched, his muscles rippling beneath his shirt. Jai's black hair, firm jaw and straight-toothed smile made him look more like a hero of a spy movie than a businessman.

Julie smiled reluctantly. "Yes, I imagine they did. But you've already told me that you don't live in the past. Why are you so determined to dislike me?"

"Distrust, yes. Dislike, no."

Julie's hands were folded on top of her closed notebook on his desk. He reached across and picked up the left one. He turned it over and pressed his thumb into her palm, stroking her skin.

"Why distrust me then?" She glanced down at their joined hands, then back to his face. She had never known a man to be so adamant and at the same time so gentle.

He shrugged. "I don't think you could understand. I'm sure I was raised very differently from you. Weren't you taught to have faith in people and try to see the best in them?"

Julie nodded. Aunt Agnes had believed in the so-called Christian virtues.

"Well, I was taught just the opposite of that. To never put my trust in others, but only in myself. I was trained to assume the worst, to look for hidden motives. You look shocked—"

"I...I just can't picture your mother teaching you such things."

"Oh, no. She had little to do with my up-bringing. Fortunately she had Priya several years later so she got to raise one child at least. But my father raised me. He was a very shrewd man. Some of his friends told him that he should let go of the old ways of bringing up first sons. But he always maintained that being a prince in the twentieth century was even more difficult than in previous ones."

"What a horrible childhood." She longed to touch Jai's cheek.

He smiled. "As a matter of fact, it wasn't. I had a wonderful time. I learned to hunt up at our summer palace in Kashmir. I had—still do have—a stable of polo ponies and racehorses here in New Delhi that is the envy of every horseman in Asia. My father took me everywhere with him. He began teaching me about the businesses he started even as he was building them up. He didn't want an idle playboy for a son. He told me that he would personally shoot me if I threw my manhood away on frivolous pursuits." He laughed at her concerned expression. "He was a harsh man. But he loved me, you see, and I always knew it. This is what counts between father and son, nothing else. Besides, he was right."

"How do you mean?"

He released her hand. "People usually do have hidden motives. Not maybe in the everyday course of their lives. But they do when they are dealing with someone who has more than they do, who can give them something. There is always something they want, something they feel it will cost me very little to give to them. An introduction to an important man. A position in my company for their nephew. Investment capital for their new business, which cannot possibly fail. Advice. Information."

Julie riffled the pages of her notebook. "I never thought of it that way before."

Jai laughed. "Well, I'm not complaining. Wealth still has more advantages than poverty. But you do learn to question people's motives."

"And here I am, wanting your help with my research."

"In your case, I think it might be a pleasure."

She smiled. "But I don't mix business with pleasure. Professional ethics, you know."

"That wasn't the impression I got last night." He got up and came around the desk to stand behind her chair. He bent down and touched her throat and the line of her jaw with gentle kisses.

"Last night was a...mistake." Julie turned her face away from his, hoping that might distract her from the pleasure of his lips on her neck. Each kiss was like a piece of kindling added to a brush fire. "Besides, I think you still suspect me of being in league with the terrorists."

"Would you prefer I pretend otherwise? I will if you like." He pulled her chair back from the desk and drew Julie to her feet as he spoke.

"I would prefer that you get rid of that horrible, mistaken notion once and for all," she replied, keeping her voice even. She tried to step aside, but his hands on her shoulders held her still.

"Why do you turn away from me? Ah, yes. I remember. You like to choose the time and place for your lovemaking. Do your men— your lovers—always let you do as you please? No doubt a woman as beautiful as you gets used to having her own way."

She pulled back from him. "I don't understand you. One minute you are halfway decent, the next minute you try to hurt me." She studied the stern planes of his face, wishing she knew what he was really thinking.

Jai's eyes never left hers. "I don't understand myself just now," he replied. He tightened his grip on her shoulders and drew her forward against his chest.

His lips nuzzled her hair like a gentle breeze. She let her fingertips slide over the muscles of his arms, marveling at his strength. He was the most masculine, fascinating, alluring man she had ever met. When he touched her, all her willpower and level-headedness slipped away. It was easy to forget his accusations—to forget her responsibility to her story. Being held by him was like diving deep into a warm pool filled with exotic underwater flowers and fish and glorious, unbelievable beauty. . . .

Julie felt his large body tremble against hers. She realized she had lifted her face to his, like a lotus to the sun. She was kissing him. A shooting star of joy burst inside her when she understood she could affect him in the same way he affected her.

Jai slipped his hands lower down her back and eased her hips against his. Hungry longing welled up in Julie—a yearning more intense than she had ever experienced in her whole life. A small sharp cry escaped her parted lips.

He gathered her into his arms, covering her hair with kisses.

"I don't care about your other lovers," he told her. She listened to his heart pounding against her body, a distant echo of her own. "We will forget them. We will forget the terrorists. We will take this moment for ourselves—for our deep pleasure—and let the world be damned."

She knew she was just a plaything for him. She knew he doubted her motives, thinking she might be a spy. She knew she must maintain a professional relationship with him at all costs. But these were vague thoughts, dreamlike and unimportant. Not worthy of serious consideration.... She felt the last shreds of her restraint drifting away, like sand slipping between the fingers of an open hand....

"No!" Julie breathed, her voice muffled against his chest. The musky scent of his body filled her nostrils.

"The best way to get rid of a desire, Julie, is to satisfy it. Let us satisfy our desire for one another." Jai's voice was soft. Loving.

She said nothing. There was no possible reply. He took her hand and started toward an inner door leading off the office.

They heard the sound of footsteps approaching from down the hallway. Jai paused, still holding on to her with his strong fingers. He turned to face the office door.

"Jai, someone is coming! Let me go." She tried to pull away. He hesitated. Then with a shrug he loosened his grasp on her hand. Julie stepped back, her heart racing from the excitement he had aroused in her. One sandal hung loose on her foot. She knelt down and pulled it back on.

Some instinct made her pause in straightening her clothing and glance at Jai's face. He seemed to be struggling with some inner emotion; she saw a look of bleak despair in his dark eyes for an instant. Then he looked down and his face became hard and impersonal, a mask shutting her out.

"Look at me, Julie."

Jai's eyes captured hers. He forced her to read the truth in them. He had wanted her. He would still have her. Julie felt a shock of recognition pass through her. She knew, as clearly as if he had spoken, that she was nothing to this man. Nothing except a means to attack his enemies. A horrible agony penetrated her heart. What she had mistaken for tenderness had really been satisfaction at getting his own way so easily. He did not doubt her motives: he thought he understood them all too well.

The wrench back to reality left Julie shaken. She felt betrayed by her emotions. Alone. Still, she could not look away. Jai let her read his gaze. When he saw that she had understood, a faint smile of satisfaction touched his eyes. So complete was his mastery that neither of them looked up when the office door opened.

"Jai! Julie!" said the maharani's voice. "I have the most marvelous idea!"

Their eyes parted, as slowly as if they had indeed been lovers. Julie felt dazed. Trying to erase all emotion from her expression, she turned toward her hostess.

"What idea is that, mother?" Jai, casual and at ease, moved over to his desk. Julie thought her legs would give way beneath her.

"Why, a party, Jai! I'm going to give a ball. A wonderful celebration. It will be the talk of the town. Just like your father and I used to do."

"A party? Why?"

"Because of Julie, of course. It will be in her honor."

"She has no honor." He spoke the words softly enough so that only Julie could hear.

THE NEXT TWO WEEKS disappeared in an uproar of confusion. The maharani and Priya turned the palace upside down in preparation for the ball. They took full advantage of the opportunity to buy new things for both their home and themselves. Priya, especially, seemed on tenterhooks with excitement.

Julie stayed as far away from the palace as possible during the daytime. Her one purpose in life became work. She wanted to work so hard that she could not think—not about herself, or the coming ball or, most important of all, not about Jai.

She spent her time in an endless round of investigations. Her days began with reading everything in each newspaper and magazine printed in English she could get her hands on. She visited all the embassies, even the Soviet mission, cultivating acquaintances in them all. She pored over government documents and political speeches. Appointments with government officials, civil servants, businessmen, intellectuals, university faculty, dissidents and leaders of the current political party's opposition jammed her schedule book. She talked with innumerable taxi drivers, shopkeepers, even beggars.

Like all foreign correspondents, Julie looked up the members of her own profession—the AP and UPI representatives, as well as journalists from the major papers that could afford to keep a permanent correspondent in India. She got a feeling for the news climate in Delhi, without revealing the real topic of her own investigations. With the help of passersbys to translate, she even scanned the tattered red-and-black political posters and crudely printed messages pasted on walls and buildings throughout the city in hopes of finding some lead as to where and when the terrorist summit meeting might be held.

Arriving back at the palace late one night, Julie collapsed on the sofa in the yellow salon. She closed her eyes in utter exhaustion, pulling a cushion under her head with a weary gesture.

"How is your work going?"

Julie opened her eyes. The prince was standing over her.

"I didn't know you were in here." Even talking took tremendous effort.

"Obviously. Had you known, I'm sure you would not have entered."

"No, I wouldn't have." Julie sat up and pushed her heavy hair back from her face. "Can you blame me?"

Jai walked away and came back with a drink. He handed it to her.

"You look like you could use this."

She hesitated, then took the cold glass. "Thanks. I can."

He retrieved his own drink and sat down opposite her. Julie leaned back against the gold velvet cushions and sipped the mellow bourbon and water Jai handed her.

"How is your work going?"

"I'm not sure it is going anywhere just yet." She traced the rim of her glass with her finger.

"No leads?"

"Maybe one or two."

"Such as?"

She glanced up at him. "Are you really interested, or are you merely being a good host?"

"I wouldn't have asked if I wasn't interested," he replied, settling back in his chair. "What have you?"

Julie found herself telling him about her investigation. The Delhi police, though at first unhelpful, had warmed up to her after repeated visits. They told her of a raid that had taken place three weeks before, a few days before Julie's arrival in India, as part of a crackdown against a recent wave of passport forgeries. One of the confiscated documents was a fake visa for a known Arab terrorist. A visa was necessary for any foreigner who wished to remain in India for up to six months.

A second noteworthy incident concerned an Indian reporter Julie had met. Krishna Rai wrote for the *Indian Express*. Over midnight-black coffee in an American-style ice cream and pizza parlor named Narula's, he recounted cases when the Indian government had killed stories it did not wish to see in print. The anecdote he related to Julie was about a dishonest customs officer who had been bribed to sanction an illegal arms shipment of Russian-made rifles and explosives. The man had been apprehended the day before a delegation of high-level Soviet diplomats was to be welcomed to the capital city by the prime minister. The government stopped the story from going into the papers, feeling it would create an unpleasant atmosphere for the reception of the Soviets. In the meantime, the rifles were stolen from the customs warehouse and never recovered. All this had happened within the last month.

"It made me think of the Kalashnikov rifle your guards found abandoned under the trees that night," Julie said. She related one or two more small leads she had come across—nothing conclusive, but enough to convince her she was on to something. Several signs pointed to an attempt to organize a terrorist stronghold in northern India.

The prince was a good listener. Julie realized she was enjoying talking to him. It was a relief to discuss her work with someone, after long days and nights of turning ideas over and over in her own head with no one to sound them out on. Somehow speaking her thoughts out loud helped to clarify them.

"You work hard," Jai said when she was finished.

"That's my job—as I keep trying to convince you," she replied.

He smiled. "I believe my mother has invited half the city to your ball," he answered, changing the subject.

"My ball?"

"In your honor, you know."

"According to you, I have none."

He paused, drink halfway to his lips. "Do you accept apologies?"

"Do you make them?"

"Well, I owe you an apology for that one, at any rate," the prince replied, his voice level.

"Keep it. I don't want it." Julie stood up. "Thanks for the drink." She would have liked to get his opinion of her finds. But she was too tired tonight to face the onslaught of accusations that would no doubt ensue if she

pressed him for information. If only she
could control the attraction she felt for him,
even now, Julie might be able to work with
him. But as it was, the less she saw of him the
better.

He took her arm as she turned to go. "Are
we fighting again, Julie?" he asked. His
gentleness surprised her.

"I hope so," she replied, pulling away
from his grasp. Her skin tingled where he had
touched her. She walked toward the door,
aware of his dark eyes following her. As she
left the room, out of the corner of her eye she
saw his tall broad-shouldered form turn away
and walk over to stare out the windows. She
felt a lump form in her throat. Why did she
feel so much like crying?

JULIE FOUND HERSELF looking forward to the
maharani's ball. Perhaps she could get a lead
on her story from one of the influential guests
who would be present. Besides, maybe an
evening away from her work would lift her
spirits.

Priya came to Julie's room the morning of
the ball.

"Have you seen the room yet, Julie?"
asked the Indian girl. "You must see it!
Come on. I'll show you."

Priya led Julie to a part of the palace she
had never seen before.

"Close your eyes," the princess commanded, pausing beside an open doorway. She took Julie's hand and pulled her forward several yards. "Okay. Open them!"

Julie looked around. She was in a huge room, standing on a beautiful parquet floor polished to looking-glass brightness. Above her a high, vaulted ceiling, with ornate molding and exquisite hand-painted murals, reflected the light of a dozen enormous crystal chandeliers. Five-tiered fountains, surrounded by exquisite pools of floating carnations, gushed forth, lending the dry Indian air a delectable moistness. Garlands of orchids, roses and lilies festooned graceful pillars and wreathed the mirror-and-mahogany walls. Beyond open arches on one side of the room Julie could see long linen-draped tables laden with china, silver and an army of crystal goblets.

"Priya! It's a real ballroom!" Julie exclaimed.

"Yes," replied the princess with satisfaction. "Isn't it marvelous? My parents used it often. But we haven't had a ball since I've been grown up."

"Everything is so pefect," Julie sighed.

"Jai said everything must be of the best quality since the ball is in your honor," Priya told her, her lovely eyes wide and sparkling.

"He did? I can't believe it." Julie felt stunned until she realized he must have been being caustic. Priya was unsophisticated enough to miss sarcasm.

"Wait until all the guests are here," Priya was saying. Her anticipation enhanced her fresh beauty more than ever. "Then it will *really* be wonderful."

"I like it just like this—so big and empty," Julie replied. "It's almost a pity to fill it up with noise and people."

"What are you going to wear?" Priya asked. "I bought a new sari—it's white satin, covered all over with gold embroidery."

"I hadn't even thought about it. I've been so busy with my work these last weeks...." Julie's voice trailed off.

"You must wear a sari, Julie! You would look so beautiful in one."

"I guess I will have to," the American woman replied. "I didn't bring an evening dress with me. I had no idea I'd need it. I'll wear one of the ones we bought at Sari Paradise. Could you come up after dinner to help me get dressed?"

"Yes, I'd love—" the Indian girl broke off. "Well, that is...I may have to help my mother with the last-minute details." She glanced down at the floor, avoiding Julie's eyes. "Sukundala can help you, though! And...if I can I'll come, too."

Dinner was a simple affair served in the maharani's sitting room. Priya was too excited to eat and left before Julie and the maharani had finished. Julie excused herself soon afterward. She returned to her room, where Sukundala was waiting for her.

"Now, let's choose the one I should wear," called out Julie as she entered the bedroom. *And pray that it doesn't fall off me in the middle of a dance,* she added to herself.

"Madam, look!" Sukundala pointed to a package lying on Julie's bed. It was wrapped in gold foil with a large white bow. A lavender orchid was entwined in the ribbon.

"Where did that come from?" Julie asked. The box was too large for a corsage, and besides, she knew no one in New Delhi who might have sent it.

"I don't know, madam. It was here when I came in. Why don't you open it? Maybe there will be a card inside," suggested the maid.

There was no card inside. Instead Julie turned back the rice-paper-thin tissue to reveal a flash of jewellike color. She lifted out the hand-painted chiffon. Bursts of midnight blue and dark emerald, touched with the glittering light of a thousand tiny silver stars embroidered with metallic thread, cascaded across the pink bedspread like ripples of a tropical ocean reflecting the starry heavens above. It was, without a doubt, the most exquisite garment Julie had ever laid eyes on. Sukundala removed a matching *choli* and slip, and flat silver sandals in Julie's size, from the bottom of the box.

Putting on the sari was like entering an enchanted dream. In a trance, Julie stared at the mirror while Sukundala wrapped the thin fabric around her and folded in the front pleats with tender care. Julie put on her mother's tiny emerald earrings, glad that she had bothered to have them reset for pierced ears. A touch of Bal à Versailles on her wrists and throat completed her preparations.

Standing at the wide door to the ballroom half an hour later, Julie wished she had thought ahead and arranged to enter with the maharani or Priya. The enormous room, so spacious when she had last seen it, was now crowded with hundreds of gala partygoers. At that moment, however, the maharani spied her and beckoned with a ring-bedecked hand.

"Julie, dear! Come in, come in! Isn't it wonderful?" she exclaimed with simple pleasure. "So many nice people, too. I want you to meet them all."

Before long Julie had the immense satisfaction of finding herself the center of a group of admiring males. Her work as a journalist had taught her to converse easily with people whom she did not know. She laughed and chatted with the other guests and, occasionally, glanced around the ballroom.

When her eyes came to rest on a knot of people on the opposite side of the room, Julie glimpsed Jai's dark hair and flashing smile.

He stood half a head taller than any of the other men. His broad shoulders and lean strength did justice to his perfectly cut tuxedo in a way that made the businessmen and diplomats surrounding him appear flabby and dull. He excused himself and moved on to another group as Julie watched.

"Miss Connell?" Julie looked away from Jai to find a pleasant-faced man beside her. "I've been looking all over for you. May I have a dance with the guest of honor?"

"Certainly. I'd love to." She whirled away in the man's arms. It was an added bonus to discover that he was a fairly good dancer.

Her partner glanced down at her after a moment. "You're quite famous now, you know," he said with a smile.

"Am I?"

"Sure. Don't you read the papers? You're a reporter, aren't you? How does it feel to get some of your own medicine?"

Julie had seen the articles in the society pages the last few days about the coming ball to introduce Miss Julie Connell, houseguest of India's most prestigious nobility, to New Delhi society. She was glad the fact she was a foreign correspondent had been mentioned only once—obviously the columnists thought such base employment lowered the tone of their article and avoided emphasizing it. Julie preferred to keep her work as low profile as possible.

As Julie danced she kept an eye out for Priya. She had expected to see the princess, with her mother, receiving guests. As though on cue, Julie saw the Indian girl slip into the ballroom from a nearby side door. Priya's face was flushed and her lovely eyes bright with excitement. Julie thought she looked flustered. The princess paused for an instant to straighten her sari and smooth back her braided hair. She gave a quick, almost furtive glance about the room, then stepped forward to blend unobtrusively with the throng of partygoers.

Julie kept up a flow of banter, which her partner seemed to feel was obligatory, throughout the rest of the dance. But her mind kept reverting to Priya. The girl's behavior had struck Julie as odd. It seemed strange that Priya would have left the ballroom at all tonight, considering how much she had been looking forward to the party. And why had the princess been so evasive about helping Julie dress for the ball? If it had been any other young woman, Julie would have supposed she had a special assignation with her favorite boyfriend. But in Priya's case, such a conclusion was absurd.

"That was great, Julie!" exclaimed her partner as the dance ended. "Say, I hope I'll get to see you again while you're here."

"I'm sure you will," she replied. He seemed reluctant to relinquish his hold on

her, so she smiled at him and stepped back. A
movement next to her made her turn. She
looked up into a pair of dark smiling eyes.

"My dance, I believe," said the prince.

CHAPTER EIGHT

JAI PLACED JULIE'S HAND on his arm and led her back toward the crowded dance floor. She could feel the warmth of his body through his sleeve and tried to ignore the tingling in her fingers.

"You are frowning. Is the prospect of dancing with me really so distasteful?" Julie looked up at him, surprised by the genuine concern in his voice. "Come, Julie, we must bury our weapons for tonight," he added.

"Oh, really? Why? Have you suddenly changed your opinion of newspaperwomen?"

"I seldom change my opinions," he replied, unruffled. "But everything in India is guided by tradition, and tradition says that we must not fight with one another tonight."

"What tradition?" she asked, her interest aroused.

"One reason we have so many holidays in my country is because we believe that social events relieve any tensions that exist between people. We think differences get resolved in a natural way when everyone joins together in celebration. For us it is like getting a fresh

start on all our interpersonal relationships."
He smiled at her, warm and for once un-
guarded. "We should do our best to help this
theory, don't you agree?"

"Yes, I do," Julie replied seriously. "You
and I could certainly benefit by a fresh
start!" To talk with him as a woman to a man
tonight would be a welcome relief, instead of
having to constantly guard against letting any
personal feelings creep into what was supposed to be a professional relationship.

"For once we are in complete agreement,"
he said, laughter flashing in his dark eyes.

The orchestra struck up a Viennese waltz.
He slipped his arm around her waist and
pulled her to him. Julie was not prepared for
the shock of sensation that flooded through
her body. She hoped the music covered her
confusion.

"We came in here to dance, or had you forgotten?" he asked. His voice was low, the
teasing words spoken close to her ear.

"Do you always notice everything?" she
countered.

"When it concerns you."

Julie was so conscious of his body close to
hers that at first it was hard to concentrate on
the smooth, lilting rhythm of the music. After
a minute or two she relaxed, however, aware
of a new naturalness that removed the self-
conscious stiffness from her body. She
swayed in time to the slow music, feeling soft

and supple in the prince's arms. The orchestra and the crowded ballroom receded from her thoughts. Instead Julie found herself noticing small things, little details that somehow added up to just the right combination of pleasant sensations.

There was the scent of the prince as he held her close to him—a faint muskiness filled her nostrils and made her want to bury her head against his chest. The broadness of that chest became more and more inviting, until at last Julie allowed her head to tilt forward just enough to brush against it.

She felt a tiny shudder vibrate through Jai's lean form. He slipped his hand up from her waist long enough to press her head closer, as though to assure her that it pleased him to have her rest against him.

A marvelous sense of well-being swept over Julie. She liked dancing like this, her head against his chest. Jai guided her through the crowded ballroom with perfect ease. They moved across the floor, gliding and swirling with such elegant grace that the other dancers paused to watch. The gossamery silk hanging from Julie's shoulders floated in the air behind her. Life seemed to take on a richer meaning for Julie, fuller and more satisfying than the narrow work-oriented existence she had forced upon herself for so long. A new world opened up to her—one of light, and music, and romance.

The prince held her close, his tall, powerful body bent over her. Julie's fingertips rested on his shoulder. She marveled at the muscles she could distinguish beneath the fine cloth of his tuxedo. A peculiar warmth invaded her limbs. She developed an acute awareness of every place her body touched his.

The warmth inside her grew more noticeable. It distracted her. Her mind began to explore the warmth, tracing the palpitating sensations that coursed through her body. The tingling swelled within her, further awakening her senses. She felt a fountainhead of hot desire pulsating through her: a dull, hungry ache in her abdomen. The inside of her thighs felt on fire. Instinct made her sway closer to the prince, who instantly gathered her tighter.

"Good," he murmured, his warm breath moistening the top of her ear as he bent over her.

Julie began to dance as she had never danced before, letting her body become an extension of the slow romantic music. She kept her eyes closed, her face pressed against his chest. She did not want anything to intrude on the wonder that was filling her heart to overflowing. They swayed together to the rhythm, sometimes swirling, sometimes barely moving.

Could this really be the same person—the cold, cynical man whom she had disliked so much, Julie wondered. Dancing with him like this, she felt a closeness between them more profound than anything she had ever experienced. They moved as if they had become one—a single impulse from the same mind. One body, one thought, one soul. Together they became a tender vibration of infinite harmony—a silent, single note of cosmic music.

He pressed her even closer to him. His stiff shirtfront rubbed against the tips of her breasts, the slippery silk of her *choli* enhancing the abrasive sensation. She felt her nipples grow tight and hard.

"You are beautiful tonight!" he whispered. "I knew you would be."

"Then it was you who sent me this sari?" she asked, withdrawing her cheek from his shoulder enough to look up at his handsome face. "Sukundala didn't know where it came from. I thought maybe the maharani.... Thank you, Jai. Thank you very much."

"The sari is perfect for you—rich and sparkling and mysterious," he said in a voice grown suddenly husky. He lowered his gaze to her breasts, as though he sensed the rebellion of flesh taking place there. After a long moment he transferred his eyes to her lips.

"Shall I tell you how beautiful you are?" he asked, his dark eyes meeting hers again. "Shall I tell you how your lips invite me? How I would make a banquet of your mouth, your luscious breasts, the tender whiteness of your thighs? How I would like to make love to you here and now, in this place at this moment, if we were alone, if such a thing were possible?''

His words seared her mind like a flame. A soundless moan filled Julie's throat. Spontaneously she brushed her hips against his body. His answering response was so immediate, so masculine, that a violent trembling possessed her. She forgot the grand ballroom, dancing couples flowing past them on either side. All else vanished except the dark man holding her, and somewhere, faraway, music.

"Tell me!" she breathed.

They danced as he spoke of his desire for her, his deep voice close to her ear fluctuating between tenderness and rough passion. Excitement tingled in Julie's lips, each nerve awakened as though his mouth really pressed upon hers. The tingling grew, spread through her, ran rampant in wild waves crashing through her body. His words were like searching, probing kisses, each one more intimate and delicious than the last. She could almost feel his tongue brushing over her mouth, tracing the outline of her lips.

"You enchant me, my precious one, even as our legends say that Lord Krishna enchants the *gopis*."

"Tell me," Julie repeated, breathing in the warm scent of his body. Her thoughts were fragmented, blissful, like the scattered, sparkling colors of a kaleidoscope. Her mind was filled with the exhilarating realization that throughout these past weeks of silent frustration, he, too, had been thinking of her as she had of him, despite every effort she had made to ignore him.

He had been thinking of her, missing her, longing for her, desiring her.... He told her all this now, as they danced together within a wondrous cocoon of their own making, quiet and alone amidst the gala throng. Every word he spoke was like a celebration of joy to her; every tender expression of love gave depth to their awakening appreciation of each other.

"The *gopis* are Krishna's handmaidens and consorts," Jai told her, his eyes alive with feeling as he looked down at her. "One day beside a river, all of the *gopis* were calling out to Krishna, pleading with him to unite with them that they might experience his divine love. Rather than disappoint any who so desired him, he split himself into many forms so that all of the *gopis* could enjoy the abundance of his cosmic love. Even as the eternal, non-changing pure awareness Krishna represents is available to all people within themselves, so Krishna became everything to all women. You, Julie, could be all women to me. I would never need another."

The sudden thrill of his words staggered her. To be loved by such a man as this dark, handsome prince! Happiness suffused her heart even as wildfire ignited in her loins, burning through her. It seemed as if the diaphanous chiffon of her sari was not between them. She could feel the smooth fabric of his trousers rubbing against her thighs. She was drowned in the beauty of the moment, lost in a raging sea of unfamiliar sensations. Feeling his growing passion, Julie longed to cling to him, to pull his hard, masculine body close against her yielding form.

Dimly she understood that Jai had guided her through one of the many arched doorways off the edge of the main ballroom and into a smaller room at one side. An intimate silence filled the chamber, signaling that they were alone. He stopped dancing. Jutting out from the candlelit room was a dark alcove. He pulled her into it in one strong movement, never letting their bodies lose contact. He kissed her long and hard, lingering over her lips. The nerve endings throughout Julie's body were so sensitive that the slightest touch produced an agony of delight. She trembled within his embrace.

"Jai," she murmured, clutching his coat. She looked up at him with wonder-filled eyes.

"How I would like to finish what we have begun, Julie," he whispered, brushing her face with the tip of his finger. She felt his heart's rapid pounding as she pressed closer to him. He bent over her, touching his lips to her ear. "The very gods would envy our love-making."

Jai's strong fingers tilted her chin upward, his dark eyes feasting on the open invitation of her parted lips. As his mouth lowered onto hers again, Julie closed her eyes in anticipation. But his lips only brushed against hers, then stopped. Julie felt his body tighten, felt his chest swell as he consciously constricted his breathing. His hands slid down to her sides. Moving nothing but his arms he lifted her up and set her flat against the alcove wall. His lips moved against her ear.

"Stay here. Don't move."

Then she heard the sound that he had already discerned. A footfall, almost noiseless, on the soft grass outside. Julie stilled her own breathing as much as she could. Her pulse pounded loud in her ears.

Jai had turned, shielding her body from view. The room's double windows, only a foot off the floor and tall enough for a grown man to step through without having to duck his head, stood thrown open to the night air. It provided the dancers in the main ballroom with a cooling breeze. Julie saw Jai reach under his coat. A large flat pistol filled his hand when he withdrew it. Julie had not realized he was wearing a shoulder holster. She wondered what kind of strange existence he must lead if he felt it necessary to go armed to a ball in his own home.

Jai reached over and snuffed the three candles on the wall next to the alcove with his moistened bare fingers. The small chamber drifted into a soft darkness, illuminated now only by the light from the ballroom that streamed into the arched doorway and mapped a semicircle on the wooden floor. Jai bent down and removed his shoes. Then he passed in stocking feet across the room to the edge of the open window. He pressed his lean form back against the wall. Julie could barely see him. A frantic pulse throbbed in her throat.

The footfall came again, right outside the window now. Julie sensed rather than saw Jai's body tense. A gloved hand gripped the molding around the lower edge of the window, only inches away from Jai. A cylinder-shaped package, about eight inches in diameter and a foot and a half long, appeared over the windowsill. Black-gloved hands hovered above it a moment, then darted in. A practiced adjustment was made, and a final shove sent the cylinder rolling forward across the floor toward the middle of the arched doorway leading to the ballroom. The hands disappeared. The sound of someone running was quickly devoured by the growing distance. Jai was already on his knees beside the package.

"Flick on the lights by the door." His calm command jerked Julie out of her frozen stance. She leaped to turn the switch, her palms clammy.

"Done!" Jai said with satisfaction a moment later. He sat back on his heels to regard his handiwork. "Too bad I had to let him get away," he remarked, turning his head to gaze out the open window. "But from the way he went running off I guessed this little present he left behind would have a short fuse. Which it did," he added, picking up his gun off the floor and putting his shoes back on. He rose and walked over to where Julie stood, her eyes gripped by the harmless-looking tubelike thing on the floor.

"It's a bomb, then?" Her voice sounded strange to her own ears.

"A homemade pipe bomb. From the looks of it, ample enough to bring down the walls of the ballroom, had it rolled out onto the dance floor as was intended. The person who planted it was counting on the fact that if anyone noticed this odd looking thing at all, they would not have time to realize what it meant or to react to the danger."

"How long did you have?"

"Let's see." He walked back to the cylinder and knelt down beside it again. He picked up one end and looked at it, then glanced over at Julie. "There were about thirty seconds left. Probably fifty to begin with. By the time this had rolled through the doorway and out far enough to be noticed, there would have been maybe five seconds left at the most. Not enough time to stop it even if you knew what to do."

"This ball has gotten so much publicity...so many prominent people are here...." Her voice trailed off. Broken thoughts jostled each other in her mind. If she and Jai had not chanced to be here in this room....

"An ideal opportunity for our terrorist friends," he agreed. "Obviously they thought so, too. I wonder how that fellow got inside the grounds without alerting my guards. I had extra men on tonight." He shrugged. "I'll have to rethink my security system. There have been too many slipups lately."

"How did you know how to defuse it?" Julie asked.

"Come here. I'll show you." He smiled as she came toward him. "In fact, in your work it might come in handy to know about such things." Julie did not return the smile; any cause for humor in the situation escaped her, although she was beginning to think that Jai Mishra would smile in the face of death itself. But she had never brushed so close against extinction before and she was having trouble regaining her equilibrium.

"See," he explained when she was kneeling on the floor beside him, "the fuse on this bomb is electrical. Each of these two wires is soldered to a hand of this pocket watch."

"Just a normal pocket watch?" Julie interrupted.

He nodded, his eyes glinting at her dismay. "That is the way of the terrorist—he uses simple materials, whatever is at hand. Anyway, to defuse the bomb I just snapped off the second hand."

"Will he come back?" Julie asked with a nervous glance at the open window."

"No," Jai assured her. "He knows by now that his bomb has been intercepted and that my guards will soon be looking for him—except it is too late to catch him. I could have caught him myself, only I didn't want to get delayed by a fight with him and have the bomb explode."

"What about those inside?" Julie's eyes traveled through the doorway to where dancers moved beneath the brilliant chandeliers.

"That depends on what explosive is packed in this," Jai replied. He unscrewed the cap off one end of the pipe and glanced at the contents. A grim anger tinged his otherwise calm voice when he answered: "I would say that out of the three or four hundred guests gathered here tonight, maybe eighty of them would have been killed instantly and another eighty severely injured, perhaps to die in the hospital later on." He stopped. His dark eyes took in her pale face.

"Come on. Let me get you away from here," he said, his voice gentle. He led her past the alcove and across the small chamber. Julie went without protest. Her legs felt weak. He felt her tremble beside him and looked down at her, but said nothing. They paused before a side door Julie had not noticed before. Here they lingered a moment, his arm around her waist, while Julie freshened up and composed herself. Her racing heartbeat slowed and the weakness drained out of her body.

"Are you all right now?" he asked in a minute or two.

She nodded. Jai smiled at her and opened the door. They stepped into a long room set with buffet tables laden with heavy trays of succulent hors d'oeuvres. Hundreds of candles in silver holders lighted the room, which had wide arches on one side opening into the ballroom.

"Stay here. I'll bring you something to revive you." He smiled at her, his tone caressing. How different Jai seemed tonight from the autocratic man she had been trying without success to work with, Julie thought, as she watched his tall form merge into the crowd. She shrank back next to the brocade-covered wall, hoping no one would notice her.

Jai returned in a few minutes accompanied by an older man. Julie recognized him. He was P. K. Dhawan, an aide to the prime minister.

"Miss Connell, may I present to you Mr. Dhawan. Mr. Dhawan, Miss Connell."

"How do you do?" Julie said, smiling and extending her hand. She liked this elderly diplomat on sight. He was tall and thin, with silver hair and an aristocratic face.

He bowed over her hand in a formal, old-fashioned way. If the prince's burning eyes reminded Julie of a tiger sometimes, this man's eyes could be compared to a hawk. The look he directed at her was swift and shrewd.

"You may leave us, prince," he said. "No doubt you think you are safe, picking the oldest man in the room to entrust with this radiant beauty while you carry out your responsibilities as a host. But you have misjudged your man. I would have to be at least twenty years older than I am for you to be sure that I won't try to steal this woman from under your nose." He smiled at Julie in a warm, fatherly way, not the least in keeping with his words.

"I have no intention of entrusting Miss Connell to anyone," Jai replied. He handed a plate of delicacies from the buffet table to Julie.

"Here, give me that," exclaimed the diplomat, intercepting the plate. "I will feed them to her one by one with my own fingers. Run along now, Mishra."

"As you wish. I do need to speak to the captain of my guards for a moment." The prince smiled at him, then nodded at Julie. He caught her eye and held it for an instant.

She read the humor, appreciation, and yes, desire in his look so clearly that she was taken aback. His eyes told her, as surely as though he had spoken, that what had passed between them in the dark alcove before the bomb incident was foremost in his mind. She knew he meant her to know that the episode was not completed, merely postponed.

Then he turned and walked through the arches into the ballroom, greeting the guests nearest him. Julie watched the retreat of his broad back, admiring the way he carried himself and the self-confidence with which he spoke to people. She turned to the man beside her and found him watching her with his careful all-seeing eyes.

"I am happy to get this opportunity to meet you, Mr. Dhawan," Julie said. "I am a foreign correspondent with the *Courier* of New York. I have been hoping to get a chance to talk with you about international terrorism while I am here in India."

"So Prince Mishra informed me." he replied. "Come, let us walk together." He held out his arm to her.

"He told you that?" asked Julie, taken off guard.

"Yes, he told me. He asked me here this evening especially to meet you. He mentioned you would be interested in any information I might have about the subject."

"Yes," Julie replied, "I would." She had

tried without success to get an appointment with some senior government official such as Mr. Dhawan for the last two weeks. "Are you familiar with recent efforts to organize a terrorist group here in north India?" she asked.

Mr. Dhawan nodded his head, then smiled at her briefly. This time the smile did not touch his eyes—they remained shrewd and appraising.

"Prince Mishra has told me about the results of your own investigation," he said. "My information points in the same direction. A rather unpleasant topic for such a splendid night, is it not?" he remarked. "Unfortunate. But necessary, perhaps." He led her to the main corridor and invited her to sit on an embroidery-covered love seat. Party guests passed up and down the hallway, brilliant in silks and satins. No one was close enough to overhear.

"We will be very cozy here," Dhawan commented when they were settled on the sofa. "That young man standing under the arch is eyeing you with positive longing," he added, with a slight nod of his head. Julie glanced in the direction indicated. A nice-looking blond man was indeed staring at her.

"You see how it is?" inquired her escort. "The young men have their looks, the old men have information. And since you are a journalist, and thereby interested in information.... Well," he said, with a shrug, "he will just have to wait."

"What information do you have about the terrorists?" Julie persisted.

His voice grew serious as he asked in turn: "You think that there are international terrorists getting together somewhere near here for a summit conference, in order to exchange ideas, loan or borrow an assassin or two, maybe set up an Indian terrorist organization? Is that what you think?"

"Well," Julie replied, slowly, trying to collect her thoughts, "that is what I have been trying to find out. That is the impression I have so far of what I might find."

"That is not what you will find," he stated with assurance. "If you, or I, or anyone find anything at all, it will not be quite that."

"What do you think it will be?" she asked. Dhawan might well know actual details of the proposed meeting—the location and the real purpose—if such information was known at all by anyone within the government.

"It will be a meeting of international terrorists," he answered, "but for a different reason. It will be a meeting to organize and develop a wide-ranging terrorist offensive to be pursued simultaneously in several places around the globe. A terrorist alliance, if you will."

"Do you believe that such an alliance is feasible?" Julie knew various national terrorist groups had vague connections with each other. They had always been linked together by a common purpose—to destroy the existing political and economic order—regardless of their individual ideologies. The State Department experts she had interviewed had emphasized that international terrorism was not a series of random happenings, but rather a methodical attempt to undermine the stability of the free world. This conference could indeed be the planning session to organize the next wave of assaults.

"Let us hope that they cannot agree among themselves any better than can legitimate governments of the countries they wish to destroy," the sharp-eyed old man replied.

"How sure are you that leaders of foreign terrorist groups are coming to, or are in India for such a meeting?" she asked.

"As it happens," he replied with a tight smile, "I am in the happy position of being completely sure. My government had the good fortune of speaking directly with one of the leaders coming to attend the proposed meeting." He paused.

"Will you elaborate?" Julie pursued.

"This morning a leader of the Red Brigades—Italy's predominate terrorist group, as I'm sure you know—was spotted by one of our undercover agents in the Delhi airport. We persuaded him that it was to his advantage to answer some questions for us. Under

interrogation this person disclosed that he
had come to India for the purpose I just explained to you. He was to be contacted personally by some unknown source about the
location and time of the meeting. Unfortunately, the Italian government, when we
contacted them, was so eager to speak with
him that he was immediately transferred to
their custody, and we did not have an opportunity to find out more details. It seems he
was wanted for questioning regarding a terrorist attack in Rome a few weeks ago.''

The train station! A wave of blinding emotion washed over Julie, leaving behind a
vague feeling of nausea in her stomach. That
day...those bodies...one of the killers here
now.... She forced herself to focus on Dhawan's next words.

''Naturally,'' he was saying, with a penetrating gaze that reminded her of the prince,
''naturally, should you decide this little tidbit
of information is newsworthy, you will refer
to me in those immortal words to which journalists must so often take recourse.''

''You mean, 'a reliable source close to the
Prime Minister,' or maybe 'a senior government official who asked not to be identi-
fied'?'' she asked, smiling at him.

''Either of those would do very well,'' he
replied, returning the smile. This time it
reached his eyes. ''Prince Mishra and I feel
that it might be a good thing, after all, to let

these subversive organizations know that their actions are not as closely hidden as they might hope. If nothing else, it will shake them up, make them doubt themselves a little bit. Self-doubt is the source of failure in organizations such as those.

"And now I see that I will have to relinquish you. The young gentleman has at last determined to his satisfaction that I am an old, unprepossessing man and therefore have no right to be taking up so much of the time of the acknowledged belle of the ball." He smiled at Julie, then rose to say with extreme heartiness, "Ah, Mr. Brunnen, so delightful of you to join us. Miss Connell, may I present to you Mr. Hans Brunnen, aide to the ambassador from Germany. Here, Mr. Brunnen, please relieve me of this plate of sweets. I was going to share them with Miss Connell, but we talked instead. Excuse me, I see an old friend I must speak to."

"Thank you, Mr. Dhawan," Julie said as the diplomat turned to leave.

"My pleasure, Miss Connell," he replied. "Please call on me if I can be of service to you again."

"Mr. Dhawan is a very important man in the government," remarked Hans Brunnen after the older man had departed. "But, of course, you would hardly be interested in such matters," he added politely. "Would you like to try one of these sweets? Prince

Mishra's cooks are renowned for their skill, you know." He gave Julie a shy smile.

"I hear the orchestra striking up a waltz," she replied. "Maybe we could dance?"

"The pleasure will be all mine," he responded, setting down the plate of sweets and offering her his arm.

The huge ballroom was still crowded with couples when Julie and her partner entered, even though it was after midnight. The young German was a good dancer. He held her as if she were made of Dresden china and guided her with polished skill around the floor. He seemed content to dance with her and did not try to talk.

Julie was relieved not to have to converse. The information Mr. Dhawan had given her was the first major lead she had gotten on the terrorist conference. The capture of a Red Brigades leader in India was news, and indicated that terrorist networks went beyond national boundaries.

Of course, she needed to double-check Dhawan's story: sometimes governments tried to feed false information to correspondents. But it should be easy to verify that an arrest was made at the airport today. Already she was writing in her mind the story she would file with the foreign desk first thing in the morning. The capture of the Red Brigades leader was fact. The details about the proposed conference Wes Harding might decide to hold until Julie had more information.

Julie kept coming back to another aspect of Mr. Dhawan's revelations, as well: the fact that Jai had arranged to introduce him to her. From what the diplomat had said, the prince had planned for Julie to have an exclusive on the capture. She wondered if Jai had finally decided to help her in her investigation. She had almost given up hope of gaining his aid. Of course, a single introduction could not be called overwhelming support—except, perhaps, when that introduction was to the one person who knew what was going on.

Julie's partner cleared his throat. She realized he must have been speaking to her.

"I'm sorry, I was lost in the music," she lied. "What did you say?"

"I believe the Norwegian ambassador is signaling to us. Would you care to meet him?"

"Certainly."

Julie floated across the dance floor in the arms of one partner after another. Elated by her progress on the story and enlivened by champagne, she enjoyed every dance. She saw the prince at a distance from time to time among his other guests, but he never came up to her again. She had to admit that dancing with him had been the highlight of her night. No matter how charming or handsome her other partners were, their respectful hands on her waist and hopeful smiles lacked the thrill of the prince's possessive, demanding embrace.

CHAPTER NINE

IT WAS THREE IN THE MORNING before the crowd on the ballroom floor began to thin, and close to five o'clock when the orchestra packed their instruments. Julie danced right up to the end. Then she helped the maharani bid farewell to the last of the guests. Julie looked around for Priya, hoping to get a word with her. She wanted to ask where the princess had been earlier in the evening.

"She has already gone upstairs," her mother told Julie. "I am going now, too. None of us will be up before noon, I suspect," she added with a laugh.

Julie noticed how happy and content the older woman looked, even after having been up most of the night. She suspected that in the maharani's married life she had been at many parties that ended in the wee hours of the morning.

"It was a wonderful ball, maharani," Julie declared. "I've never attended anything to compare with it!"

"Yes, dear, it was nice, wasn't it? It is so pleasant to have the palace full of guests again and to use the ballroom once more. Maybe now that you are here we will do this more often," she added, her eyes sparkling.

"I'm glad you could use my visit as an excuse for the ball," replied Julie. "I hope you can entertain more, since you enjoy it so much," she added, as she accompanied her hostess to the grand staircase. "You do a beautiful job of it!"

"Thank you," replied the maharani. "I enjoyed making the arrangements," she added, with a casual wave of her hand to indicate the remains of the elegant buffet and the confetti-strewed ballroom. "But all these people came to see Jai, not me. Except maybe for a few old... what is your word?"

"Admirers?" supplied Julie.

"Yes, that is it. The romance of a ball never dies, you know, even at my age. Good night, dearest Julie," she added, giving the American woman a warm hug.

"Good night," Julie echoed.

When the maharani had gone, Julie turned away. Despite the late hour, after all the excitement of the evening she did not feel ready to go to bed. She wandered through the empty ballroom, enjoying the stillness following so much noise and confusion. She dragged her toe through the layer of bright-colored confetti covering the dance floor, then bent down and removed her sari slippers.

"No celebration in India is complete without confetti," said a male voice.

Julie looked up to see the prince leaning against one of the arches, watching her. He had stripped off his dark jacket. Somehow his shoulders looked broader than ever in the white shirt.

"Well, it adds a feeling of festivity," she replied, picking up a handful of bits of colored paper from the floor as she stood up. She let the confetti sift through her fingers, then threw the last part up into the air. "You don't even look tired!" she added, as he walked over to her.

"A life of dissipation obviously suits me," he replied. "You seem to have held up very well, also, considering your inexhaustible list of partners tonight."

"I have always heard that expression about dancing the whole night through, but this is the first time I have really done it. Thank heavens sari sandals are flat—I never could have made it if I'd been wearing high heels!"

They stood facing one another in the middle of the huge room. She looked up at him from under her lashes, searching his face for some sign of the old mockery and distrust. It was not there. For an instant their eyes locked. She studied with care the infinitesimal flame smoldering in his dark eyes. She felt bewitched by those burning points of light.

"Shall we walk out onto the terrace?" he

asked, disturbing the silence that hung between them like a silver thread. "Dawn is breaking."

He reached out and took her hand. They wandered through the vast rooms, empty but for the debris of the night's festivity. Being alone together seemed odd, after the crushing throng of people earlier.

"It was a wonderful ball," Julie said, turning her head to look at him. Why did it seem so natural to be walking hand in hand with this silent, mysterious man, she mused. And why did her palm start to tingle the moment those steellike fingers wrapped around it?

"I'm glad you enjoyed it." He sounded like he meant it.

"You are lucky to have so many friends," she remarked, aware of the warm sensations spiraling through her.

He glanced down at her. "Friends? You are so refreshing, Julie," he observed, a little smile playing at the corners of his mouth.

"But they were your friends, weren't they?"

"Acquaintances, maybe. Business associates. Politicians. Social climbers. But friends? I'm not sure."

"I would think Mr. Dhawan is your friend, at least," she suggested quietly.

He smiled. "You are right. Dhawan is a friend. Some of the other old-timers who were here tonight are, as well, now that I

think of it—people who have known and respected my parents over the years.'' He
paused. ''What of your own parents, Julie?
You have never spoken of them.''

She glanced up, surprised that he should
ask. ''My father was killed in a small-plane
crash when I was a baby,'' she answered.
''My mother died when I was twelve. I was
their only child. I was raised in my aunt's
house,'' she added.

''I'm sorry. On both counts—that you lost
your parents so early and that you are alone
without siblings.''

She shrugged. ''I guess it's not as bad as it
sounds, really. Being on my own is a challenge. But I can't help missing my parents
just the same. No one to turn to, no one to
confide in.... I can't believe I'm telling you
all this,'' she added, attempting to smile.

''I am glad you are.''

They reached the terrace then. Jai slipped
his arm around Julie's waist and guided her
over to the marble railing. They stood side by
side, barely touching, yet each acutely aware
of the other's body. Beyond them stretched
the broad lawns. The growing light revealed
the outlines of leaves and flowers. In the distance black trees loomed huge against the
gray silver sky. A pregnant silence hung over
the majestic scene. Then a bird burst into
song. Another answered it.

''I always wonder how they know when to

begin singing," said the prince. "Look, that was the leitmotiv to herald the sunrise." He pointed toward the horizon beyond the silhouette of the treetops. A faint pink glow had appeared there—a long rosy line of color above the black branches.

"It's beautiful," Julie whispered in awe.

He turned toward her. "So are you." He drew her closer. Julie stiffened in his hold, not so much opposing him as resisting the sudden trembling of her own body.

"Have you forgotten how much you enjoyed our dancing?" he murmured, his warm breath brushing her ear. His strong arms wrapped around her. There was no hesitation in his movements, no doubt. His long fingers spread across her back, pressing her to him.

Julie raised her palms against his chest. No, she had not forgotten. The sudden tremor of excitement rushing through her veins would have reminded her, even if she had. She realized she was hoping he would kiss her again. Dismayed by her own eagerness, she pushed hard against his broad chest. She might as well have pushed against a mountain of stone. The only effect of her struggle was to heighten her awareness of the steellike strength of his arms.

"Julie," he asked gently. "Why do you resist something you so obviously want?"

She pressed her hands against him again. Julie wanted to tell him that she could not get involved with someone she had to work with. To do so could create a conflict of interest—she might lose her objectivity as a journalist, depending too much on his evaluation of events in India and not enough on her own observations. But she could not find the words. The strength seemed to have gone out of her arms. Her fingertips hesitated as they distinguished thick, curling hair beneath the fine cotton of his shirt. An image of his bare chest, of how it must look covered with coarse dark hair, flashed into her brain. The musky scent of his male body, blended with the heavy fragrance of flowers opening to the dawn, delighted her senses.

She became aware of his shortened breathing. A thrill shot through her: she was doing this to him! Invincible man that he was, he still trembled at her touch. She affected him as intensely as he affected her! Julie realized she had a magnetism of her own equal in strength to his. An exquisite sense of power—of respect for her own womanliness—overwhelmed her. A yearning, wild and compelling, arose within her.

Her hands, with which she had meant to push him away, wrapped around his neck instead. She heard his sharp intake of breath. Then he was pulling her to him, closer and tighter, molding her body against his own with strong, domineering hands. She shuddered: her body was racked with longing so intense that she wanted to cry out. A marvelous sense of wonder invaded her.

What was it that Jai touched in her that no one else had? Her life, full enough until now with her career and friendships, had taken on a deeper richness since meeting him. It was as though knowing him provided the wash of color across what had been the well-composed, black-and-white portrait of her life. His dynamic personality gave her own purposeful existence other dimensions—drama and passion—and chipped away at the cold professional exterior she had built around her feelings when Eddie died.

The touch of Jai's fingers aroused her, as he explored the curves of her hips, her waist, her shoulders, seeking out the sensitive places on her body with excruciating slowness. She locked her fingers in his thick hair and pulled his dark head down, her mouth lifted in anticipation. He towered above her, immovable, his dark eyes drinking in her upraised face. Then his mouth descended on hers, covering her lips with kisses of exquisite sweetness. His tongue invaded her mouth with deep, thrusting strokes—gentle and suggestive. He leaned over her, intensifying the contact between their bodies.

A low, wailing noise rose in Julie's throat, like a whispered scream. "Oh, Jai!" she moaned. "I want...." She felt as if she was glowing, on fire with a strange, undefined desire. His strong male body next to hers seemed the only real thing in the world.

"Yes, my sweet darling. I know what you want." His arms encircled her waist. Keeping her body pressed against his side, he crossed the terrace. He guided her down a narrow stairway that twisted off from the corner of the wide porch, almost hidden by a screen of shrubbery. At the bottom of the stairs a tall stone wall blocked their path. Jai glanced down at Julie standing silently beside him, her cheek pressed against his shoulder. A slow smile spread across his face.

"Now I'll show you a boyhood secret of mine," he told her, brushing his lips across the top of her head.

"A secret?"

"Not really a secret, but I liked to pretend that no one else knew about it." He was moving along the overgrown stone wall, taking care that low branches did not sting her face. Julie listened to the rise and fall of his breathing. She had a strange sense of having come home at last, of being somewhere she would never have to leave again, where she would always be welcome.

"Here it is." Turning her head, Julie saw that they had stopped before a heavy metal door in the stone wall. Beaten into the gray metal was the tiger emblem of the Mishra princes. Jai pulled away some vines to reveal a metal latch. "I haven't been here in years," he murmured, half to himself.

"What is it?" she asked, as he lifted the latch and pushed against the door. It swung open on stiff hinges.

"My hideaway. A secret garden." He led her though the doorway then, and Julie caught a glimpse of high walls and a luscious overgrowth of flora abounding with vines, shrubs, trees and flowers.

"I'm not the only one who seems to have forgotten it," Jai remarked with a low laugh as he paused to glance around. "It doesn't look like the gardeners have touched it in years."

"I like it this way," Julie whispered.

"It was always less formal than the rest of the grounds," he replied. "I came here to be by myself, because I could bolt the door from inside and no one could bother me." He slid shut a rusty bolt as he spoke. "And now no one can disturb us," he added, his low voice filled with deep satisfaction. He led her across the garden and into a small gazebo grown over with climbing roses. He pulled her down beside him on a wide marble bench covered with soft, faded cushions.

A vague panic possessed Julie. "Jai," she whispered hoarsely. "I don't think...." The words slipped away, lost in the onslaught of kisses he rained on her hair, her eyelids, her mouth. His lips sensitized her skin, arousing a torrent of rapture.

"Julie," he murmured, his voice husky. He wetted her ear with short, brushing tongue strokes. "Haven't you wanted this, as I have, since the day we met? Haven't you longed to feel my lips on your lips, your neck...your breasts...."

He lowered his mouth onto hers, preventing any further objections. Julie sank beneath his weight, a fever of excitement obliterating her fear. She journeyed beyond herself, carried along by the rising ecstasy within. Her excitement grew, distracting her mind from all else save the feel of his lips sliding down her neck, brushing her collarbone. She felt delirious. A deep-seated joy swelled her heart until she thought it would burst. His tantalizing kisses left behind a trail of burning, molten gold.

"Jai," she whispered, "what...are you doing to me?"

"I'm letting you be the woman you are, letting you become the woman you were meant to be." His lips moved against hers as he spoke. "You are so filled with beauty, Julie, my love," he whispered.

He took hold of the flimsy fabric of her sari and gave a short jerk, undoing in one motion the pleats that Sukundala had put in with such painstaking care. The gauzy silk floated free from the confining slip, like a mist in the air around them. The prince pushed the material off the bench with an impatient thrust.

The next instant his hand was at her *choli*, sliding over the form-fitting silk. His dark eyes glittered with appreciation as he watched the outline of her nipples become visible beneath the smooth cloth.

The need in Julie forced her to cry out. She watched as he lowered his mouth to her breast with the deliberation of a gourmet. She arched her back to hasten the moment of contact. Then his lips were on the breast nearest him, kneading the nipple through the thin layer of silk. His hand came up to cup the ripeness of her other breast, embracing its fullness as he stroked the sensitive tip with his rough thumb. A terrible ache grew in her loins as, with one soft bite, he brought the supple roundness of that nipple to hardness.

An enervating sweetness stole through Julie—her body, her mind, her heart. She felt so close to Jai, as if all the barriers between them had dissolved. She felt included in the mystery of his life, as if she was a special part of his existence; no longer on the outside peering in wistfully through shuttered windows. Her consciousness became an intrinsic part of his. Their natures fused, merged, melted together in the velvety feeling of closeness they were creating together.

"I did not know it was possible to want a woman as I want you," he told her, his eyes smiling and tender. "I want all of you, Julie. Not just your beautiful body." His lips closed

over her mouth again. She sucked in her
breath, trembling uncontrollably as his hands
swept over her.

She wrapped her arms more tightly around
his lean, powerful body. She felt him shudder
with desire, and she triumphed in her newfound power. He trailed his hand along the
inside of her thigh, pulling up the sari slip as
he went. A tidal wave of pleasure swept over
her, and she writhed with building passion on
the soft velvet cushions.

He undid the hooks down the front of her
choli, releasing her swollen breasts, and gently, reverently, he touched them. For one timeless moment he held his hand still, dark upon
white, male upon female, his flesh upon hers.

Julie shuddered wordlessly against him, unable and unwilling to protest. Far from protesting, she would gladly have begged him to
continue. But he needed no urging. Slowly he
rolled the hard tip of her breast between his
gentle fingers until Julie's body turned to fire.
Sensations of pleasure erupted from some hidden source deep within her and flowed
through her body. When his lips burned into
the hollow between her breasts, she clasped his
dark head against her, savoring the roughness
of his cheeks against her flesh.

"You are so soft, and round, and perfect,"
he mumbled, his mouth against her breast.

"Jai...Jai," she whispered, loving the
sound of his name on her lips. She pulled her

body closer to his, that he might know her eagerness. She knew then that what she wanted was to unite with him, to be a part of him, and have him be a part of her forever. She wanted to be of one flesh with him, as in his embrace they had grown to be one heart.

His dark eyes, glistening with desire, filled with understanding. His hands dropped to her waist and untied the sari slip. She raised her weight off the couch as he slid the confining fabric over her hips, watching his face soften with appreciation as the curve of her thigh and then her shapely legs were revealed. His large hand slipped beneath the wispy white lace of her panties. These he removed with a slow, deliberate motion, so rigidly controlled that Julie could only guess at what it was costing him to restrain his own passion.

His eyes never left her as he removed his own clothing. Try as she might, Julie could not match his patience. With a moan of relief she welcomed his naked form down beside her own, thrilled by the full glory of his perfect, muscular body. She buried her hands in the hair on his chest, dark and curly as she had once imagined it would be.

He gathered her to him, his strong arms holding her pressed against his body in a gentle, loving embrace. They lay still a moment, wrapped in each other's arms, suffused with a vast contentment yet quivering with unbearable expectancy. When their stillness at last became intolerable for both of them, Jai began a new, intimate exploration of her with his hands and mouth, seeking out the most responsive parts of her body with exquisite sensitivity. His touch aroused in Julie a throbbing, all-encompassing desire greater than anything she could ever have imagined.

"Jai!"

The sound of her high-pitched, breathless cry snapped the last shreds of his restraint. He lowered his large body onto hers, pressing her slender form deep into the cushions. His burning eyes locked with hers as he entered her. The tiger flame in the depths of his eyes flared bright as he watched a wondrous glow transform Julie's face. Then they were lost in an unquenchable fire of their own making. Two souls merging in a mutual spiritual awakening, the glorious beauty of which would last until the end of time.

How long they lay together afterward, Julie had no idea. She would have been happy to spend eternity here beside this man who, in the midst of such ardent passion, had made her life—for the first time—complete.

At last Jai raised himself up on one elbow and tilted his head to one side. Then he looked at Julie, a smile of pleasure but also regret on his face. A heartbreaking sense of loss swept over her as she felt him drawing away. Her protesting fingers dug into his well-muscled back.

"It is time to go," he said quietly. "Listen. The morning servants are arriving to begin cleaning up after the ball."

"No. Don't go," she whispered, shutting her ears to the distant chatter of servants, arriving fresh and energetic to begin a day of work. "Please."

"There will be other times," he murmured, his deep voice full of promise.

As a diver surfaces from the bottom of a pool, so Julie returned to a sense of her surroundings. She found that the gray sky of dawn framed by the tall walls of the neglected garden was rapidly lightening to blue, and that the single thread of pink on the horizon had splashed vibrant colors across the entire sky. Even as she watched, the sunrise began to fade.

Last of all she looked at the man lying beside her. He was still propped up on one elbow, his eyes lingering on the curve of her breasts. The early-morning light glinted off his black hair. The thought came into Julie's mind that never before had she cared for another human being as she cared for this handsome dark-haired prince. The beauty of this final moment with him—before she must rise from this bench and face the coming day—was something she would never forget as long as she lived.

Jai raised his head to watch her. The last lingering flame of passion in his dark eyes died away slowly, to be replaced by amusement. "Welcome back to the world of mortals, sweet Julie. You look like a traveler just returned home from a very long trip."

She smiled. "Does it show so much? That's how I feel."

His eyes met hers. "We soared far together," he said. "We will fly again. Come. Get up." He sat up and stretched, then swung his legs over the edge of the bench.

Julie rose, also. "Oh, Jai!" she cried in alarm, "I don't know how to put my sari back on!"

He laughed. "You had better just wrap it around you as best you can. You don't need to cross the terrace to get to your room," he added. "Follow the path outside to the left, and it will take you to the back hallway. There won't be any servants there yet." He stood up, his dark form towering over her. "Oh, Julie," he whispered, his voice rougher, "what a pity we can't stay here forever."

She stared up at him, unable to answer. Could it really be that she had fallen in love with this enigmatic man? Nothing else could explain the bliss she had found in his arms just now—or the wild abandon that had possessed her.

But what a fool she was! She knew he distrusted her. He believed she was a pawn of the terrorists—a morsel of flesh with which to tempt the appetite of the tiger prince. Hadn't he told her point-blank that he intended to take full advantage of her "assignment"?

She turned away from him, a wave of self-recrimination flooding her mind. Regardless of the prince's misplaced distrust, she had her own professional standards to maintain. Letting herself be seduced by one of her sources was no way to maintain her standards.

"Julie?" He touched her shoulder. "Come here."

She faced him. "Yes?"

"What were you feeling just now? Your face changed."

She tried to smile, tried to make light of something that she did not feel the least light-hearted about: "I was feeling that I shouldn't be feeling what I'm feeling. Really, Jai." Her voice grew serious. "We can't be together like this. It's not fair to my work, or to me, or to you."

"Why isn't it fair to you and me?" he asked, his dark eyes intent on her face.

"Do you trust me yet?" she countered. "Ask yourself that, Jai. Do you really trust me?"

He did not reply. A look of pain filled his eyes as he, too, realized the dilemma in which they found themselves. That one look was answer enough for Julie. She clutched her *choli* together and snatched the fragile material of her sari from the floor, wrapping it around her. She ran down the steps of the

rose-covered gazebo and jerked back the bolt
on the garden door. A moment later she was
running down the back hallway to her room,
her bare feet flying over the cool marble.

CHAPTER TEN

THE SLOW PROGRESS OF HER TAXI down Netaji
Subhash Marg gave Julie ample leisure to
study the massive stone structure on her left.
The Red Fort, a famous Indian landmark, was
built by Moghul Emperor Shah Jahan in the
1600s at the same time his workmen were com-
pleting the Taj Mahal in Agra. Amazement at
the immensity of these undertakings without
modern construction equipment ended Julie's
preoccupation with her own affairs.

It was afternoon of the day after the maharani's ball. The telephone's shrill buzz had
woken Julie at noon with her call to the foreign desk. After confirming his arrest, she
had dictated her story on the capture of the
Red Brigades leader at the airport, and then
spoken briefly with Harding. Unable to get
back to sleep, she decided to take the afternoon off and explore Chandni Chowk, Delhi's oldest marketplace. She wanted to get out
of the palace before the maharani and Priya
were up. Most of all, she did not want to see
Jai just yet, not until she collected her
thoughts.

Easier said than done. From one day to the next, rational thinking had become an impossible exercise. Usually calm and observant, Julie discovered that the reliable logic that had ordered her life in the past had scattered with the four winds. She could not tear her thoughts away from the almost mystical beauty she and Jai had shared at dawn.

Now, scrunched against the corner of the taxi with her eyes half-closed, Julie could feel Jai's lips against her skin, on her mouth, her neck, her breasts. It was hard to accept the fact that she had succumbed without resistance to him, knowing as she did how he felt about her. Yet the memory of his touch, of the joy and desire coursing through her entire being in that enchanted interlude in the secret garden as the sun came up, made her realize that her surrender had been inevitable. Honesty prevented her from blaming the prince. She had wanted him as much as he wanted her. . . .

The cab driver turned onto Chandni Chowk, the biggest and richest street of old Delhi. The maharani had told Julie that Indians nicknamed this crowded thoroughfare "the silver street" because of the ornate gold and silver jewelry sold there. Each side street leading off Chandni Chowk had its own specialty—one street for shoes, one street for brass, one street for shawls. . . .

A dense flow of pedestrians pushed past

the cab as Julie paid the driver and stepped onto the sidewalk. She paused a moment to watch as the crowd in the street parted before a towering wall of gray flesh. An elephant decked in red velvet lumbered along with innate majesty, setting each gigantic round foot down with a forward swaying motion. The smell of animals and humans mixed with spicy aromas from street vendors' carts, and fragrant incense wafted out of stores that had fronts opening like stalls right onto the sidewalk.

Julie stepped aside to avoid a large, cream-colored sacred cow that had wandered out of an alleyway. Shopkeepers called out to her, inviting her into their stores. During the next hour she explored several streets packed with shops featuring hammered-brass lamps, carved-wood screens and tables, inlaid ivory ornaments and jewelry, and endless arrays of gorgeous silks, cottons, wools and cashmere. She had just purchased a bag of cashews in a shop lined with shelves containing hundreds of glass jars filled with exotic nuts and spices, when, stepping out of the shop doorway, she saw a familiar outline.

Twisting back toward the street she recognized Priya's lovely profile. The young princess was leaning against a granite pillar several yards away. She looked radiantly happy. As Julie watched, the Indian girl lifted her head to speak to a man at her side.

Julie pressed back against the building without taking her eyes off Priya. She knew that Jai would never have allowed his sister to go out alone with a man. It was indicative of the tremendous influence of Indian culture that Julie found herself almost equally as shocked by Priya's behavior as either Jai or the maharani would have been. A young Indian woman of Priya's status simply did not go out unattended with a man.

Julie's attention shifted to Priya's companion. He was slim and tall—undeniably good-looking. His eyes never left the young princess's face. That he was a suitor—an infatuated one, at that—there could be no doubt.

After a moment's hesitation Julie worked her way through the strolling crowd toward Priya. The Indian girl's face was a study in dismay when Julie greeted her. The princess's lovely eyes widened in alarm: her consternation was obvious. She threw her companion a mute, imploring glance of acute distress. He, however, seemed unperturbed.

Priya had no choice but to present him to Julie. His name was Lal Delal. He acknowledged the introduction with polished charm. In fact, the unmistakable glance of fiery appreciation he ran over Julie's shapely figure made her revise her first impression about his interest in Priya. Yet no man in his right mind would risk a clandestine meeting with Prince

Jaiapradesh Mishra's sister unless he was
very much and hopelessly in love.

Julie, once she had forced the introduction,
could think of little to say. She made small
talk with Delal for a minute or two and then
excused herself. Priya, twisting the end of her
sari nervously, said nothing at all.

Julie returned to the palace deep in
thought. When the battered taxicab she had
hailed in Chandni Chowk deposited her at the
tiger-guarded veranda, Julie was still thinking
about the princess. What Priya did was her
own business, of course. Yet Julie realized
that she felt protective of the young woman.
She did not want Priya to get hurt, and that
seemed to be the only possible outcome of
disregarding all social and cultural conven-
tions by meeting a man in secret.

Lal Delal had appeared charming and well
educated. There was no reason to suppose he
would not make a suitable husband for Priya.
Yet Julie found him too smoothly ingratiating for her own taste. Also, the fact that he
chose to ignore the danger these meetings exposed Priya to did not augur well for his
character. To be fair, though, Julie had to admit that Priya had the sort of exquisite,
unbelievable beauty that could make an
otherwise responsible man throw aside all
other considerations, especially if he thought
courting her in secret was his only hope of
winning her. Julie wondered why Lal had not

made a push to be introduced to Priya through conventional channels. Of course, if his social standing or caste was different from the princess's, it might be impossible to meet her.

Julie paused inside the circular entrance hall. The beauty of the hand-painted tile floor beneath the high sunlit dome never failed to soothe her nerves, no matter how preoccupied she was. Her thoughts turned to the man whose home this was. Whatever reservations Julie had about the new intimacy in her relationship with Jai, she could not deny the contentment she had felt throughout the afternoon. The most remarkable man she had ever met found her attractive, desirable. . . worthwhile. This knowledge filled her with a deep, simple pleasure.

Propelled by these thoughts, Julie found herself heading down the long hallway toward Jai's office. He had told her not to interfere in his family life, but Julie felt that Priya was running a risk more dangerous than she realized. In a society where conventionality and obedience were prized traits in a prospective bride, an indiscretion would not be treated lightly. . . or forgotten. And, as Priya had pointed out, marriage was her only viable option for a happy life. Julie did not want to tell tales on the young princess. Yet, having become involved through no fault of her own, she now felt a certain responsibility to the Indian girl.

The door to Jai's office stood open. As she approached, Julie heard a rapid exchange in Hindi. Then a small man, dressed in the ill-fitting nondescript clothing common among the working classes, stepped into the hallway followed by Jai. The man said something in Hindi, nodded one final time and turned away. Seeing Julie he hesitated an instant, then passed by her in the corridor with his eyes lowered shyly and his face turned slightly away. Julie glanced at him with curiosity before he turned the corner, deciding he must be an outdoor servant or perhaps a worker in one of Jai's factories.

When the man had disappeared she transferred her gaze to the prince, who stood leaning against the doorway. She literally stopped in her tracks, too stunned tc speak. He was glaring at her with unmasked contempt. One look at his handsome face and burning dark eyes told her how foolish she had been to consider discussing Priya's clandestine romance with him. It did not seem possible that this was the same man who had held her with ardent, exhilarating desire in the early-morning hours—had held her and cherished her as though it were their divine destiny to share the dawn together.

She searched his face, seeking any trace of the appreciation, tenderness or acceptance he had shown at their last meeting. There was none. His countenance reflected only disdain as he watched the telltale signs of bewilderment, hurt and anger flit across Julie's features. His mouth twisted in an unpleasant, self-deprecating smile that said more than language ever could.

Without a word being spoken by either of them, Julie turned and walked back down the hallway. Unshed tears burned her eyes. She had no idea why he had changed his mind about her just when they were beginning to reach some kind of an understanding. But change his mind he had obviously done.

Julie was not surprised when, later that evening, a quiet knock sounded on her bedroom door. Even with her own concerns, she had spared some thought to Priya's predicament. The princess came up to the edge of the bed where Julie lay propped up on pillows surrounded by unread newspapers. Seeing Priya's face streaked with tears and her usual grace inhibited by tension, Julie could only be glad that Jai's cold reception at the door to his office had prohibited her from disclosing the purpose of her visit.

"I didn't tell Jai, Priya," Julie stated. She had no doubt what was uppermost in the Indian's girl mind. If Jai had been her own brother, she would have been sick with apprehension.

Priya fell on her knees beside the bed and grasped Julie's hand. "But...are you going to? Please, don't tell my brother about Lal!"

she pleaded. "He would never understand! He wouldn't let me see Lal again, I know. And without Lal, I might as well be dead."

The princess's ethereal beauty and agitation robbed her words of melodrama. Looking at her, Julie could almost picture such a scene taking place centuries before when Priya's desperate plea would have been a matter of life or death.

"Get up off the carpet, for heaven's sake, Priya!" Julie exclaimed. "I promise not to say a word to Jai about your boyfriend." She patted the silk coverlet at her feet. "Sit here and stop worrying. But how did you ever meet Lal and what are you going to do?"

Priya seated herself on the edge of Julie's bed and proceeded to indulge in a hearty bout of tears, whether from relief or hopelessness Julie could not determine. At any rate, after she had finished with her cry, the Indian girl divulged the entire story of her secret relationship with Lal Delal. She told Julie she had met Lal by accident one day while she was out shopping. Priya had dropped a box on her way out of a shop. Lal, who was loitering outside admiring a window display, retrieved the package for her. Somehow before they parted a meeting had been arranged for the following afternoon.

That was about a month ago. Since then Priya had met Lal several times. The princess admitted she had even used the excitement of

the maharani's ball to cover an illicit rendezvous with Lal in a distant corner of the palace
grounds. Like any woman, she had wanted
her admirer to see her dressed in her finest.
That explained the princess's late entrance the
night before and also her reluctance to help
Julie dress before the ball. Julie felt, as she
listened, that the adventurous nature of this
attachment and the challenge of using her
own wits appealed to Priya almost as much as
Lal himself. Still, he was obviously adept at
making himself agreeable to an overprotect-
ed, romantic young woman.

The uneasiness that had prompted Julie to
consider consulting Jai was not alleviated by
Priya's recital. Long after the princess had
left, Julie turned the problem over in her
mind. The manner of the lovers' first meeting
especially bothered Julie: she knew that meeting by accident was almost unheard of in India. All introductions between males and
females of marriageable age were arranged
through family or friends. For Priya to have
agreed to meet Lal again was an astounding
breach of convention. Delal must be persuasive in the extreme to have managed the
meeting with a girl brought up as strictly as
Priya had been.

"Julie, you fool, you're making much ado
about nothing. You're getting as suspicious
as Jai," Julie muttered, pushing the newspapers she had meant to study off the bed

onto the floor. "As handsome and polished as Lal is, it's not a wonder they fell head over heels for each other at first sight." Except Lal Delal had not struck Julie as the kind of man to lose his head over anything. She had sensed a certain aloofness underneath his warm, witty sophistication.

She slid off the bed and crossed to the sitting room, resolving to put Priya and Lal out of her mind. She had her own work to attend to, and there was nothing she could do to help Priya except, perhaps, try to be a sympathetic friend. For her part, she believed Priya should be able to marry Lal if she wanted. No one else was going to see it that way, though. Priya had chosen a heartbreakingly difficult path, but maybe true love was worth it. Julie did not know. Her one consolation was that each meeting with Lal had apparently been in a public place, except for the brief outdoor rendezvous the night of the ball. Julie was sure from Priya's innocent enthusiasm that whatever passion might be stirring in her suitor's heart, Lal had at least had the good sense not to attempt a physical relationship yet for fear of frightening the young princess away altogether. Or maybe he really did care enough to want to protect Priya from the consequences of her rashness.

Why can't I learn to show equally good sense, Julie thought. *Then I could have spared myself the humiliation of succumbing to a man who refuses to even speak to me the next time he sees me!*

She lifted her slim briefcase onto the writing table in the sitting room and rummaged through it in search of a particular pamphlet she wanted to study on the automatic conversion of Indian commercial airports into military bases in cases of national emergency. She was trying to put together a list of probable terrorist targets, each of which she intended to research briefly, in order to be prepared for any breaking stories. But the frustration, anger and, if she was honest, disappointment at the prince's reaction in the hallway still rankled enough to make concentration next to impossible. The only explanation she could think of was that his initial mistrust of her motives for being in Delhi still overshadowed his growing feeling for her.

She forced herself to focus on her work. How long she sat bent over the small blurry print typical of Indian publications she had no idea. But when the phone buzzed—a sudden irritation of noise in the otherwise still night—she discovered she was stiff as she rose to answer it. Glancing out the windows, Julie realized that the lights in the opposite curving wing of the palace were all out and that the sky was dark black. It must be past midnight. She picked up the receiver.

"Hello?"

"Come to my office," commanded the prince's voice.

JAI ROSE FROM BEHIND HIS DESK when she entered. His white shirt was open at the neck, revealing his tanned throat and a tuft of curling dark chest hair. Julie, still dressed in the orange sundress she had worn to Chandni Chowk, noticed his suit coat and tie thrown in a careless heap on a needlepoint upholstered chair nearby. The clock on the mantelpiece said it was one-thirty in the morning.

The prince stared at her for a moment, as though he had forgotten having sent for her. His dark eyes, slightly bloodshot from long hours of reading reports, roved over her. She heard his sharp intake of breath and saw his long-fingered hands clench and unclench. Abruptly he turned his back on her and walked over to a well-stocked liquor cabinet.

"You wanted me?" Julie asked, her tone one of professional indifference.

He poured a drink from a heavy crystal decanter and turned around. His powerful form cast a threatening shadow across the room. "I did," he replied. "God help me if I still do. Read the printout on my desk."

Julie walked over and picked up a thin sheaf of telex paper covered with square computer type. She was aware of Jai's eyes on her face, of the intense, potent vitality of his nearness. She riffled through the papers in her hands. They seemed to be a series of reports. The locations, printed at the top of each page followed by different words that might be code names, were various cities in India. She glanced up to meet the prince's intent gaze.

"Intelligence reports?" she asked.

He nodded once in assent.

"Government agents?"

"No, my own men," he replied.

Julie slipped into a chair beside the large desk. She laid the papers on the polished mahogany surface. Julie lowered her forehead onto her hand and closed her eyes a moment, guessing what was coming. Then she turned back to the beginning of the reports, reading the complete text this time. Jai watched her in silence for a few minutes, then paced with restless strides around the large room until she had finished.

"Oh, no!" she whispered at one point, raising her eyes to Jai. "Not Mr. Dhawan!"

The prince's cold expression softened slightly. He set down his glass and crossed over to stand on the opposite side of the desk.

"Dhawan will probably pull through. He's in intensive care but listed as serious rather than critical."

When Julie had read the whole report carefully, she shuffled the pages together and pushed the neat stack into the center of the desk. The reports contained accounts of a series of brutal assassination attempts that had taken place simultaneously in several of India's largest cities within the last two hours. Reading them had reawakened the horrible, numbing revulsion she had experienced in connection with other terrorist events she had covered. She stood up from her chair, leaning on the corner edge of the desk. Her head hung down, spilling the thick mass of her golden blond hair forward in disorder; she tried to get a grip on her emotions.

"What do you know about this?" Jai asked, coming to stand beside her. His face was an expressionless mask, but his dark eyes burned with fiery alertness. Julie glanced up at him.

"You could make me hate you, Jai," she answered. "I knew nothing about this. I had nothing to do with it." A slow, involuntary shudder racked her body, ending in a dry sob that strangled in her throat. Another soundless sob escaped her, then another. She turned her head away, so he might not see the wet tears sliding over her smooth cheeks. She closed her eyes, trying to stop the flow.

She felt his arms come around her. He pulled her tight against his chest. In spite of her resolve, a fit of crying overcame her. She clutched his body, gripping the crisp cotton of his shirt with desperate hands. She could not hold back the flood of tears. A sense of universal sorrow pervaded her heart, as though all of mankind was lamenting this latest terrorist incident, as well. Every one of the targets had been—like Dhawan—wise, venerable people; Julie had met several of them at the ball. Jai held her close, stroking her hair as she wept.

When she was finished the prince stepped away from her, his face inscrutable. Julie moved back to the desk and sat on the chair beside it again. She pushed tear-dampened strands of blond hair back from her face and raised her eyes to his. Drained by that tidal wave of feeling, she could feel almost detached from the whole situation.

"I'm sorry. I lost control. Where were we?" she asked. "Why did you show me these reports?"

"What is your opinion of them?" he replied after a pause. A curious, probing expression glinted in his eyes. Otherwise his face and voice was impassive. It was as though nothing had happened just now, nothing had passed between them.

Maybe he considers himself weak for wanting to comfort me, Julie thought. She found she did not care. Somehow, compared with the terrible violence of the reports, nothing else much mattered.

"Has anyone claimed responsibility for these attacks?" she asked.

"Not yet. Maybe they will have by morning."

Julie considered the matter, unconsciously pulling the reports back across the desk toward her and idly sorting through them. "Do you think the assassinations could be a way to announce the formation of an official Indian terrorist organization, so to speak?" she asked after a couple of minutes, watching his face to catch any reaction he might have to this suggestion.

"I think it very likely."

"That would mean that the terrorists must have already met together and gotten organized. We missed our chance," she said, her voice bleak.

"Not necessarily. It's probable that this co-ordinated attack has been in the works a long time. One of the hallmarks of terrorists is that they never kill on impulse. Every move must be carefully researched, planned and carried out. To act on such a large scale as this must have taken months of preparation. Especially to be able to move against all their victims at the same time."

"Very dramatic," Julie murmured.

"Of course. You know as well as I do that, in order to be effective, terrorists must achieve a theatrical effect. That is the only way they can make their activities appear different in some aspect from ordinary crime.

"But these assassinations, though extensive, all took place in India. I have not heard any word of similar events in other countries tonight. I would have by now, had anything happened," he added, seeing Julie's amazed look. His lips twisted into a tight smile. "It's not really that I'm so addicted to international intrigue, you know. It just happens that being instantly informed of foreign events often helps me make a sounder business decision. World events have a direct and immediate effect on international trade and national economies."

"So you think these attacks tonight do not represent any alliance of terrorist groups, such as Mr. Dhawan talked about," Julie interposed.

"That Red Brigades leader just arrived yesterday morning," the prince pointed out, sitting down at his desk and leaning forward a little. "Nothing could have happened that fast. I think these assassinations are a show of strength by some newly formed Indian terrorist group, partly to announce their existence to the world and partly to impress upon visiting terrorist leaders that Indian terrorists must be taken seriously at the coming convention." He sat back in his chair, his dark eyes clouded with speculation.

"What a coup de grace to catch them all together," Julie murmured, half to herself.

"I hope to be there," he said, his voice soft with repressed anger.

"So do I," the woman opposite him replied.

Julie checked the information Jai had given her by phoning police stations in the cities where the attacks had occurred. Then she used the prince's telex to send the story to the foreign desk in New York, rather than wait for an overseas phone line. Jai offered to wake his secretary, but Julie assured him she knew how to operate the machine. She keyboarded the *Courier*'s telex number, typing in the story as she composed it in her head. She used the intelligence reports in front of her to supply the necessary details. The assassinations made a good peg on which to hang a general story that included all her observations and information about terrorist events in India to date, so it took her some time to complete her work.

At last, satisfied that she had covered everything and that she had managed to convey at least to some extent the horror of the assaults, Julie sat back from the machine exhausted. Not all of the attacks had been successful. She knew she would have to write a new lead for the following day's edition to update the readers about the survivors' conditions. The victims had been either high-level government officials or influential business leaders—representatives of the order of society terrorists found repugnant. She knew that, thanks to Jai, she was in all likelihood the first foreign correspondent to file the complete story of the coordinated terrorist strike.

Julie closed the door to the telex room, which connected with the prince's office. He had returned to his desk. Hearing her enter, he lifted his head from the large chart he was studying. A lock of dark hair fell forward across his brow. His white shirt was wrinkled, and he had opened two more buttons in the front.

"I'm sorry if I kept you up," Julie said, realizing she should have arranged to lock up after herself. The light from the desk lamp shone on her bare arms and shoulders, giving her skin a rich golden hue. Her cotton sundress, limp and mussed after the long night, clung to her lean thighs and full breasts, revealing and provocative. "It is very late." She felt dead with fatigue.

"It doesn't matter." He pushed the chart across his desk and leaned back in his chair, stretching. His shirt pulled open to reveal more of his broad, muscular chest. "I had plenty to keep me busy," he added.

Julie moved across the room toward him, almost staggering with weariness. She stopped several feet away, as though fearing to step within the field of his powerful, seductive attraction. The strain of the last hours had left her weak and vulnerable. She could feel the strong flow of magnetic current that swirled around him and made her long to try to reawaken his passion for her.

"Why did you show me those reports, Jai?" she asked, standing before him.

"Does it matter?" he replied slowly, his eyes taking in the luscious curves of her body revealed by the clinging sundress.

"It matters to me. Have you finally decided to cooperate with my investigation by making reports like those available? Or were you trying to surprise me into revealing my supposed involvement with the terrorists?"

"Let's just say I decided I can play the game either way," he answered after a moment, glancing down at his hands. "I will help you regardless of your true motives. If you are sincere in your efforts as a journalist, then by reporting the true story of terrorist activities you will invariably expose the hypocrisy of their methods and motives. If, on the other hand, you hope to benefit the terrorists by infiltrating my industrial organization, I will turn the tables on you and use you to lead me to them. I prefer to attack first, rather than wait for them," he added, rising from the chair.

Julie bit down hard on her lip, swallowing the urge to tell him what he could do with his offer of assistance. So he agreed to help her, but not to trust her! Well, she would take the half loaf offered to her for now. Her first concern must be for her story. But in the end she would somehow make him admit his mistake.

"We understand each other very well, I believe," he said, watching her with a cynical expression.

"You are mistaken, Jai," she retorted, turning away. "You don't understand me at all." She walked across the room and out the door, despising herself each step of the way for physically wanting a man who doubted her integrity.

CHAPTER ELEVEN

JULIE STUDIED HER REFLECTION in the mirror with critical eyes. She had intended a more professional look. The lightweight, soft gray summer suit was her standby for important interviews and business meetings. Maybe her favorite ruffled pink blouse was the problem. Too late to change the blouse for a crisp white cotton shirt, she settled for twisting her thick curls into a punishing chignon, set smooth and chic low on her neck.

Her preoccupation with her appearance stemmed from having worked with the prince every day the past week. She had discovered nothing escaped his scrutiny. She did not want him to think for a moment she was dressing to please him. As he favored soft, feminine clothing on women, she had deliberately begun to create the most severe, professional outfits she could from her limited wardrobe. The pink blouse was a definite mistake, she thought with regret, as she flung down her comb and grabbed her notebook. She made it a point never to be late for her ten-o'clock daily appointment.

Jai glanced up as she entered. He was dressed casually in white slacks and a short-sleeved navy shirt, so Julie guessed he had no appointments away from the palace scheduled for the morning.

"That will be all, Hari." The thin, slight Indian man rose, nodded politely to Julie and left the room.

"You're slipping up, Julie," the prince said, once his secretary had gone. His eyes brushed over her once, then returned to the map spread open on his desk. "Or have you decided to quit mimicking an elderly dowd?" he added without looking up. "I admit it's a relief. I was afraid you had taken wearing color in permanent aversion."

"I'm sure you didn't schedule this appointment in order to discuss my wardrobe," Julie replied, irritated.

"No? How little you know me." He glanced up, his eyes lighted with amusement.

"What are you doing?" Julie asked quickly, indicating the map on the desk. The warm teasing note in his voice made her uncomfortable because she knew it could not lead anywhere. Jai's lack of trust in her was an unspoken, insurmountable barrier to any real feeling of friendship between them, no matter how well they might work together.

Which they did. Julie had found the prince a brilliant partner in investigation. She usually spent about an hour each day in his office, discussing intelligence reports or leads she had uncovered. The rest of the time she continued with her own research. She felt she was building up an accurate picture of the international terrorist scene. It was rather like fitting together pieces of a jigsaw puzzle. It was only a matter of time before she would uncover the piece she was seeking—a clue as to the date and location of the conference of terrorist leaders.

"This map shows the places where the assassination attempts took place," Jai was saying, his voice thoughtful. "What do you notice about it?"

Julie came around to the other side of the desk. Bright red dots were scattered across the map of India.

"The attacks were more concentrated in the southern half of the country," she said after a few moments.

"Yes. In fact, except for Dhawan here in New Delhi, almost every assault happened in the south. By the way, Dhawan went home from the hospital today."

"That's good news! I liked him so much the time I met him." She walked back around the desk and sat opposite the prince.

"He liked you, too. Did you know that?" Jai caught her eyes across the polished wood surface. He gave her a measured, appraising look.

Julie flushed. "Is that so hard for you to accept?" she countered.

"My compliments. Dhawan is not an easy man to take in."

Julie half rose from her chair, her hands gripping the edge of the desk. "So help me, Jai—" she began.

"Sit down and be quiet, Julie. You and I will never agree on that point. Believe me, there is no use in trying to convince me." His voice was bored, indifferent. "What about this map?"

Julie sank back into her chair. She closed her eyes and forced her mind to count to ten. After all, what did it matter what Jai thought about her? He was helping her track the terrorists and that was all that counted. Her boss hadn't sent her here to win a popularity contest. Which was fortunate—her ratings were disappointingly low.

"I think if I was planning a terrorist conference," the prince said slowly, glancing down at the map again, "I would want to make sure that all available antiterrorist police squads were searching for terrorists in some other part of the country."

"You mean we should look for an area with a lack of terrorist activity?" she replied, her anger forgotten. It made sense.

"Lots of activity down in Maharashtra, Tamil Nadu, Andhra Pradesh," he continued, naming some of the south Indian states. "Nothing up north in Punjab, Himachal Pradesh or Kashmir. Well?"

"It seems simple enough," Julie conceded. "Drawing away the police with a false scent. But would the terrorists really stage all those assassinations just to divert attention from their conference grounds?"

"The attacks were probably multipurpose. A step toward forcing political change. A trap for the government, trying to force harsh reprisals—such as massive arrests—that will harm the innocent along with the guilty and thus raise public outcry against the administration. An attempt to jockey for power among other terrorist groups to strengthen their position at the coming conference. Did you read the news, by the way? A group called the Black Band is claiming responsibility for the assaults."

"Yes, I heard that. I sent a 'new-top' to my editor about it."

"Anyway, why not distribute the attacks evenly across the nation? That would have served the other purposes just as well. But in the latest reports, the police and newsmen are referring to the Black Band as a new South Indian terrorist group. So of course the police are searching for them in the southern states."

"Meanwhile, they hold a conference in a northern state."

"Right. Didn't your stringer say his source said the rumor indicated a meeting in northern India?"

"Yes...." Julie considered the question. "At the time I guess I assumed New Delhi would be the logical spot."

"Well, Delhi is north. And the national capital. Also, terrorists these days tend to stick to large cities rather than rural areas. It is easier to hide in a city, and they would have a bigger group sympathetic to their interests. But there are other large cities in the north: Chandigarh, Simla, Srinagar."

"You know, the northern states *are* closer to Afghanistan," Julie suggested. "If some of the terrorists were on good terms with the Russians, they might be able to get aid in crossing into India that way, even though the Pakistan border is heavily guarded." She kept a careful watch on his face. Usually the prince's reactions appeared only a brief instant in his expression. She had never known a man who guarded his thoughts and feelings so closely.

"Yes. I have wondered at the carelessness of the captured Red Brigades leader. He deserved to be caught. Airports are easy to watch. Most of the terrorists will come in by train, or ocean freighter, or even on foot. Crossing over from Pakistan or perhaps Nepal would be ideal, if they could arrange it."

"Isn't Kashmir a big tourist spot here?" Julie asked after a pause.

"Yes. The upper-class Indians who can afford to travel flock to the hill stations—the towns and cities near the Himalayas—as soon as the hot weather hits. I have a summer palace in Srinagar, the state capital, myself.''

"What about foreign tourists?" she probed.

"I think Kashmir is a famous vacation spot the world over. It is very picturesque." He regarded her with interest. "What are you getting at?"

She dropped her eyes, then raised them to meet his. "I was just thinking that the majority of the terrorists will not be Indians. They will need to be able to blend in with their surroundings. It is late spring now. With the temperature over a hundred degrees and rising like it has been here the last few days, I can't imagine that New Delhi does much tourist business a month from now. The conference would need to be held where foreigners were too common to excite any speculation. Doesn't that just leave Kashmir?"

"Very good, Julie!" He leaned back in his chair and regarded her with something akin to approval. Then he picked up a phone, dialed and spoke in Hindi for three or four minutes. When he hung up he said:

"We don't want to narrow our search down too far yet, in case you are wrong. But I've just now ordered a team of my best intelligence people to go to Kashmir to see what they can find out. I also told them to check and see if there are any sports, cultural or religious events planned anywhere else that would involve a large influx of foreigners. Kashmir is mostly a Muslim population,'' he added, a speculative gleam in his eye. ''I can't think of a better way to disguise a person than to cover him from head to foot with a purdah veil.''

''Do they really still wear those awful black things?'' Julie queried.

''But of course!'' The corners of his mouth twisted with a teasing smile. ''Imagine seeing the world through a tiny patch of black netting for your whole life. Just be glad I am Hindu instead of Muslim, or I might feel it my sacred duty to veil you.''

''I think I'd rather be dead than cooped up under all that cloth,'' Julie responded. ''It must feel like a walking cage.''

He laughed. ''Well, in your case I think a Muslim husband would be wise to make you wear purdah. It would probably save him a lot of bloodshed in the long run.''

''Bloodshed?'' The flame had sprung into his eyes.

''Do you think a man who married you would not be willing to fight to keep you?'' he asked softly. ''You underestimate your own beauty. Or else the passions of Asian men.''

''It isn't like that anymore,'' Julie declared with a smile. ''People just get divorces nowadays, you know, and tell everyone that they are still the best of friends." She jerked back as his hand slammed forward and caught her wrist against the desk, the loud clapping noise ringing in her ears.

"Don't ever marry a Mishra descendant, then," he growled, "or you will find out differently to your own sorrow. Having once had you, I think a man would rather kill you than lose you."

She turned to stare at him, her eyes locked with his own. "Well, as you are the only Mishra descendant I know," she managed to say with assumed calmness as she slipped her hand out from beneath his loosened grasp, "I think we can safely dispense with one worry at least, don't you?"

JULIE RETURNED TO HER ROOM to find Sukundala arranging a large bouquet of fresh roses on the bedside table, something she did every day after cleaning the bedroom suite. Before she left the maid imparted some unwelcome news: Priya's fiancé was coming to the palace tomorrow to meet the young princess for the first time.

Julie fingered the satiny blossoms as she digested the information. She realized this meeting was a concession on Jai's part, as some Indian brides and bridegrooms did not even see each other until their wedding day. Since he knew nothing about Lal's existence, he must be hoping Priya would take a liking to Prakash and become reconciled to the approaching marriage.

But Julie wished Jai was not pushing the matter along so fast. She could imagine how frantic the princess would be, feeling that even to meet Prakash Das would be betraying her love for Lal. Sometimes Julie wondered if, left to her own judgment, Priya would come to realize that she would be happier in the long run by not alienating herself from her society. Or maybe she would even discover that Lal was not the ideal lover she had thought him to be. It seemed to Julie pretty cravenhearted on his part that he expected Priya to find a way to stop the wedding.

For some reason her mind shot back to the scene that morning in Jai's office, when he asserted his willingness to fight for the woman he would someday love. She felt sure *he* would be able to find a way to keep the woman he wanted from marrying someone else, no matter what the obstacles.

A faint smile curved her lips. Working with Jai had given her new insights into his complex personality. For one thing, she had been amazed at the subtlety he could use to gain his ends, and at the enormous amount of political and economic clout he could bring to bear when he wanted. His backing had made her own investigation a thousand times easier. Suddenly Julie wondered what Priya would think if she could see Lal Delal face to face

with her own brother—surely the too-polished
suitor must suffer by the comparison, even in
Priya's besotted mind.

Julie went into her sitting room to pore
over a new batch of research documents—
newspapers, speeches, opposition propagan-
da and police logs. She found it hard to concentrate on her work, however. Her thoughts
kept reverting to the problem of Priya's marriage.

For the umpteenth time she considered
breaking her promise to the princess and lay-
ing the whole matter before Jai. Despite her
own antagonism toward him at times, working in his office in the past week had forced
her to recognize the high values and fierce
loyalties of her host. Time and again, while
she was using the telex or perusing some
terrorist-related intelligence report he wanted
her opinion on, she had overheard him make
a business decision based on loyalty or compassion rather than pure profit. Such as the
time he had agreed to accept much-delayed
payments on a shipment of steel beams after
a construction project had caught fire. He
had told the speaker on the other end of the
telephone—a financial advisor, Julie had
presumed—with asperity that he had no intention of foreclosing on a friend of his
father's, so not to bring the matter to his attention again.

Yet, even though Julie worried about Priya

seeing Lal in secret, she could not bring herself to broach the matter to Jai. She was afraid he might not show the same compassion to his own sister as he did to others. His sense of family pride was such that Julie feared he might react with harsh reprisals against Priya, feeling she had humiliated the Mishra name by loving someone beneath her station.

Irritated, Julie swept aside the text of a speech by a pompous, ingratiating politician. How did the wire services ever get any facts about this news-repressive country, she wondered. Would she ever get used to a society that did not respect the concept of a free press? She rose and strode out onto the balcony, the hot marble burning her feet through her thin-soled sandals. Heat waves shimmered in the distance, lacing the trees on the horizon with wavy ripples of light.

Julie leaned over the rail, gazing out across the palace grounds and letting the bright noonday heat sink through her clothing and warm the tight muscles in her back and neck. She was constantly aware of the enormous contrast between Asia and the Western world. She was beginning to feel that on the exotic stage of India's high plains, the greatest tragedies and the greatest glories were both possible.

A vision of Jai—the sharp, handsome planes of his face; his burning intelligent

eyes; that broad-shouldered, powerful, alluring body—formed before her eyes. He seemed
to embody the contrasts of East and West: the
most urbane, charming, cosmopolitan man
Julie had ever met, yet more passionate, more
hauntingly attractive than she ever could have
imagined. She found herself drawn to him
with a primitive force that was impossible to
resist.

Julie's hands tightened on the smooth marble railing. She must not give in to this
ungovernable desire. To do so would be to in-
sure a tragedy, for herself at least, that would
be beyond bearing. He would use her and
then discard her. Hadn't he said as much,
when he accused her of being a terrorist spy?
She must conquer the thrill of discovery she
felt growing inside, the blossoming appreciation for such a complex, fascinating man.
Her eyes focused on the distant trees without
seeing them. She felt as though through resolve alone she could banish the heat waves
Jai excited in her mind.

SUKUNDALA BORE A MESSAGE to Julie from
Priya the following morning. Although it was
graciously worded, Julie nevertheless caught
the underlying note of panic. She slipped into
the crisp blue-and-white sundress she had laid
out, leaving the white blazer to wear over it
on the chair back for the time being. She
planned to spend the day checking with her

contacts in Delhi's many embassies to see if they had anything new to report. But first she would stop in to see Priya.

Julie entered the princess's room to find the maharani there, also, helping her daughter prepare for the interview with her future husband. Priya twisted around when she heard the door open, jerking away from the pleats the maharani was tucking into the front of her slip. Pale lilac folds of chiffon silk laced with sparkling gold threads cascaded to the floor.

"Oh, Priya, what a wonderful sari!" Julie exclaimed without thinking. "I have never seen you look more beautiful. You really do look just like a fairy-tale princess."

"I don't care how I look!" wailed the girl. "I wish I looked horrible! Then no one would want to marry me."

"Really, my child," interposed the maharani, "you must compose yourself. You are behaving with extreme lack of consideration for Julie's feelings. I am sure she did not come here to witness a scene. Jai gave his sister this sari," she added to Julie. "I agree with you; it is the most beautiful one I have seen, and I've seen many."

"Julie," interrupted Priya in a pleading tone, "talk to Jai for me. He will do anything for you! Beg him not to make me go through with this. He could still stop it! When Prakash Das comes here this morning, Jai could meet with him and tell him there has been a mistake!''

The maharani looked up from straightening Priya's sari, a concerned look on her face. "Why don't you talk with Jai, Julie?" she said slowly. "He *does* listen to you. Priya is right. I should have thought of this myself. I'm afraid she is going to get ill with all this excitement. What is the hurry, after all? She is still young enough that she doesn't have to marry this instant. Why not let her wait another year if she wishes it so much. By then she will realize how happy marriage will make her. Of course, Prakash Das might not be willing to wait so long,'' she added with a regretful sigh. "But I suppose it doesn't matter so much after all. Jai can find a husband equally as good when the time comes.''

"Yes! Yes! Let me wait a year!" Priya cried. A year was as good as eternity as far as she was concerned.

"But Jai won't listen to *me*,'' Julie protested, looking from one eager face to the other.

"He does listen to you!" Priya asserted. "I've watched him when he joins us for dinner. He treats you like a person he respects.''

"His attitude toward you is unique, Julie,'' the maharani agreed. "Surely you must have noticed? I have often thought perhaps it is because you are interested in the things he is—politics, and India's future, and such. He enjoys talking with you—he laughs more.''

"But that is business. In private we always argue," Julie objected.

"Ah, well." The maharani lifted her shoulders and extended her palms in an eloquent shrug. "Mishra men like to argue. Believe me, I know! Please do go talk to him, Julie, while I try to restore Priya."

Julie was knocking on the library door before she recovered from her surprise. That the maharani and Priya could think that she had the power to sway Jai was absurd. But in the face of their joint entreaties she had had no choice but to try, hopeless though she knew her efforts to be. Because Jai might respect her opinion on work-related topics did not mean he would welcome her advice.

"Come in!" a familiar voice invited.

Jai was standing beside a tall bookshelf, a leather-bound volume in his hand. The dark coolness of the library and the rich smell of wood and books delighted Julie's senses. The prince paused to mark a passage with his finger, then looked up, raising his eyebrows when he saw Julie. He wore a white shirt of fine cotton, loose with wide sleeves and a deep V down the front that exposed most of his powerful chest. His pants, of sturdier black cotton, were cut wide and sashed with a heavy black belt. His feet were bare. Julie sensed a new physical alertness about him— never had she felt such primitive, masculine power radiate from someone as she did now.

Yet on the surface, at least, he appeared relaxed.

"Did Hari forget to tell you that I would not be available for our usual consultation this morning?" he asked. "I was under the impression that you planned to visit the embassies today, so I made other arrangements."

"He told me, thank you. But that's not why I am here. What are you doing?"

"I don't leave all my protection to my bodyguards, you know," he answered, an amused half smile twisting one corner of his mouth. "I've been working out in my gym. But a phrase from one of the great martial-arts masters—Taisen Deshimaru, if you have heard of him—kept eluding me. Finally I had to come up here and look up the exact passage. But what can I do for you? Have you uncovered a new lead?"

"I'm not here on business." She felt the attraction from the dark man before her like a tangible force in the room. Julie wished she had not agreed to come.

The prince laid aside the book he was holding. "Am I to assume you came here for pleasure, then?"

"I came because of Priya," she replied.

"Ah." His voice relaxed. "An emissary from the sacrificial victim."

"Jai," Julie said, moving to his side, "it really is cruel. You know she doesn't want to get married—at least not now. Your mother thinks that if you would give Priya a little more time—say another year—she will naturally become reconciled to marriage."

"Tell me, what do *you* think, Julie," he said, the words almost a sneer.

She dropped her eyes. How could she answer that question truthfully, without revealing the existence of Lal? Perhaps the maharani was right. After all, a lot could happen in a year. Priya might lose interest in Lal. At least she would not be forced into marriage.

"What can a year hurt?" she asked. "I think your mother is right."

"The sooner Priya marries, the better," he replied, enunciating each word with deliberate force. "I have no intention of allowing my sister the license Western women have," he added.

"Of choosing their own husbands?"

"Of choosing their lovers."

"Priya? I really don't think she would do that, Jai."

"I wasn't thinking of Priya just now. I was thinking of you."

"Are you condemning me for what happened in the garden?" she asked, meeting his eyes squarely. "The situations are entirely different. A woman in my culture who takes a lover doesn't face the total social ostracism one encounters here."

He took her chin between his long fingers.

She could smell the sweat from his workout in the gym—a clear, musky odor not the least bit unpleasant. He tilted up her face. "I could never censure you for what happened. Don't ever think that, Julie. What we shared together can never be taken from us, no matter what the future brings."

Julie's heart lurched in her chest. She had almost given up hope of ever hearing that special undertone of tenderness in his voice again. She sensed that, beneath that masculine reserve, he wanted to reach out to her, communicate with her, share a little in words of what their hearts had shared in the secret garden. A warm current of desire awoke in her body in response to his need. For perhaps the first time she could see him not just as a man but as a friend, another human being struggling to live according to his own code of honor, as she tried to live according to hers.

"What worries, you, Jai?" she asked, reaching up and touching his bare chest with her fingertips. "What does the future hold that troubles you so much?"

His eyes searched her face as though trying to read the truth to that question in the clearness of her gaze. "I've told you before that Indian princes live longer if they mistrust the motives of those around them. I was raised to trust no one." He paused, letting his hand drop away from her face. "I find myself wanting to trust you."

"Then do."

"If I could. . . ." His breath caught. The flame shot forth from the depths of his dark eyes. "Sometimes I feel that my destiny lies with you, Julie," he murmured, his voice low. "This much I do know: whatever was between us before will be better still. Whatever pleasure I gave you, I will give more. Believe me, Julie, a thousand times more."

He pulled her to him then. She did not resist. His words, his nearness, the glow of his dark eyes. . . they aroused her past caution, as though she knew in her heart of hearts what he said was true. She sensed the destiny of which he spoke: that he alone could give her the fulfillment her soul craved, could satisfy the deep desires that had cried out in her since the night of the ball. She lifted her eyes away from his dark chest to meet his own glittering gaze.

A brilliant, laughing smile flashed across Jai's face. His strong arms released her. He jerked the fine cotton shirt over his head and tossed it aside. Julie stared at his hard sinewy muscles. Black hair curled into a dense mat in the middle of his chest and ran down the center of his flat stomach in a dark vertical line. He had the broad-shouldered, narrow-waisted, iron-hard physique of a professional athlete. Julie longed to be initiated into the mysteries of that perfect male body—to learn each smooth contour of muscle, each spot of pleasure. To please such a man. . . .

Jai withstood her riveted gaze without self-consciousness. With adroit fingers he began to undo the tiny flowered buttons down the front of her sundress. She trembled at his touch, shaken by a tremor deep within the inner recesses of her body. She moaned with anticipatory pleasure as his strong hands worked their way down the tight bodice. She reached out tentative fingers to touch his arm, tracing his massive biceps.

"So chaste a touch, Julie?" he asked, his voice tender. "I will not show similar restraint." He brushed the strap of her sundress off her shoulder with a gentle motion, then slid his hand beneath the open bodice. It came to rest on her left breast.

A wave of joy washed over Julie. The tone of Jai's voice filled her with a strange sweetness, even as it struck a dissonant note of confusion in her brain. Did he still distrust her? No. Surely not. He was pulling her against him now. He slipped the sundress off one shoulder, revealing her breast. He pressed her close.

The hair on his chest grazed her nipple, bringing it to a delicious hardness. Julie moaned again, a husky groan that ended in a whisper of need. His body hardened in sharp response. He bent over her, his mouth fastened to hers, as he slid his left hand up under the skirt of her dress, tracing the slim length of her well-shaped thighs.

His hand slipped beneath the lace of her

panties and gripped the curve of her buttock. He pulled her up and forward so she could feel for herself his answer to her urgent desire. Her teeth sank into his neck to stifle the scream of pleasure in her throat.

"Delight of my life," he murmured, a soft growl of satisfaction rumbling in his chest. He lowered her to the carpet in one smooth movement. "To think I have my little sister to thank for this moment!"

"Priya!" Julie exclaimed, stricken. "I . . . I forgot!"

"Forget again," he admonished her.

But a vision of the heartbroken princess in the bedroom awaiting her return flashed through Julie's mind. She opened her eyes to stare at the man lying on his side next to her, watching her face through half-closed eyes. Did she need any better reminder of his ability to use people for his own ends? He was willing to sacrifice the happiness of his own sister to preserve his family's position in the world! How easy it would be for Jai to use her only to satisfy his own desire.

Julie pushed him away with a violence that surprised even herself. A quick twist and she was out of his arms and on her feet. She buttoned the front of her dress with trembling fingers. He rolled over on his back, regarding her beneath languid, hooded eyelids. But she did not miss the deadly flash that leaped into his eyes. She jumped back, ready to flee.

However, the prince merely rose up on one elbow, then pushed up onto his feet with an easy gesture. He stood beside the bookcase looking down at her as he straightened the black belt around his naked waist. Barefoot and dressed only in loose black cotton pants, he towered before her like some primitive warlord. Awe crept through Julie's numb brain, despite herself.

"You use people for your own purposes!" she accused. "Your sister. Me." She choked back a dry sob of frustration and humiliation.

"You do have your uses," he agreed. She knew him well enough to recognize the anger beneath that quiet voice. "Why did you stop? Surely your comrades expect you to do all that is necessary to placate my suspicions!"

"You...you!" In blind rage, she reached out and grabbed the first thing she found—a heavy blue-and-cinnamon vase on an end table beside her. Grasping it with both hands, Julie heaved the antique porcelain at him with vicious accuracy. He stepped aside. The vase hurled into the bookcase with a deafening crash, scattering out beautiful brightly colored fragments in a wide semicircle across the carpet.

The silent aftermath of tinkling china filled the room. Julie stared at the bookcase in dawning horror. The tidal wave of fury that had swept through her when Jai accused her of being a terrorist drained away, leaving her weak. Why did everything about him affect her so strongly? Why could she never keep her equilibrium around this man? Why did she always have to either love him or hate him, with nothing in between? She gazed down at the broken vase appalled.

"What do you do to me!" Julie stormed. She whirled and rushed from the library.

CHAPTER TWELVE

JULIE HEARD A CAR coming up the long driveway to the palace. After informing the maharani that her mission of mercy had failed, she
had escaped from the oppressive atmosphere
of the princess's bedroom for a brisk walk
across the grounds. Now she sat slouched on a
bench beneath a mango tree, head in hands,
unable to work or even to think clearly. She
felt utterly defeated, not so much by the prince
as by her own attraction to him.

For the first time since coming to India, she
doubted her ability to successfully complete
her story. More and more, her thoughts gravitated to Jai Mishra. She was used to function-
ing with her mind completely absorbed in her
work. Now she found herself torn apart. Part
of her strove to maintain her usual brisk pro-
fessionalism. But the clearheaded efficiency
she had always relied on had been shattered by
the tumultuous, irresistible, wanton emotions
and sensuality that the prince aroused. Despite
her best effort, the distinct line between objectivity in her work and involvement with the
prince was becoming blurred.

Then there was Priya. Julie's heart went out to her. She had seen the princess's pale face turn toward her as she reported on her visit to the library. Julie knew, if no one else did, that the Indian girl was not resigned to her fate. She had seen Priya set her mouth in a straight, determined line as she listened to Julie's words. For the first time the resemblance between brother and sister, other than physical attractiveness, was strikingly clear.

Julie rose and returned to the palace. She needed to get some work done. She reached the top stair of the veranda just as a dark blue Porsche pulled up. Even as the driver jumped out and started toward her, Julie realized who he was.

The man ascending the marble stairs with a light step was younger than the prince and not as tall. But as he paused a moment to glance about him she saw that, if rumor lied, it was only not to do him enough justice. He was the most handsome man Julie had ever laid eyes on. A vision flashed through her mind's eye of Priya and him together: she could see at once why Jai had supposed they would suit.

Prakash Das had classically perfect features—too manly to be beautiful but without the cynical harshness that characterized Jai's own more roughly cast face. The young man on the stairs looked cheerful, friendly, sensitive, and more than a little dashing. He was trim with strong, broad shoulders—any broader and he would have been stocky. His well-built body lacked the prince's tigerlike grace, but he certainly appeared to be in perfect condition.

"Hi!" Julie accompanied her greeting with a smile, extending her hand. "I'm Julie Connell, a houseguest of the Mishras."

"How do you do. I'm Prakash Das." His boyish grin conveyed the information that he knew, as did Julie, that every person in the palace from the lowest gardener's assistant to the maharani would be watching for his arrival.

"I guessed," Julie replied with an answering smile. "Please don't let me keep you."

"Thank you. I don't want to be late. It's nice to have met you!"

Watching him walk away, Julie felt sure that if Priya had not formed a previous attachment, Prakash Das could not have failed to please her. He radiated a certain peacefulness that would have complemented Priya's own romantic sweetness. As it was, nothing could come of the match. But Julie felt a sudden charity toward Jai: he certainly had done his best by his sister. No doubt he had arranged this early meeting between the betrothed couple for the sole purpose of setting the young princess's mind at rest, never guessing how much distress such a course of action would cause her.

Julie returned to her room. A slow hour

ticked by. As her embassy appointments were
scheduled later in the morning, she stayed
at her desk trying to work. She found herself
listening for Priya's soft step outside the
sitting-room door. The American woman
fully expected to hear a tearful account of the
whole ordeal as soon as the princess's un-
wanted guest left the palace. Julie prepared
herself to listen with at least assumed patience
as Priya recounted the superiorities of her
own chosen suitor, vowing not to try to interfere with Priya's determination to stand by
Lal Delal, despite the invincible forces moving against Priya.

Eventually the hum of the car engine outside started up and moved off toward the distant trees. To Julie's surprise, Priya did not
come to visit her. Nor was the princess at
lunch when Julie went downstairs. The maharani told Julie that her daughter had gone
directly to her room as soon as her caller
departed, without speaking to anyone. She
had remained there alone, allowing admittance to no one. Julie left for the embassies
without seeing her.

A creamy white envelope propped up on
her dressing table caught Julie's eye the moment she entered her suite several hours later.
Casting aside her notebook, she grasped the
card and tore it open, her heart lurching in
her chest with a sick feeling of apprehension.

Her fear proved to be unfounded. The note

was not from Priya. Instead, the prince's bold, sloping scrawl leaped out at her surprised eyes. He requested that she attend a dinner party with him that evening at the home of one of New Delhi's reigning industrialists.

Julie stared hard at the flowing black words, reading the short note twice. She could discover no subtle sarcasm underlying the prince's polite phrasing. He did not even specify that he invited her to accompany him purely for business reasons, although after the morning's scene in the library Julie could not delude herself into any other explanation for this signal honor. If appearing with Prince Jaiapradesh Mishra as an escort *was* an honor, which she rather thought it was. She had noticed that whenever Hari phoned a response to the prince's numerous engagements, he RSVPed for only one person. Which was not to say there were not other, more intimate occasions not left to the jurisdiction of the prince's efficient secretary....

Whatever the case, Julie found herself dressing with great care. A glance at the mantel clock assured her she had time enough to get ready, despite her late return from the embassies. She wondered why Jai had not told her of the engagement earlier. But as a journalist, she was used to moving quickly. If there was any chance of news gathering at this party, she was glad for the opportunity to attend. The last-minute nature of the note only confirmed what she knew: it was a business, not a social date.

Still, forty-five minutes later as she examined herself before the three-way dressing-room mirror, the tingle of pleasurable anticipation that brought a warm flush to her cheeks had nothing to do with journalistic investigation. She had chosen a black cocktail dress of lustrous satiny silk. Cut with almost severe simplicity, it looked incredibly chic on Julie's elegant body. The sleeveless dress, gathered at the shoulders, plunged in both front and back all the way to the wide V-shaped black satin belt that clasped her tiny waist. The skirt flared out over her hips, then converged tightly around her knees, the long slit up one side revealing a glimpse of a well-shaped thigh and emphasizing the long line of her leg.

She wore high-heeled black satin sandals, purchased especially for this dress. A single pearl drop—a relatively inexpensive solution to the problem of evening jewelry—glowed on her neck. She carried a black silk evening bag with a tiny pearl clasp. At the last minute she decided to leave her hair loose, only lifting it away from her face on the sides with matching combs.

She brushed her lips with a raspberry gloss, using a soft violet blusher to highlight her high cheekbones. A connoisseur of expensive perfumes—her one real extravagance—Julie dabbed her wrists and throat with Jean Patou's Joy in a valiant gesture to the promise of the night to come. She could look forward to an evening in the prince's company tonight since in such a public setting she would be safe from her own treacherous desire.

Jai was waiting for her in the domed entrance hall. The skylights that infused this circular room with sunlight during the daytime now appeared as star-studded panels of deep black in the white marble ceiling. Hidden lights illuminated the room. Standing on the richly colored tile, his tall form dominating his surroundings, Jai reminded Julie of a man of bygone times. He looked every inch the royal prince he was as he watched her approach.

"You look very distinguished tonight," she said with assumed lightness. She was aware of a sudden shyness that had nothing to do with the awkwardness of their last meeting. She felt as if she were seeing Jai for the first time—seeing him *whole*, as if she were beholding the full force of his masterful personality shimmering in the air around him. A rush of acknowledgment, of recognition for what he was, passed through her.

"You received my note," he said. "I'm sorry I didn't ask you earlier. I had forgotten the engagement until Hari reminded me this afternoon. It occurred to me that you might find this party enjoyable. I'm glad you could join me on such short notice." His eyes moved over her with peculiar languor, taking in each detail of her appearance as he spoke.

"Thank you for asking me," Julie murmured, watching his face from beneath her long lashes. His eyes flashed to meet hers. He held her gaze—his eyes intense, bright, flickering with flame—until she expelled a long-held breath. What other man could look at a woman so that she forgets to breathe, Julie wondered, shaken.

"You are beautiful tonight," he stated. "You will make me the envy of every other man there."

"You probably already are," she replied, laughing. An answering smile curved the corners of his mouth, softening the harsh lines of his face. "If they knew the whole, they would think differently," he assured her.

"Like having to deal with inquisitive reporters?" she teased. She was willing to forget their contretemps of the morning, as he obviously intended for them to do. It would make the evening much more pleasant. She felt relieved just to talk with him for a change. So often their encounters had been disagreeably intense.

He looked down at her. "Any man in his right mind would desire to deal with you—reporter or not." His hand reached out. He touched the pearl on her neck. "Why this?"

"Don't you like it? This is my favorite necklace with this dress."

"I would have thought a woman would wear diamonds with a dress like that," he replied, his face inscrutable.

She laughed. "You must be a mind reader. I've always thought so, too. But one of the few disadvantages of my chosen profession is the pay. What a pity my editor doesn't recognize my true value. Whenever I've just filed an especially good story, I feel like I must be worth several million a year."

Julie saw a curious flicker appear and disappear in his eyes. "Does your work bring you that much pleasure?" he asked, his dark eyes intent on her upturned face.

"Yes, it does, Jai," she replied, meeting his look. "It really does."

"You're fortunate," he stated after a pause.

"I know."

He took her arm and smiled down at her. They went out through the double doors, held wide by liveried servants, and down the marble stairs. The prince's red sports car awaited them, engine running. Jai helped her into the passenger seat, then went back around the car. For some reason Julie felt pleased that he intended to drive them himself tonight, rather than use Gunam Singh and the Mercedes.

The party was in full swing when they arrived. Their host, an English textile-mill owner and exporter named Leon Calvert, greeted Jai with enthusiasm and then turned to Julie, a look of inquiry on his face too obvious to be missed. Jai performed the introductions.

"So, Julie, for once Jaiapradesh will do more than talk business at one of my dinners. I have you to thank for that. I owe you a favor, indeed!"

"I will be sure to collect it in that case," Julie replied, laughing. She liked Leon on sight. In fact, she liked Jai's taste in friends in general.

A peculiar rush of pride flowed through Julie as she entered Leon Calvert's living room on Jai's arm. Her fingers rested lightly on the sleeve of his dark suit. She was keenly aware of him beside her. A quiver of excitement stole through her: she felt that familiar stirring within her body in spontaneous response to his attractiveness. Her senses became alive, alert, totally receptive. She felt relaxed. Happy.

"Can I get you a drink?" Jai asked. He looked relaxed, too, at home among friends. "Leon's predinner cocktail hour can last indefinitely."

"In that case, I won't overlook those delicious hors d'oeuvres," she replied.

"I'll bring you some."

As she watched him walk away, Julie became aware of someone beside her.

"Quite a man, Jaiapradesh Mishra," boomed Leon Calvert.

"Do you always call him by his full name?" Julie asked, turning to her host with a smile. He fitted her image of an English country squire. She wondered why he chose to live in India.

"Good heavens, no!" he exclaimed with mock horror. "You should hear his full name! Takes half an hour to say it all, including all the titles."

"Titles? I thought his title was just 'prince.' "

"It is now. I'm talking about the traditional way he would have been addressed, had things not changed. You know: 'Protector of the People,' 'The Intelligent Praiser of the Gods,' 'Grantor of Abundant Boons,' 'Oppressor of the Foe.' "

"You're making those up," Julie accused.

"Maybe I am, maybe I am." He winked. "You should read some of the old literature, though. You'd see what I'm talking about. Besides, Jaiapradesh strikes me as that type, if you know what I mean."

Julie thought she did. Jai had a unique, innate dignity deserving of such expressions of respect.

"Besides, he never depends on his title to get him what he wants. He has already made his own fortune, young as he is. I know. I'm in the same business, you see. Textiles. Although Jai has enormous holdings in steel, as well."

"But didn't he inherit his fortune for being a prince?" Julie asked.

Leon Calvert fixed his alert eyes on her face. "No, my dear, he did not. It is true that the Indian government bought the land of the states from the ruling princes. But many of the old Indian aristocracy live today in deplorable poverty. Jai, and to some extent his father before him, are among the few aristocrats who were able to adapt to the new structure of life and become successful in the modern industrial society.

"It's always the same, Julie, in any culture. Some people add to what they inherit. Others continue to sell off bits and pieces of their inheritance—land, jewels, antiques—throughout their whole lives in order to keep going. Jai is the first type. He could live in a primitive tribe in Africa and still succeed. Why, he'd end up chief!"

"You know," replied Julie, laughing, "I think you're right."

"Trust me, I am right. I make a habit of being right. Beautiful dress, m'dear," he added, before moving off to greet some new arrivals.

"With what lies was Leon regaling you?" Jai asked, returning with two drinks. A servant followed him with a plate of hors d'oeuvres, set it on a side table and walked away.

"As a matter of fact we were talking about you," Julie replied, taking one of the drinks.

"Were you, indeed?" His voice had deepened. He stood in front of her, closer than was necessary. "Did he tell you that I have a rapacious desire to get to know you better?"

"No, he didn't." Julie smiled up at him.

"I do."

"Well, we have all evening," she reminded him.

"I wish we had all night. Besides, when I invited you here, I didn't realize what a distinct disadvantage it would be to have all these other people around," he replied, smiling.

"Believe me," Julie countered, "I realized what a distinct *advantage* it would be!"

Jai laughed, his dark head tilted back, his eyes on her face. "In that case, come and let me introduce you to some of the people here." He took her hand and led her forward into the crowded room.

Julie gave herself over to the social delights of the evening, aware that she and her escort were the most observed couple at the gathering. She liked the people Jai introduced her to. It was a relief to forget all about her work for one night and just enjoy the company of the other guests. Away from the camaraderie of her co-workers in the newsroom, it seemed like a long time since she had relaxed and conversed with people as people, not as news sources. Jai seemed bent on exerting the charm for which he was famous. Julie admitted to herself that his reputation was justified. He made her feel beautiful and special: she had never enjoyed an evening more.

It was late in the night before the elaborate dinner was served and much later still when Jai told the doorman to have his car brought around.

"Did you have a good time?" he asked, as the red sports car cruised through the light traffic at high speed.

"Wonderful!" Julie leaned back in the seat, enjoying the cool breeze from her open window. She wondered if she could ever get used to New Delhi's heat: night always came as such a relief to her.

"I'm glad." He did not speak again until they reached the palace gatehouse. As the car paused for the iron gates to swing open, he glanced over at her. "Could I interest you in a walk? We could leave the car here and go the rest of the way on foot."

Julie turned her head to look at him, surprised. Several times tonight it had been borne home to her that his invitation had, after all, been purely social. The prince had not mentioned a word about work the whole evening. Instead he had done everything in his power to make certain she enjoyed herself. She had never had a more considerate date.

"I'd like to walk," she answered. She glanced down at her high-heeled sandals. "We'll have to stay on the grass so I can go barefoot, though."

He looked down at her skimpy sandals. "Women's shoes always amaze me," he said. "They seem designed to prohibit movement."

"Men must design them," Julie agreed, sliding the straps off her ankles. "No woman could do this to her own kind."

Jai got out and opened Julie's door. He spoke a few words in Hindi to the gatekeeper, who pointed at the car and nodded several times.

Then they were alone, strolling over the soft grass beneath blossom-laden umbrella trees. The star-filled sky, illuminated by an almost-full moon, flowed a dark, midnight blue above them. Faint rustling sounds touched their ears. The night breeze brushed against some feathered pampas grass, causing each tall stalk to quiver like an ostrich plume. Julie carried her sandals in one hand. Jai's strong fingers closed over the palm of her other one. They sauntered in the general direction of the palace, prowling away from the pathway now and again to search out an elusive night songbird or to pursue an enticing fragrance.

"Tell me about your fiancé—the man in Los Angeles you almost married."

Julie glanced up at him. She had wondered, after that day in the bookstore when Priya asked about Hollywood and Julie had mentioned Eddie, whether or not Jai would ever ask about him. But now that he had she didn't know what to say. How could she explain what Eddie had meant to her, the role he had played in her life as a substitute for any real family.

"How did he die?" Jai asked. He squeezed her hand as though to encourage her. "Or does it hurt too much to discuss it?"

Julie smiled her appreciation for his understanding of how difficult it was to talk about it. "He...he died in a car crash. He was a stunt man in the movie industry. The best one."

Somehow the whole story poured out, starting with Eddie's death and working backward. It was as if a dam had burst inside her. Julie realized with a jolt that she had never really spoken about Eddie's death to anyone. She had quit her job and left L.A. within a few weeks after the funeral. Her new friends and co-workers in New York hadn't known Eddie, so naturally they didn't ask her anything about him or realize the adjustment she was going through.

All that unexpressed grief, bottled up inside for so long, came rushing out now. Julie realized she *wanted* to talk about Eddie, that she *could* talk about him. Enough time had passed. It felt good to tell Jai about him—what a kind, loving person he had been. Once she started talking, Jai listened without interrupting, as though realizing that talking was a necessary part of her grieving, a relief that she had denied herself for too long. His silent sympathy and understanding gave Julie the strength she needed to face the final encounter with her own feelings about Eddie's death.

"At the time I'm sure it was right for you, Julie," he said when she at last stopped talking. "I could never resent anyone in your past who gave you as much support as this man apparently did." He paused. She felt the tension in his fingers as his hand gripped hers more tightly. "But I'll always be grateful," he continued at last, "that you weren't married when I met you."

They walked on together without talking any more, lost in their own private reflections. Julie felt a peculiar light-headedness, a sense of magical gaiety. Jai cared about her! And he was glad she was single! The night world passed by on either side of her, but Julie's awareness was all for the man next to her.

He paused at the curve in the path, then stepped over to a low bush. Bending over, he took a snowy blossom between his fingertips.

"Smell this."

Julie knelt down and sniffed, her senses attuned to the night. Jai towered above her.

The moonlight shone on the planes of his handsome face. His dark eyes glowed with intelligence. Was there ever a man to equal him, she wondered. Her mind plunged forward into a sudden, blinding minisecond of clarity, as though her thoughts tottered on the brink of a great revelation. She felt drugged by the fragrance of the flower, moved by the whirling star-bright galaxy above.

"Get up, Julie," Jai was saying, his voice patient, as though he had had to repeat himself. "The grass is probably damp and your legs will get cold."

She rose, obedient to the gentle tug he gave her hand. He slipped his arm around her waist.

"Come on, I'd better get you home. It's very late, I'm afraid."

They walked the rest of the way in silence. Jai kept his arm about her, and Julie reveled in the closeness of his body. It felt so natural to be beside him. As though she belonged. . . .

Two servants were waiting to open the palace doors for them.

"Don't they ever sleep?" Julie questioned, stooping over to slip on her sandals before mounting the marble steps.

"They work shifts, you know," he replied, a soft laugh in his voice. "It's not as if I make them stay awake twenty-four hours a day."

"Oh. Are they guards?"

"Well, let's just say they are doormen who

happen to be very able to use their ornamental swords as well as other less obvious weapons concealed on their persons," he replied with grim satisfaction. "Come inside."

They stopped in the center of the circular entrance hall. Placing his hands on her shoulders, Jai turned Julie around to face him.

"Thank you for a wonderful evening, my beautiful one," he said, his eyes on her face. He bent over her. She felt the fleeting touch of his kiss on her lips. He released her and moved away, toward the doorway on the left, which led in the direction of his office. He paused at the threshold, lifting a hand in a gesture of leave-taking.

"I'll see you in the morning," he said.

"Yes. Good night," Julie replied.

Julie stood there a moment longer repressing a vague feeling of letdown. She had gotten what she wanted—a chance to enjoy the prince's company without the thunderstorm of passion that usually accompanied their meetings. Certainly nothing could have been less threatening than his good-night kiss. So why did she feel disappointed? It was only after she had returned to her own room and was crawling beneath the inviting fresh sheets, which Sukundala had left turned back, that the irony of her situation struck Julie. Jai had released her without making any demands; she wished she had been asked to give more.

JULIE WOKE EARLY the next morning despite going to bed late the night before. Sukundala was in the room, arranging a large vase of fresh camellia blossoms and hanging up Julie's evening clothes.

"Did you wear this last night?" asked the serving girl in halting English. She eyed the skimpy black cocktail dress in her hands with disbelief.

"Yes, I did," Julie replied, laughing at the Indian girl's expression. "Western clothes are very different from saris, aren't they?"

"Yes. *Very* different." She stroked the smooth satiny silk as she fitted the garment onto a padded hanger. "But very pretty, also," she added after a moment's thought.

"Yes, each is nice in its own way," Julie agreed. She leaned back against the pillow, enjoying the bright sunlight that filled the room as the drapes were drawn back.

"You have a...a present," said the maid, releasing the curtain cord and pointing to a tray table near the bed. There was a silver pitcher and china cup and saucer on the linen tray cover, along with a matching napkin in a silver ring, a white gardenia and a thin black velvet box.

"When did that come?" Julie asked, regarding the box.

"A car delivered it to the palace this morning—about half an hour ago. I was told to bring it to you with your morning tea."

"Who told you to?" Julie noticed the little maid's suppressed excitement for the first time. This explained why Sukundala had begun her morning chores without waiting for Julie to ring.

"Hari told me. So it must be an order from Prince Mishra himself," she answered, with obvious awe.

"Oh." Julie's heart gave one quick thump and then returned to a normal rhythm. "Tell me, has the maharani eaten breakfast yet?"

"Not yet. She is going to dine in the breakfast room in a few minutes."

"Good. I'll get dressed and join her there. So you don't need to bring any breakfast up for me."

"Do you want your tea?" asked the girl, with another glance at the tray.

"Yes, thank you. That is all for now."

Julie sat on the edge of her bed after the Indian girl had left, staring at the black box. She reached out and picked it up. She closed her eyes, opened them, then lifted the hinged lid. A slow gasp escaped from her lips.

Lying inside the box, reposing on red satin, was a necklace. Three rows of diamonds—each stone the size and quality to do justice to a solitaire ring—had been styled to form the most magnificent choker Julie had ever seen. She picked up one end, letting the necklace dangle in the air before her eyes. Sunlight flashed from the clear white gems, bursting

into a million rays of sparkling fire. She tore
open the enclosed note. Jai's scrawl covered
the small card: "To Julie, who was born to
wear diamonds."

CHAPTER THIRTEEN

THE MAHARANI WAS RISING from the table when Julie entered the breakfast room half an hour later. It had taken her that long to compose herself. Never in her life had she received such a present. She felt sure she should not accept such an expensive gift. She felt equally sure she could not bear to part with it.

"Oh, Julie dear," exclaimed the maharani, her face brightening with pleasure. "I am just finishing my breakfast. But Priya just sat down. And here Jai is now."

Julie felt his presence behind her even as the maharani spoke. She turned quickly. He was smiling down at her, incredibly handsome in a short-sleeved beige shirt and blue jeans. His black hair gleamed, still damp from his morning shower. He looked casual and relaxed. Before Julie could speak, he lifted one eyebrow in a faint look of inquiry and said:

"You're up early. Did you get enough sleep?"

"Yes. And Jai—"

"My note said everything, Julie," he interrupted. "Nothing more or less. Don't worry and don't thank me. I was only remedying an...inaccuracy in your setting. Good morning, mother. Priya." He nodded to each family member, then took Julie's arm and led her to one of the white wicker breakfast chairs. He seated her, then took his own place across the table from her.

"So nice to see you, Jai dearest!" exclaimed his mother. "Aren't you working today?"

"I thought not."

"Really! Have you any plans? Maybe we could all do something together," the maharani suggested in her gracious way, including Julie with a warm smile.

"I rely on you to think of something." He glanced across the table at Julie. "Something special," he amended. His mother nodded, smiled and left the room.

Faint color stole into Julie's cheeks. Jai's look had been a caress. To hide her confusion, she turned to Priya.

"Good morning, Priya," she said, noting the girl's pallor. With a start Julie realized she had not yet spoken with the princess about her first meeting with her future husband. So much seemed to have happened in Julie's own life in the last twelve hours, she had not spared a thought for Priya.

That the princess had troubles was ob-

vious. After murmuring a greeting to Julie,
the Indian girl lapsed into silence, refusing to
meet the eye of either her brother or Julie.
She toyed with her food and looked miserable. Julie tried once or twice to engage her in
conversation, but desisted after realizing that
Priya needed all her strength to hold back a
threatening flood of tears. Midway through
the meal the young princess's self-control
gave way. She burst into gigantic, racking
sobs. Pushing her plate aside, she mumbled a
hasty excuse and rushed from the room.

Julie's heart went out to the beautiful girl.
It seemed impossible that Jai could remain
unmoved by his sister's suffering, but meeting his dark eyes across the table, Julie saw
no trace of remorse in them.

"Jai," she began, "don't you think—"

"No, Julie, I don't," he interrupted, his
voice firm. He pushed a plate of toast toward
her.

"Have some."

Julie took a slice. She occupied herself with
spreading on a lavish layer of imported black-
berry jam, her forehead puckered with a worried frown. She was still debating whether
anything she could say—even just a hint that
Priya's affections might lie elsewhere—would
do more harm than good when the maharani
reentered the room.

"I have thought of the perfect outing for
us," she exclaimed, beaming. "I can't imag-

ine why we haven't done it before now. Jai, we must take Julie to Agra to see the Taj Mahal!''

He turned from his mother to look across the table at Julie. His eyes gripped hers. "A monument to lovers," he murmured, his voice filled with satisfaction. "By all means, mother. Let us go today."

"My work..." Julie protested.

"Oh, Julie!" the maharani pleaded. "Surely you can take a little time off. We can be back by tomorrow night!"

"Who knows," Jai agreed, "maybe the terrorist meeting is scheduled to be held in Agra. All the tourists visiting the Taj Mahal would certainly provide an excellent cover for the conference."

"I could make some inquiries," Julie conceded. Even though she knew Jai was teasing her, it was actually a good idea. Agra was close enough to Delhi to be convenient, and all the tourist traffic would be perfect protection for foreign terrorist leaders who wanted to lose themselves in the crowd. Besides, she had no specific lead to follow up on here in the capital. No matter where one was, no journalist could be free from the ever-present anxiety that a big story would break somewhere else—in the spot he had just left, or the place he had decided not to go to.

An hour later the black Mercedes was speeding along the narrow two-lane highway to Agra. Julie leaned back in her corner of the limousine, cool and comfortable. She scanned the brush-covered plains of northern India through the deeply tinted window, marveling to see these endless open spaces in such a populated country.

"This scenery reminds me of America's western plains," she remarked to the maharani, who was sitting beside her. Jai was on the other side of his mother. Priya had elected not to join the expedition—Julie had no trouble guessing why. "Those bluish gray bushes look just like our sagebrush."

"I thought we would stop at Vrindaban on our way, Julie," the maharani said, smiling. "It is a very small village, quite different from New Delhi. It is also reputed to be the birthplace of Lord Krishna, the greatest of all the Hindu gods. There are many traditions attached to Vrindaban, which you might enjoy learning about."

Julie was ready to get out and stretch her legs by the time they reached Vrindaban. Even in a luxury automobile such as the Mercedes, travel in India could be tedious. Gunam Singh had to drive slowly due to the deep chuckholes in the road, and it was hard to pass the many oxcarts, buses and horse- or camel-drawn wagons on such a narrow road.

"I'm surprised they don't widen this stretch of road between Delhi and Agra," she said, as the driver opened her door for her.

"There must be a lot of traffic from people going to see the Taj Mahal."

"For India this is a *good* road, madam," Gunam Singh assured her, a big smile on his face. With his bushy full beard and merry eyes he reminded Julie of a beaming, not-yet-gray Santa Claus. "Besides, the *dacoits* would steal all the road equipment at night."

"Who?"

"The *dacoits*," the maharani corroborated, getting out on the pavement beside Julie and shaking out the folds of her sari. "They are notorious along this stretch of road. They attack cars and buses and rob the passengers. No one drives between Delhi and Agra at night if they can help it."

"Do you mean *highwaymen*?" Julie asked, incredulous.

"Yes. Wicked, isn't it?" the older woman said, patting Julie's arm with a plump hand.

"It doesn't seem possible in this day and age," Julie marveled.

"You forget that in some places India's 'day and age' is centuries in the past," Jai admonished her as he came around from the other side of the car. "You'll agree with me when you see Vrindaban. Come on." His light touch on her arm sent a cool thrill of arousal down her spinal column.

Jai had changed into a white cotton shirt and white slacks before leaving Delhi. His dark hair and tanned skin contrasted with his clothing and the white heat shimmering off the pavement and the sides of the buildings. Striding ahead of Julie and the maharani down the sleepy streets of the squalid village, he looked exceptionally energetic and virile.

Julie watched him from beneath the white umbrella she had brought along. She still had a low tolerance for India's dry heat—the thermometer had reached 110 degrees yesterday. Today might be even hotter. Before leaving the palace she had twisted her heavy hair into a soft chignon to keep it off her neck. Her square-necked white sundress, with its purple-and-orange flounce, was chosen with coolness in mind, as well.

Jai led them through a labyrinth of narrow cobbled streets. Tall adobe buildings with ruinous stone doorways—often adorned with beautiful carved friezes that were crumbling—blocked the view on either side. The path led steadily downward, growing tighter and narrower so that in the end it was nothing more than an alleyway.

Jai stopped at last. As Julie caught up with him, she caught the smell of moisture in the air. Then her breath exhaled in a slow sigh of appreciation. The alleyway ended at the top of an ancient stone stairway. A wide, winding river stretched out below them, flowing into the distance with calm beauty reminiscent of the chanting of a Vedic hymn. Indeed, the measured, delicate rhythm of a pundit's song floated up to Julie on the clear air.

"The river Yamuna," said Jai's deep voice beside her. "Hindus consider it a holy river. Devout worshippers pilgrimage here to bathe in its purifying waters."

"This same river flows on to Agra. You can see it from the Taj Mahal," the maharani added.

"What is that tree down there?" asked Julie, pointing past the foot of the stairs to a gigantic banyan tree with branches as thick as a man's torso. Bright-colored scraps of cloth decorated its lower boughs.

"Come on, I'll show you," Jai exclaimed. "I'd forgotten all about that tree! I haven't been to Vrindaban in years."

"You go ahead," the maharani interjected. Her pleasant, musical voice seemed to Julie to fit in perfectly with these harmonious surroundings. "I'll wait here at the top of the stairs. I don't want to have to climb back up."

"Are you sure, mother?" the prince asked. "We could return by a lower road."

"Go ahead, Jai. Take Julie. I don't need to touch the river to immerse myself in the peace here."

"Your mother is very religious, isn't she?" asked Julie, following Jai's broad back down the steep stairs.

"Let's just say that, aside from Priya's and

my happiness, her priorities now are spiritual,'' he replied, glancing over his shoulder at Julie. "Are these stairs too rough for you?''

She shook her head. Fortunately her open-toed sandals had low heels.

"Why is Lord Krishna considered the greatest of the gods?'' she asked, pausing on a narrow stone landing to catch her breath. Jai stopped, too, leaping the two steps back to the landing in one easy bound. He stood beside her, and they looked out over the flowing river sparkling in the afternoon sunlight.

"Krishna represents pure consciousness— that unbounded, eternal, all-pervading 'glue' of creation that underlies all existence. To experience pure consciousness all the time even while engaged in the activity of daily life is the goal of all Hindus. They call it enlightenment, or cosmic consciousness, or *moksha*— liberation. The pundits say that in that state of enlightenment, a man could do no harm to others. He would be in perfect harmony with natural law.

"But the Vedas tell lots of stories about Krishna himself,'' Jai continued, taking her hand and leading her down the last flight of stairs to the ground. "This tree is one of them. As a child Krishna was supposed to have been very mischievous. One day the *gopis*, Krishna's celestial handmaidens, were bathing here in the Yamuna. While they were in the water, Krishna stole their saris and hung them on the tree beyond their reach. Now people come here and hang a piece of cloth to make a wish.''

''Could I make one?'' Julie asked.

''That depends on what you intend to wish for,'' Jai replied, his powerful body suddenly beside hers. He smiled down into her heat-flushed face, his dark eyes burning. Merely to be near him stirred her senses almost beyond bearing. To say nothing of when he touched her! A rush of memories—of the times he *had* touched her—sprang to mind. For the first time she wondered what really had prompted her to take this trip. Was it to see the Taj Mahal? Or had she been thinking of tonight, the two of them together, away from re-sponsibilities. . . away from restrictions?

Jai signaled to a vendor nearby who was selling bits of cloth for a rupee. Julie stood on tiptoe and tied the gay cloth to a small limb of the huge tree. Her mind on Jai, she forgot to make any wish at all.

Then they walked together down to the river's edge. Jai rolled up his trousers and waded out into the muddy current while Julie, hesitant to get her dress wet, sat on a rock under her umbrella and watched a group of naked youngsters playing catch with a large beach ball. Their shouts filled the air as they splashed in wild pursuit of the ball. One shot went wide, out toward Jai who sent it spiraling back in a high arc, which made the children shrill with delight.

"Maybe I should take Julie to Krishna's garden," Jai said, as they rejoined the maharani at the top of the stairs a little later. "Krishna is said to come to this particular garden each night to play with the *gopis*," he explained. "The people in Vrindaban say that a human would go mad if he actually saw Krishna, so the gate to the garden is locked every night at twilight. But we could still see it this afternoon, if you wanted."

"I don't think I had better go," Julie replied. She could not recall when she had last felt so at peace with herself, or with Jai. "I feel mad enough as it is!"

"In that case let's go on to Agra," the maharani said, laughing at her American guest. "Tonight is the full moon, when the Taj Mahal is most beautiful."

CHAPTER FOURTEEN

LIKE EVERY OTHER AMERICAN, Julie had seen postcard-type photos of the Taj Mahal since childhood. In fact, she had seen so many glossy representations of the great marble tomb, complete with sunrises or sunsets in the background, that she would not have been surprised to view the real structure with a sense of blasé familiarity. Nothing she had ever seen or heard, however, prepared her for the reality.

To see the Taj Mahal was to experience beauty—a pure, serene, all-encompassing beauty that lifted one above the narrow confines of human existence to touch eternity. She had walked through the gigantic stone gateway to the park surrounding the Taj with the casual interest of a tourist. She stood at the top of the stairs descending into the park in breathless awe.

Threads of mist floated in the air. A lustrous globe—the full moon—hung like a wondrous, huge pearl low in the black sky. In the distance, across a park of pools, shrubs and fountains, white marble rose out of the mists.

The dome glowed in the moonlight; slender prayer towers on each corner of the platform base spiraled high into the wispy clouds. Even from that distance Julie felt the impact of the massive tomb and was charmed by the magical design that gave a fairylike delicacy to the structure.

"You are very quiet," Jai remarked. He was standing close beside her, his eyes on her face. The maharani had met a party of old friends in the hotel in Agra, and she had sent Jai and Julie on alone to see the Taj.

Julie glanced up at his tall form beside her, searching his handsome face with somber eyes.

"How can it be so beautiful," she said. "It . . . it touches one very . . . deeply."

"It is a monument to love," he answered.

She started down the stone stairs. He walked beside her without speaking. Communication required no words—each was fully aware of the other. A current of electric excitement flowed through the air between them, a strange connecting force. Julie wondered at it. She felt so open, so receptive to this masterful man at her side, as though she had folded back the covers of her thoughts for his perusal.

He took her hand in a light hold. The Taj Mahal loomed above them as they drew nearer. Jai helped her climb the steep stairs of red sandstone that led to the marble platform of the tomb. They walked around the outside first, admiring the carvings of flowers and script.

"What does this say?" Julie asked, kneeling down beside the wall to study the hand-cut stone. She traced the unfamiliar letters with the tip of her finger.

"I don't know." He stood behind her, his hands resting lightly on her shoulders. Warmth radiated from his palms into her back. A longing stirred in her abdomen. She ignored the warning alarm registering in her brain.

"This is a Muslim tomb, you know. I believe these decorations are passages from the Koran."

"The man who built this was Indian, wasn't he?" she questioned, rising. The prince slipped his arm around her waist. They continued their exploration around the base of the shrine. His hip brushed her as they walked.

"His name was Shah Jahan. He built this in memory of his favorite wife, Mumtaz-i-Mahal, which means something like 'pride of the palace.' The Taj Mahal takes its name from her."

"I wonder what she was like," Julie mused.

"Something like you, I imagine."

Julie laughed. "You flatter me."

"I flatter her," he responded, his voice

husky. The smile curving his lips was disarmingly tender as he looked down at her, his face awash with moonlight.

"Let's go inside," Julie said, turning away. He marked her flustered haste and chuckled.

"As you wish."

She didn't look at him again. Somehow she felt the viewing of the interior was in the nature of a reprieve. These precious minutes, here among a scattering of other tourists, seemed like the last outpost of safety. The intensity of her attraction to the prince increased the longer she was with him. What of the long night ahead?

Inside the sepulcher two gem-encrusted marble coffins lay in state on the main floor, which they viewed through a carved screen of alabaster as delicate as a lace curtain. Jai showed Julie the stairway that led into a deep vault on a lower level. Here lay two much simpler caskets that did in fact contain the bodies of the emperor and his wife. The actual tomb was not as appealing as the rest of the shrine, and Jai and Julie soon returned to the outdoors.

Leaving the lovers emtombed in the glowing white marble, Jai and Julie crossed back through the wide park. Jai's arm tightened around her waist, holding her body molded against his side. He shortened his long stride to her steps, then shifted his hold from her waist to her shoulder. She heard him draw in a soft breath as his strong fingers closed on her bare skin. Her own heart caught in her throat.

When they reached a curve in the path, Jai stepped aside onto the night-damp grass. Turning toward her, he pulled Julie to him. It seemed so natural for him to take her in his arms that she came without hesitation, yielding her lips to his. His mouth closing over hers was the inevitable conclusion to the evening. The moonlit Taj Mahal dominated the background, its slender towers wrapped in high dark clouds. A supreme peace invaded Julie, as though in this fantastic, unreal setting she had found her true self. Yet when Jai at last released her, she discovered she was trembling with barely restrained passion.

"You know, don't you, that I will come to you tonight, my love?" He spoke with quiet certainty, leaving no room for vain protests. Julie felt no desire to argue.

She looked up at him, losing herself in those mysterious, burning eyes filled now with reflected moonlight. Deep in her mind a paradox struggled to resolve itself: how was it that she came to both simultaneously lose herself and find herself in this one man? She gave a slow, mute nod. Yes, she knew that tonight he would come.

Voices reached them. A group of late-night tourists, who came like themselves to view the

Taj Mahal in the moonlight, was approaching down the path. Jai touched Julie's arm with his fingertips. They stepped back on the path and returned to the entrance gate without speaking again.

Back in her own room at the hotel, Julie sat on the edge of the king-size bed and dropped her head into her hands. Why had she stood passively by when Jai declared his intention of joining her in this bedroom tonight? Of course he would interpret her silence as acquiescence. She should have made her position clear right then. It would be much more difficult now, when he was standing in the doorway expecting admittance, to tell him she could not—would not—succumb to the moonlight madness that threatened her good sense.

She rose and paced the large room. The bedside lamp she had turned on cast her shadow across the floor and up the wall, a gigantic mimic of her own tense motions. Oppressed, she went to stand on the little balcony that overlooked the hotel pool. Leaning out over the balcony railing, she watched the tiny ripples on the empty pool below without really being aware of them. She forced the image of the golden-glow bedroom behind her out of her mind. She would never share that bed with Jai Mishra. Or any other bed.

She had not forgotten that he still suspected her of collaboration with the terrorists. Never once in the weeks they had worked together had he indicated a change of attitude toward her. Perhaps he was growing to respect her as a professional. He even appeared to enjoy her company sometimes, like last night at Leon Calvert's dinner party. He respected her. He worked with her. But he did not trust her. He still intended to use her.. . .

Five minutes later Julie walked briskly past a sleepy hotel doorman, overnight case slung on her arm. She knew she could not resist Jai Mishra's advances tonight. But she could flee them.

Getting a taxi to New Delhi in the middle of the night proved to be more complicated than Julie had anticipated. Only a few cabs remained at the taxi stand not far from the hotel entrance. The drivers of these old-fashioned black automobiles lay sleeping in a circle around the burning coals of a small fire, curled up under lightweight blankets. Julie roused the sleeper nearest her.

"Madam," he exclaimed, when he was at last made to understand her request, "I take you in the morning. Where you stay? The hotel? I meet you at the front entrance at eight o'clock."

"I must go now, sir," Julie persisted. "I know it's late. I will pay you well."

The driver sat up and rubbed his eyes. Other sleepers around the fire awoke.

"In the morning, madam." He smiled widely. "You can pay me in the morning."

"I can't wait until morning." Julie looked at the other huddled forms. "Will any of you drive me to New Delhi now? I will pay double your usual rate," she added rashly.

A man bent over to stir the coals with a stick. The firelight illuminated his face for an instant.

"It is not safe to go now," he told her. "Danger. *Dacoits*."

"Dacoits?" Julie repeated. "Oh! Do you mean the highwaymen?" she asked, remembering the maharani's mention of bandits.

"Dacoits," he repeated with a solemn nod. The other men nodded, as well. The speaker pulled his tattered blanket up over his body and prepared to go back to sleep.

Julie hesitated. She had two options: to get a room in another hotel in Agra tonight or to return to New Delhi. She was fully awake, overstimulated from the adrenaline coursing through her body at the thought of confronting Jai. She just could not face the idea of tossing and turning all night long in some strange hotel room, wondering what to say to Jai on the ride back to the palace in the morning. Better to go back to Delhi now. She could stop along the way and call the front desk to have a message taken to Jai's room saying she was called away on a lead. If she left immediately she would get to bed in time to put in at least a half day of work tomorrow....

"I will pay *triple* the usual rate," she stated, quelling a wave of trepidation. Even if some risk was involved, she could not help feeling that a far greater danger lay in allowing Jai to find her in Agra tonight.

"I go."

The speaker was an emaciated gray-haired fellow, more ragged than any of his companions. He rose from a rickety cot set a little way back from the fire, moving with painful stiffness. His narrow face seemed kind enough, but his bearing in general did not inspire confidence. He would certainly be no match for bandits if they did encounter any, Julie thought, her heart sinking a bit.

His fellow drivers were arguing with him in their own tongue. He replied with a few words that silenced them. Julie got the distinct impression that he had a greater need for the cab fare than the others, and for that reason alone was willing to undertake such a grim journey. His taxi, by far the oldest and most decrepit, corroborated her interpretation. Ignoring the leaden weight of apprehension in her stomach, Julie pulled open the squeaky rear door and climbed inside.

CHAPTER FIFTEEN

RATTLING ALONG DOWN THE NARROW ROAD two hours later, a draft chilling her feet, Julie hunched farther over in one corner of the back seat. She glanced at her watch. Two in the morning. She estimated they were about halfway to Delhi, although the taxi's pace was enough slower than the limousine she had travelled in yesterday morning that it made it hard to compare travel time.

Her thoughts drifted back to Jai. Try as she might, she had not been able to shake the image of his face from her mind. That he would be angry when he discovered her flight she had no doubt. Would he feel hurt, as well? She had no idea. That depended on whether or not he had meant to merely use her, or if he truly cared for her, as well. At least she had no fear of his pursuing her. For one thing, he had the maharani to think of. For another, his pride would certainly not allow him to go chasing after a reluctant bed partner. Would he guess that the reason she had fled was because she was *not* reluctant?

She removed the cotton jacket she had

brought to cover her sundress and wrapped it around her numb ankles. She was too uncomfortable and nervous to sleep. A half smile flitted across her lips—how quickly she had grown used to Jai's luxury automobiles!

In an attempt to give her buzzing thoughts a constructive turn, she concocted and discarded various excuses to explain her flight to the maharani. A rumor overheard from a taxi driver of a possible newsbreak in Delhi? An urgent telephone call from the stringer in Bombay? Whatever she told her hostess, it must serve as a reason for leaving the prince's palace. Wes Harding was just going to have to accept the fact she could complete her story better in a hotel.

Proximity to the prince had become too dangerous. Even here, in this drafty, noisy taxi, Julie felt surrounded by Jai's presence. Thoughts of him intruded, refusing to be vanquished. So immersed was she in imagining what might have happened if she *had* stayed in Agra tonight, she paid little heed to the taxi driver's sporadic mutterings of foreboding. His sharp, unintelligible cry came as a complete surprise to her.

The cab careened to a halt as the driver pumped hard on the weak brakes. Julie lurched against the front seat. She untangled her jacket from her legs and rolled down the window. Peering outside, she saw a roadblock looming out of the darkness ahead. Several dark shapes leaped up from a dry roadside ditch and rushed the automobile.

She rolled up the window again and sat back against the torn seat. Despite the pounding of her heart, she felt still inside, as though garnering together all available resources to deal with the impending crisis. It came as a surprise to realize that she was not afraid. In fact, her mind seemed unusually clear, so that she was able to comprehend and evaluate every detail of her situation in a calm, unhurried fashion. These few precious seconds of reflection allowed her to compose herself. Then the door beside her jerked open and dirty hands pulled her out of the taxi.

She faced her captors with assumed calm, keeping her back against the car. Four wild-looking men formed a semicircle in front of her; they were more ragged and filthy than any of the beggars she had seen in New Delhi. They had remnants of cloth wrapped around their heads—odd how Indian men seemed to feel the need for a headband or turban of sorts—but no masks covering their faces. She could not make out their features in the darkness. Out of the corner of her eye she saw that two more *dacoits* had dragged the cabdriver to the edge of the road and were forcing him to turn out the pockets of his old coat.

"Rupees," Julie said, trying to make her voice casual. She held out her purse to the men, glad that it did not contain her passport or return airline ticket.

The bandit nearest her snatched the handbag. His hand dived inside and came up with her wallet. Pleased murmurs of anticipation spread through the group as her captors took note of the thick sheaf of bills inside. She had brought more money on this trip than she usually carried, in hopes of finding some interesting mementos of Agra. When she had decided to return to Delhi by herself, she had been glad to have the extra rupees in order to be able to afford the taxi fare. She hoped she could convince her driver to continue on to Delhi once the *dacoits* left—she had more money in her sitting-room desk with which to pay him and reimburse him whatever the highwaymen stole.

The *dacoits*, having counted the money in her wallet and searched the rest of her purse, now spoke heatedly among themselves. From the frequent glances cast up and down the highway, she knew they feared the approach of other vehicles. It seemed likely that the military police would patrol that section of road, notorious as it was for highwaymen. She wondered why the bandits delayed, now that they had her money. She felt confident they would not harm her—robbery might be overlooked by the Indian government; assault would not be. Just then the men became silent, as though they had reached an agreement.

"Madam," said one of the men, stepping toward her, "you come." He took hold

of her arm. Julie jerked away from him.
"What do you mean?" she exclaimed, the
first cold shiver of fear touching her spine.
"You have my money! Now go away!"

The other men moved closer. The two bandits who had been frisking the cabdriver
released him. The old man hurried back to his
taxi and got inside. He started the engine.
Metal scraped as he put the car in gear.

"Wait!" Julie cried out, appalled to realize
that several bandits had edged between herself and the automobile. The *dacoits* shouted
at the driver. Their tone carried an unmistakable threat. The taxi jumped forward before
Julie could move. A moment later she was
standing in the middle of a deserted highway
surrounded by her enemies, all escape cut off.

This time she did not try to pull away when
grimy hands grasped both her arms. She was
too frightened to protest. Besides, logic told
her it was pointless to instigate a struggle she
could not possibly win. She sensed her safest
recourse was to maintain—at all costs—an
unconcerned, dignified calmness. Therefore
she moved forward with firm steps when the
men holding her indicated she was to leave
the roadway and cross the dry ditch.

She marched between her captors across
the dry plain, a sharp eye on the ground to
avoid stumbling. The men hurried her along,
no doubt wanting to get as far away from the
highway as possible. That the highwaymen
meant her no immediate harm was obvious.

They were too close to the thoroughfare to be safe. Besides, she thought they were taking her to some particular place.

She looked around to get her bearings, trying to ignore the hollow feeling in the pit of her stomach. Bright moonlight illuminated the plain. Even so, she found it difficult to judge her progress. The ground, which had looked so flat from the highway, was in fact filled with washed-out gullies and low hills. The bandits seemed to know this semidesert region like the back of their hands. They moved with smooth certainty farther and farther from the road, often altering direction to accommodate the lay of the land.

Soon Julie was completely lost. She realized with a sinking heart she would have no idea how to get back to the highway even if she did manage to break free. She wondered if the taxi driver would report her abduction to the police. She had to acknowledge the possibility that he might not. After all, she was just another tourist as far as he was concerned. His first consideration must be his own peril if he betrayed the *dacoits*—the bandits undoubtedly threatened him to keep him silent.

If the old taxi driver did not report her capture, no one in the world would have the faintest idea what had happened to her. She winced to think what Jai would believe about her— that she fled India without so much as a goodbye. That she was a tease, or a traitor. . . .

She became aware of a deep pain in her side.

Her mouth felt unbearably dry. On and on the tortuous march continued across the plain, the dry sand swishing into her sandals and rubbing her feet raw. Her legs had grown numb with exertion. Just as Julie felt she must stagger to her knees in the dirt and collapse, a faint golden glow ahead signaled the journey's end.

Her companions led her around a thick stand of brush on the crest of a low hill. They went down a steep bank into a wide gully, and the glow became a campfire. Dark figures, moving here and there, paused to watch the arrival of Julie's party. Exclamations of surprise greeted the sight of a prisoner. Several men came forward to inspect her. Her captors, however, led her directly to the fire.

Cross-legged in front of the fire, a dismantled rifle in his lap, sat a swarthy man with the broadest shoulders Julie had ever seen. He was of medium height, so that he seemed almost as wide as he was tall. A red brocade vest covered his otherwise bare chest, revealing muscles worthy of a weight-lifting champion. A cloth of royal blue bound back his black hair, headband style. His square face, as he looked up, struck Julie as handsome in a fierce, primitive way. His wide-set eyes flicked over her from head to toe, then focused on the man holding her right arm.

She realized her companions were waiting for the man beside the fire to speak. He did—

one terse bark of interrogation. He did not
seem particularly pleased, but he listened
without interrupting what Julie's captors had
to say. When they had finished he laid the rifle parts on his lap aside on a blanket and
rose. Standing, he was only a few inches taller
than Julie. He spoke and a cushion was
brought and placed at Julie's feet. He was obviously the leader of the *dacoit* band.

"Please sit, madam," he said, smiling for
the first time to reveal yellow teeth. He pointed at the cushion.

Julie sat down with relief. He reseated himself across the small fire from her. The other
men ranged themselves on either side, hunched
down on their heels in that posture Indians
could hold for hours. A quick glance around
showed her that the entire camp was gathering
by the fire.

Water was brought, and she drank deeply.
The man across from her said nothing until
she had finished and returned the clay jug to
its bearer. He motioned it should be placed at
her side, which it was.

"What is your name?" His English was
good, though stilted.

"Julie Connell."

"You are American?"

"Yes."

He studied her as though puzzled.

"Where is your husband?"

Julie hesitated. Would it be wiser to pretend to be married so he would think there was someone to protect her?

"I don't have a husband." She decided to play it safe. Lies could backfire.

A murmur ran through the crowd around the campfire.

"No husband?"

"No," she repeated firmly. "American," she added, as though that explained the matter.

His smile flashed. "In India you would be married and the mother of sons by now." He had a certain rakish charm Julie decided she would quite enjoy under less tension-filled circumstances. She watched him carefully. He seemed nonplussed to discover she had no man with whom he could deal.

"In whose home do you live?"

Julie felt she was following the drift of his questions. One possibility was that he wanted to assure himself there was no one to come to her aid, and then—but that did not bear thinking of. The other possibility—by far the most likely one, she felt, since he must know she was protected by the American Embassy if nothing else—was to hold her for ransom. He needed to locate someone who would pay for her immediate safe return. It must be someone close by, for not even this bold *dacoit* would dare to try to hold a foreigner hostage very long for fear of government involvement.

"I have no friends here," she said calmly. "I am a journalist—a newspaper reporter. Reporter?" Julie wondered if he understood that word. He gave no sign either way. She tried again. "I'm here by myself. Alone. I work in New York City in America. I'm only in India for a few days."

"Yes, madam, but I am asking you where do you live in India?" His voice was harder. Also, his command of the language was better than Julie had anticipated. She would have to be careful. She sensed he was immensely crafty—no doubt a necessary quality for a man who lived by his wits.

"I live with an old woman."

"What old woman?"

Julie maintained a prudent silence. She felt sweat break out on her brow. A cold, cruel fear gripped her. An image of Jai's face flashed before her eyes. How angry he would be when he discovered that she had not kept their rendezvous! In fact, he had probably learned of her absence hours ago and was congratulating himself on being well rid of her. He would never forgive such an insult to his masculine pride.

An ironlike hand shot out and caught her wrist, which banished all other thoughts from her mind. The stocky fingers exerted bone-crushing pressure. With cool deliberation, the bandit drew Julie's arm toward him. He stopped when her wrist was directly over the fire. Her skin flushed red from the heat of the flickering coals.

"What is the name of the woman with whom you are staying?"

She met his eyes over the fire. How had she ever thought him handsome? He was a beast.

"She is a very old woman. She has no money." Julie clenched her teeth as the *dacoit* pushed her arm an inch closer to the fire.

"Why has she no money? She must have money if an American comes to stay with her. You do not live in a hut!" he hissed.

"Her. . . her son keeps her money for her!" exclaimed Julie, with a desperate glance at the fire. Her skin was starting to blister.

"Who is her son?" he shouted at her. He made as though to press her arm onto the coals.

"Jai!" Julie shouted back. "Prince Jaiapradesh Mishra!"

Instantly she was released. She clutched her arm to her, scowling across the fire at her tormentor. The highwayman leaned back on his blanket. His eyes gleamed with delight. At once his urbane manner returned.

"Prince Mishra," he murmured under his breath. "Prince Mishra is a very rich man."

He spoke a few words in his own language. A man beside Julie leaped up. He returned in a moment with a glass jar filled with dark grease. He motioned for Julie to spread the ointment on her arm. She was amazed to discover that her arm was not badly burned at all—it had felt so hot! The balm relieved her skin with its sweet coolness.

"Where will I find the prince at this moment?" asked her captor, as soon as she finished doctoring her wrist.

"He is in Agra," Julie revealed reluctantly. She named his hotel. "But you don't understand. The prince dislikes me. He thinks. . . he doesn't like journalists. He will never give you ransom money. He would rather see me dead!"

"There are worse things than death, madam," the bandit king said crisply.

"Did you wish to speak to Prince Mishra?" said a deep voice from beyond the firelight. "Prince Mishra comes to you."

Julie's eyes had been fixed apprehensively on the man across the fire. In the split second before the full meaning of the interruption dawned on her, she saw the bandit freeze as he rose to his feet. The swarthy face she saw in the light from the coals changed suddenly to ashen. He cast an instinctive, sideways glance at Julie's singed arm where it rested in her lap. Then Julie was on her own feet and turned toward the sound of Jai's voice.

The prince stood on the outermost edge of the firelight, flanked by four machine-gun-armed guards. His tall, broad-shouldered form rose up out of the black desert, outlined

by cold, silver moonlight. A sudden flare
from the campfire illuminated the handsome
planes of his face. A cruel smile twisted one
corner of his mouth, making him look more
dangerous than any bandit.

A collective gasp of dismay could be heard
from the twenty or more men gathered. And
a name, whispered with respect bordering on
awe. Later on Julie would learn the translation of the people's name for Jai—the Tiger
Prince.

Now, though, her total attention was focused on the man facing her across the camp.
His flintlike eyes met hers and held her gaze
an instant. Then, to her complete surprise, his
whole face softened. The snarling curl of his
mouth was erased by a warm smile. His eyes
shone with something that, had she not
known better, she would have mistaken for
relief. He gave no indication at all of the
anger he must be feeling at her desertion.

Instead, he walked toward her, holding out
his hand. A path opened before him like
magic as the highwaymen moved out of his
way, well aware of the machine guns leveled
on them by the wary guards who followed in
the prince's wake. When he reached her, Jai
slipped one arm around Julie and drew her to
him with a gentle tug.

"Are you all right?" he asked.

"Yes," she managed to reply. She buried
her face in his broad chest, fighting against

an overwhelming desire to cry. The calmness that had sustained her up until now dissolved. She began to tremble as the reaction to her ordeal set in.

"You are safe now, Julie," Jai told her. His deep voice was infinitely reassuring. "Sit down." He pulled the cushion she had used before back a short way from the fire and seated her on it. A blanket was handed to him and he wrapped it around her shoulders.

"You handled yourself very well," he told her. "Forgive me for not getting into a good attack position two minutes earlier." He knelt down beside her and drew her sore arm out from beneath the blanket. He turned it over and examined the underside for a moment, then released it. Standing up, he turned to face the bandit leader.

"How fortunate her arm is not badly burned." His voice held a note of intense, sinister menace Julie had never heard before—and hoped never to hear again.

The *dacoit* bowed briefly. "I quite agree. Will you join me at the fireside, prince?" he suggested.

Jai inclined his head in assent and a cushion was brought. Julie was not surprised that the *dacoit* addressed Jai in English. India had more than 180 languages and 700 dialects. Ironically, the only language Indians from different regions had in common had been imposed on them from outside by the

British during their two-hundred-year occupation.

"May I ask how you found the lady so quickly?" said the *dacoit* leader, as soon as Jai was seated.

"My guards alerted me the moment she left Agra. Did you imagine I would allow a woman such as that one to go anywhere unprotected?" the prince replied calmly.

Julie sucked in her breath. Jai had guards following her! Did he always do so? She felt an odd mixture of anger at his interference and pleasure that he had concerned himself with her well-being.

The *dacoit* leader nodded. Then, in a casual way, he began to discuss the overall state of Indian affairs. Julie sat at an angle from the men, just beyond the first bright circle of golden firelight. Recovered from her shock, she watched the faces of the two men with great interest. She was aware of a certain tension in the *dacoit* camp—the machine guns never wavered in the hands of the vigilant guards. Julie sensed that the *dacoit* leader intended to try to bargain for leniency. He began to speak at length, making vague references to "enemies of the state."

Julie sat back and listened, letting the words flow over her, striving to follow the conversation. She regretted the loss of her purse—she would have liked to record the meeting on the mini tape recorder she always carried. As it was, she listened and made mental notes, trying as much as possible to memorize everything about the *dacoit* camp. A firsthand account of the daring Indian highwaymen would go well in the Sunday section. Maybe it would disguise the fact that she had filed no terrorist copy with the news desk for several days now. . . .

"You yourself, Prince Mishra, are known to be a champion of the poor, so I know you are fully aware of their problems, and their . . . vulnerability," the swarthy *dacoit* was saying. Despite his muscular build, he looked insignificant compared with Jai. "You pay your workers the highest wages. You educate their children. The working conditions in your textile and steel factories are pointed to by the government when foreign dignitaries come to India. You gave generous gifts of land to the landless peasants of your state—" He broke off with a laugh, as Jai's face remained impassive.

"You wonder that a wretched *dacoit* concerns himself with all this?" the bandit queried.

"I imagine you have your reasons," Jai replied. "Go on."

Julie rocked back on her cushion and clasped her arms around her knees under the blanket. A weight slipped from her shoulders as she heard about Jai's actions. It had been impossible for Julie to spend time in India without contrasting the living conditions of the rich and the poor. She felt happy to know that Jai was doing what he could for the working classes. The more she knew him, the less possible it seemed that he would take advantage of those weaker or less fortunate than himself.

Julie's eyes traveled to his face. How wonderful it was to be able to study him like this, to enjoy the play of shadow and fire glow over his fine, aristocratic features. Her mind went back to the moment he had first appeared on the edge of the camp, looming like an avenging angel—or demon, more like. Her heart had leaped to see him, with more than just relief. She had felt *warmed* somehow. Joyous.

Julie struggled to define her feelings toward Jai, yet feared to do so. She realized that a subtle change had taken place in her attitude toward him. Despite their conflicts—his unfair accusations—she had grown to trust him, even to rely upon him. Deep in her heart, regardless of his anger, hadn't she hoped against hope that somehow Jai would help her? And didn't she seek him out when she had problems with her work, as someone whose judgment she could respect? Julie enjoyed discussing things with him. He was always willing to listen and in spite of, or because of, an occasional caustic remark, he often stimulated her own mind so that she could discover the answer she needed.

Could she possibly have fallen in love with

him? Julie shied away from the idea, wrapping the blanket more tightly around her body. She felt unable to face caring for a man who, regardless of his increased friendliness, retained a basic distrust of her. And what about Eddie? Julie realized she didn't think of him lately. Was she willing to forget him? Did she really want passionate, dangerous Jai Mishra to replace sweet, affectionate Eddie Bryce in her life? If she wasn't careful, she would find herself more miserable than even poor Priya—at least Priya's sweetheart returned her love.

"My time is limited." Jai said abruptly. "Say what you have to say and I will decide how I shall deal with you." Jai's guards moved closer to him, rifles cocked, as if to emphasize his point.

"I merely tell you what you already know," replied the *dacoit*. His voice took on the smooth tone of a politician preparing to make a sweeping conclusion guaranteed to win over his audience. "Certain factions would like to see the current political party defeated. They foster discontent among the poor, creating damaging strikes, marches and so forth.

"I, myself, have been contacted by these people." He spread his palms upward in a gesture of submission. "I am just a humble *dacoit*, harming no one. I am content with my lot in life, poor as it is. I desire no more. I have no wish to become a *guerrillero* in their cause. Besides," he added frankly, "it is too dangerous. You have enemies both within and without."

"How much contact did you have with them?" Jai asked, his eyes boring into the man opposite him. Julie felt quite certain that the *dacoit* leader would not risk lying.

The highwayman dropped his voice. "Enough to learn that these terrorists are going to meet in the near future to make plans with their counterparts in other countries."

"When and where?"

"Is it worth my freedom and the safety of my men?"

"You cannot bargain with me," Jai replied coldly. "Tell me what you know."

The *dacoit* shrugged. Julie had to give him credit—he had nerve. "In Kashmir, then. In five days."

"Where in Kashmir?"

"I do not know for sure." The bandit hesitated. "My own guess would be Srinagar, but I cannot be positive."

Jai leaned back on his cushion. He appeared satisfied. "Good," he said. "It is enough. I will find them." He rose to his feet and held out his hand.

The highwayman rose, also. Surprise at Jai's gesture registered on his face, but he reached out and grasped the prince's hand in a firm shake.

"I would not have taken the lady, had I

known she was yours," said the *dacoit*. "I know you to be a friend of the people."

"I don't doubt it. You also know me to be a dangerous enemy," Jai responded with cool humor.

The *dacoit* bowed. "Yes. The Tiger Prince. No word will come to the *guerrilleros* that their plans are known."

"Not if you value your life." Jai turned his back on the fire. Seeing Julie, he approached her.

"Sorry to make you wait when you must be longing to leave. But you will agree it has been worthwhile," he said in a low voice as he bent over her. He gave her his hand to help her rise.

"Are you sorry I'm not punishing your captors?" he asked as he led her through the camp. "As long as you are safe, I don't feel it's my responsibility. Let the police do their own work. But if you wish it, I could still do so."

"Oh, no!" She smiled up at him. "I've grown irrationally fond of our highwaymen, for some strange reason."

He squeezed her arm. They walked on together for a minute. Julie began to chuckle.

"What is it?" Jai asked, smiling down at her.

"Oh, I was just thinking of his face when he said he did no harm to anyone. He looked so innocent and sincere I almost believed him, despite the fact I know he's a notorious robber!''

Jai joined in her laughter. Behind them, the *dacoit* camp came alive with chattering voices. Jai and Julie climbed the embankment, their retreat covered by watchful guards.

"There should be a Land Rover somewhere close by to meet us," Jai told her when they reached the desert plateau. "I had one sent out from Delhi as soon as I heard you had gone, just in case. The guards will have directed it here with their radios."

"Really? That's wonderful news. I was dreading the walk back," Julie admitted.

He glanced at her sundress and sandals. "You are hardly dressed for it. We are not too far from the road, though. A lot of the distance you walked was an attempt to throw us off the trail."

"It didn't confuse you?"

"No. I was fortunate to have one of my trackers with me." He turned to point out one of his guards to her. "Munshi always goes with me on my hunting trips. Or did, at least. I don't hunt much anymore."

One of the guards shot off a flare. In a minute or two the headlights of the Land Rover came into sight. In no time at all it seemed Julie was back on the asphalt highway. Gunam Singh held open the door of the limousine for her as she climbed inside.

"How did you know where the roadblock was?" Julie asked, as Jai slipped onto the seat beside her. He gave orders to the chauffeur to drive to New Delhi, then closed the glass divider.

"We were not far behind you," Jai replied. "When we saw a taxi coming back in our direction, we stopped him. It turned out he was your driver. He took us to the spot where the *dacoits* abducted you."

"That poor old man! How frightened he must have been to be stopped twice in one night! Besides, the *dacoits* robbed him and I think he must have really needed his money."

"He was generously reimbursed for his cooperation with my men," Jai assured her. "Don't give it another thought."

"Oh, thank you, Jai! I'll pay you back whatever you gave him. It was all my fault."

"On the contrary, the fault is mine. Only—" He broke off. She noticed his self-mocking smile in the dark. "Only I had no idea you were so opposed to my. . .courtship. I got the distinct impression at the Taj that you would welcome me to your bed tonight with open arms." His dry, humorous voice ended on a faint questioning note.

Julie, struggling to find the right words, was grateful for the darkness. After all, he was right. She *had* wanted him. That was why she had run away.

"Never mind, Julie." His hand covered

hers in the dark. "Let's talk of something else. Or perhaps you would rather rest."

"I wonder how many people missed their night's sleep because of me," Julie said a few minutes later. "You, your bodyguards, the Land Rover driver, Gunam Singh. . . . Oh, no! What about your mother, Jai? She'll wake up to find us gone!"

"No she won't. I left her a note and I'll call her in the morning. I arranged for a car and driver to be available to her, but I think she'll come back with the friends she met last night."

"Were you very angry when you heard I was gone?" Julie glanced at Jai's dark profile.

"At first—yes."

"Why. . . why did you rescue me? All things considered—our. . . differences, my leaving like that—I really didn't think you would come."

He turned his head to look at her, his expression enigmatic. "Didn't you? I told you I take care of my own."

Neither of them spoke again on the long ride home. The full moon shone above the deserted highway, a beacon of hope in the black desert night. Julie pondered Jai's last words, eventually falling asleep on his shoulder. Dawn was breaking over the city when they arrived at the palace.

CHAPTER SIXTEEN

JULIE SLEPT LATE the next morning. When she awoke the palace seemed peaceful and still. Apparently Sukundala had orders not to wake Julie after her ordeal in the desert. Rather than ring for the maid to bring her breakfast, Julie helped herself to the fruit arranged in a basket on the table in her bedroom.

She peeled a ripe mango with a fruit knife while she considered what to do next. Rather than transmit her undated feature on the *dacoit* over expensive overseas telex or phone lines, she decided Harding would prefer she send it via air. She spent the next two hours typing the final version of her copy, not giving in to the temptation to sensationalize about the bandits' way of life in order to make the story more dramatic. She adopted a stark, simple style of writing that matched her impression of the clear, open desert. Several times she paused, searching for words to convey the rough camaraderie of the highwaymen or the particular way the moonlight washed the sand with a cool silver glow.

When she shuffled her finished pages together at last, Julie was aware of the sense of
well-being she always got when she wrote
well.

Julie addressed a large envelope to the
paper. She would ask Gunam Singh if he
could find someone to take the dispatch to
the airport. Knowing India, it might take
hours of standing in different lines and filling
out long forms to send the story by air.

Today she was eager to see Jai and discuss
the *dacoit* leader's revelation of the terrorist
plans. As she slipped into a cool beige cotton
suit, she wondered if the prince would accompany her to Kashmir. She wanted to follow
up the new lead as soon as possible.

Five minutes later Julie briskly rounded the
corner to the hallway leading to Jai's office.
After waking up so late and writing the *dacoit*
story, the afternoon was already half gone.
Julie considered different plans of action,
hoping she could still leave for Kashmir late
in the afternoon. She wanted as much time as
possible to track down the exact location of
the terrorist conference. Thus preoccupied,
Julie practically collided with Priya before
she noticed the princess.

"Priya! I feel like I haven't seen you in
days!" Julie exclaimed. "I've been thinking
about you. Is something wrong?"

The Indian girl stood stock still, staring at
Julie with eyes glazed with shock. Julie

stepped forward impulsively. A convulsive movement of Priya's hands drew the blond woman's eyes downward. She saw the princess was clutching a variety of papers and folders. A bold red stamp on the uppermost manila envelope read, "Private and Confidential." Behind her, Jai's office door stood ajar.

Julie raised her eyes to Priya's, meeting her stunned look with a cool, penetrating gaze. An unspoken question hung in the air between them. Then Priya dropped the papers and burst into tears.

"Priya, Priya!" Julie murmured. "What in the world...."

"Oh, Julie!" The Indian girl threw herself into her friend's arms, pressing her sleek dark head against Julie's shoulder. "I am so unhappy!"

"Don't cry, Priya," Julie soothed, stroking her hair. "Stop crying." She held the Indian girl away and peered into the beautiful tear-stained face. "Tell me what is going on. Are you in some kind of trouble?"

"My life is ruined, Julie," replied the princess in a hoarse whisper. "Ruined!"

"No. It can't be that bad! Here, sit down." Julie led the young woman to a straight-backed antique love seat at the end of the hall. She retrieved the scattered papers from the floor. A quick glance through them confirmed her first impression.

"Do these belong to your brother?" Julie asked gently, as she seated herself beside Priya. The Indian girl was bent over, sobbing quietly into her hands. "Come, Priya. You must talk to me! Maybe I can help you."

"Can you?" The princess lifted her tear-streaked face. "But you will hate me when I tell you what I've done!"

"No. I could never hate you, Priya, no matter what you've done. Does this have something to do with Lal?" she asked on a sudden intuition.

"Lal!" Disgust flashed across the girl's fine features. "I hate Lal! He...he lied to me! Julie, you won't believe this, but...but he never cared for me at all!" Her eyes—eyes that could have belonged to a hurt child—focused on Julie's face.

"Oh, I believe that all right." The memory of how Lal had looked at her in Chandni Chowk that day flitted in and out of her mind. "What has he done?"

Having broken her long silence, the distraught girl poured forth the whole torturous story. It all began the morning of her interview with Prakash Das. When she had at last met the fiancé her brother had chosen for her, Priya had found him to be all a woman could ever hope for. Contrasted to Prakash's soft-spoken kindness and natural light-hearted dignity, the young princess suddenly discovered how superficial the charms of her il-

licit suitor were by comparison. After the
meeting with Prakash ended, Priya had fled
to her own room, aghast at having en-
couraged Lal Delal's affections. She had
burned incense on the altar in her *puja* room
and prayed to her patron goddess.

In the end she determined to break off her
secret relationship with Lal Delal so that she
could marry Prakash Das. With this in mind,
she arranged a meeting with Lal while her
mother and brother took Julie to Agra. But
when Lal discovered he had lost his hold on
Priya's heart, his true reason for the court-
ship came to light. He threatened to reveal his
relationship with Priya to her future husband, unless Priya agreed to bring him some
papers from Jai's office.

"And I did as he asked, Julie," the princess concluded in a low voice. "I went against
my own brother! But, Julie, if I don't give
Lal these papers, he will tell Prakash that he
met me in secret. My reputation will be
ruined! Prakash Das comes from a very good
family. He would never be allowed to marry
me after that, even if he *wanted* to. *No one*
would ever marry me if such a story were
known."

"Have you ever given Lal any information
or papers about Jai's businesses before this?"
Julie asked.

"Oh, no!" Priya's hand touched Julie's
arm. "Jai was right, wasn't he, Julie?" she

whispered. "He told me there would be people who would try to use me for their own purposes while pretending to be my friends. But I thought Lal *loved* me!"

"It happens to every woman, Priya, even those who aren't princesses," Julie replied with a little smile. "But don't be discouraged. For every person who betrays your trust, there will be many others who sincerely care for you." Julie knew that feeling of being used. During her years as a journalist, politicians, performers and businessmen had tried to date her, only to discover that she would not write an article supporting their interests in exchange for dinner at a posh restaurant or a dozen long-stemmed roses delivered to her modest apartment.

"Is this blackmail?" Priya asked after a minute.

"Yes. And there are ways to deal with it," Julie answered, her voice firm.

"But Lal is so...so evil, Julie! I could see that at last, when he was talking to me, sneering at me, telling me what I must do. And I must do it, Julie, or else...." Priya began to sob again.

Julie tried her best to comfort the princess. Julie had been in India long enough to recognize the intense social pressure for a woman to marry. An unmarried woman was considered useless. She bore no sons to perform the religious rites so necessary for the spiritual well-being of herself, her parents and her ancestors. Her life had no purpose. There was simply no social niche for single people in India, unless they chose a life of religious celibacy. An unmarried woman who had no religious vocation remained in her parents' home, the bane of their existence.

Knowing how terrible such a fate would appear to Priya, Julie did not blame the young princess for giving in to Lal Delal's demands. Julie wondered how Lal would use the papers. Her mind raced with possibilities. Industrial espionage? Did he intend to try to blackmail Jai? It occurred to her that if she could discover why Lal had wanted these papers, it might be possible to counterblackmail him into silence. He was undoubtedly involved in some kind of illegal activity.

"Priya." Julie shook the Indian girl gently by the shoulders. "Priya, listen to me. Everything will be all right. How did you know which papers to take from Jai's office? Did Lal tell you what to get?"

"He said...he said to find out where the... confidential reports and plans...and things like that were," replied the girl, choking back her sobs. "I found a file that had lots of sealed envelopes and folders marked 'private.' I just took everything from there. He also wanted maps showing where all my brother's factories and businesses are, and any other maps I could find."

"I wonder why Jai didn't have those things in a safe somewhere," Julie puzzled.

"The palace is so guarded. No one could possibly get to his office, do you think?" said the girl, wiping her eyes with the back of her slender hand.

"You are probably right. He wouldn't think it was necessary. Or maybe he does have a safe, for that matter. Anyway, everything must be put back where it came from."

"Oh, Julie! I'm so frightened! I don't want to go back in there! What if someones comes?" Priya cast an anxious glance up the hallway. "I don't know where my brother is, or Hari."

"Jai would have been at work by now if he was coming in today," Julie replied. It was her turn to blush. "He...he stayed up very late last night—all night, in fact." Fortunately, Priya was too absorbed in her own problems to feel curious about that statement. Julie felt relieved not to have to reveal her own folly.

"Listen, Priya," she said, "you go back to your room." The girl looked on the verge of collapse. "I'll put the papers back in your brother's office. Then we'll think of how to deal with Lal. Only tell me which file you took the folders from."

A few minutes later, having sent Priya off to bed, Julie closed the office door. The click sounded loud in the stillness. She crossed the wide room quickly, her feet noiseless on the deep maroon rug. She would have liked to look through the papers in her hand in hope of gaining some clue to Lal's purpose, but there was no time. Even though she did not think there was much danger of someone coming to the office this late in the afternoon, she was more nervous than she cared to admit.

She was on her knees before the bottom drawer of the filing cabinet Priya had told her about, intent upon replacing the folders in what she hoped was their original order so as not to draw attention, when a cold shiver crept up her spine. She paused, reluctant to turn around.

"Eyes in the back of your head, Julie? How useful in your profession. I thought I came in rather quietly."

She pivoted on her heels. Jai's eyes reflected the same cold anger she heard in his voice. She stared up at him, dismayed.

"How did you know to come in quietly?" she asked when she could speak at all.

"I heard the door to the office close as I came around the corner of the hall," he replied, his dark eyes boring into her. "Satisfied?"

"Oh." She stood up. "Believe it or not, Jai," she said, stretching out one hand to him in an unconscious gesture of supplication, "it's not what you think."

He reached out and took the papers from her other hand without replying. He sorted through them quickly, pausing once or twice to scan a particular page. Then he tossed them onto his desk with a careless flick of his wrist.

"It's no go, Julie." His face contorted. "Spare me the story you no doubt have prepared. These papers contain exactly the information that would be most useful to the terrorists. Need I say more?"

Julie stared at him, stunned. "The terrorists! Then...then...." She stopped, her mind whirling. So that was Lal's game! Right under their noses all this time, if she had only known.

"Don't bother to look so surprised." His eyes never left her face. "Names and addresses of my closest business associates. The identities of my security people. Floor plans of my factories and office buildings—essential for planting bombs or planning kidnappings, of course. Personal information about key employees."

Each word was like a blow to her. It could not have hurt worse if he had actually hit her. He looked as if he would like to. His fine mouth was drawn back in disgust; his eyes filled with rage.

Yet Julie could not defend herself without revealing Priya's indiscretion. It would have been one thing to tell Jai that his sister was seeing a man in secret. Julie had been tempted more than once to do so. But it was another matter altogether to divulge that Priya had joined forces with the terrorists at the expense of her own brother. Julie could not betray the young princess. Maybe when Jai's anger abated she could explain to him in a rational manner how helpless Priya had been to do otherwise. But now was not the time for such a disclosure: he looked like he would be happy to wring Julie's neck if she dared to utter a word.

"Of course I was a fool not to lock these files up. Everything I have learned about you pointed to this. But the more I got to know you—" He broke off and turned away.

Julie stared at his back. A violent shock went through her as she recognized how much his good opinion meant to her. She realized now how precious a part of her life her growing intimacy with this man had become—those days of working together, the nights of dancing, the ever-present desire that even now in his anger he aroused in her. . . .

"I guess I should be grateful," he stated. He had turned toward her. The emotion was gone from his face. His voice was cold. Only his eyes revealed his true feelings. "You see, Julie, despite my suspicions about you I could not help feeling attracted to you. I imagined you had a certain bravery that I found irresistible. Yes, another man made a fool of by your beauty! How useful your comrades must find you. But how fortunate for me that I discovered you here today. Without this proof of your guilt, I was in danger of falling in love with you.''

"In love with me?" Julie repeated his words in a whisper.

"Does that please you?" He was smiling at her—a hateful, mocking smile. But as he watched her the smile faded.

She stared at him as though she had never seen him before. Her mouth was dry. He cared for her. He had been falling in love with her. He saved her from the *dacoits* because he—he, Jai Mishra—had worried about her, *wanted her safe*. Suddenly something occurred to her.

"The guards, Jai." She forced her constricted throat to function. "Last night. In Agra. The ones who told you I had gone. Were they there to spy on me—or...or to protect me?"

He glared at her. "To protect you, more the fool I!" he snapped. "You have had my guards near you since the day you joined my household. Just like my mother and sister do, without knowing it. I told you I take care of my own," he added, sardonically. "Oh, Julie!" His voice was anguished. "Even *now*, after *this*—" he gestured at the papers on the desk "—I still wish you *were* mine!"

It was then that she knew. She had known

without recognizing it for weeks now. Maybe since her first few days at the palace. She loved this man—this dark, intelligent, fascinating, autocratic, protective prince. She loved him with all her heart. All her mind. All her soul.

She knew now that there was no question of him taking the place of Eddie Bryce. Eddie was...well, Eddie. Wonderful and sweet. But that relationship had been a first awakening, a prelude. What she felt for Jai was so entirely different it was no threat at all to her fond, loving memories.

Maybe because she was older now, Julie was capable of a greater love. But what she felt for the man before her—his eyes blazing with anger and contempt—filled her to overflowing. In that moment of recognition, her life became complete. Pure, pristine joy surged through her. To love Jai Mishra seemed the greatest blessing on earth.

"Don't look at me like that, Julie!" His voice shook with fury. "Save the playacting!"

She smiled into his anger. "I didn't do it, Jai." A new thought struck her. At last she understood the overpowering attraction she felt for him. Deep love gives birth to deep desire. "I didn't steal these papers for the terrorists or anyone else."

Julie's voice trembled, not with fear but with a sudden, melting passion born of her love. Her whole body flamed, and her senses ignited with the exhilarating speed of an oil refinery caught in an explosion. Understanding at last the limitless depth of her emotions—of her love for Jai—she longed more than anything else to share her newfound bliss with him. Suddenly even being in the same room with him was unbearably stimulating.

"I. . . I'm going, Jai. We. . . we can discuss this another time." She moved toward the door.

He stepped forward and caught her shoulders. *"We'll discuss it now,"* he told her through gritted teeth. He wrenched her around to face him. One glimpse at her face and his eyes narrowed. He felt the heated excitement quivering through her body beneath his hands.

"Ah. . ." he breathed. His eyes glinted. "So that's it. So that part at least wasn't a fake." Cold wrath flooded his handsome face. "You want to be made love to, do you? I'm happy to oblige you! I'm sure any man would do for you—you will find I won't disappoint you."

Before Julie could protest, the prince grabbed her wrist. He strode across the office and kicked open a connecting door with one foot. He dragged her after him down a short hallway. Julie absorbed the fine detail of the hand-painted wallpaper in the narrow corridor. Then another blow with his foot sprang

open the door at the end of the hall. She
glimpsed the room beyond. It was the
prince's bedroom. . . .

"Jai, no! Not now!" Her hands clutched at
his shirt.

"Oh, yes, Julie!" he replied in a grim
voice. "Now! You are through with your
games. You can start *earning* the information you carry back to your friends. Believe
me," he added, a speculative look in his
eyes, "in the end you'll enjoy this as much
as I will."

He flung her down on the huge bed. Warm
sable touched her skin. She cast a frantic
glance around. Lush, cream-colored carpet
covered the large expanse of floor. The walls
were white marble flecked with black. Black-
and-gold lacquered furniture—priceless antiques—vied with luxurious sable throws in
the contemporary black-on-white decor. A
large cinnabar vase on a black marble coffee
table provided the one splash of color.

"Take off your clothes." He pulled his cotton knit shirt over his head as he spoke and
began to unbuckle his belt.

Julie stared at his naked torso, fighting her
own rising passion. Awakened to her love for
him at last, she discovered she had lost her
will to resist the erotic delirium that had tor-
mented her since meeting Jai. Her limbs
melted with desire for him. The blood burned
in her veins. *Want him! Oh, yes, how she*

wanted him! Her whole body throbbed with an insatiate thirst for him.

Watching her face, Jai smiled. He let the belt drop through his fingers onto the carpet.

"Here, I will help you." He joined her on the bed, his body long and broad next to hers, weighing down the mattress.

He removed her clothing with rapid skill, lingering a moment only when he reached the red lace of her bra and panties. These he removed also, but slowly, so that Julie felt a wild impatience growing in her responsive body. He laughed softly as she struggled to keep from rising to meet the touch of his hands. With a final pull, he slipped her panties over the smooth curve of her hips and off her feet. She lay back upon the sable spread, gloriously naked before him. He removed his pants and lay beside her, pulling her close to him.

"My God," he whispered, touching the spill of her golden hair with reverence. "You are more beautiful even than I remembered."

"You have thought of me...like this?" she asked, her voice low, throaty with passion.

"Every night, my love. Every long, lonely night since we were together in the garden."

He began to stroke her, drawing his hands over her body in feather-light caresses. She quivered, losing herself in this new world of sensations. A fire burned in her loins, so that every touch of his fingers inflamed the urgency of her need.

The prince was not immune to the desire he was arousing in her. His hands were cool against her skin, but she heard his raspy breathing and the pounding of his heart. She marveled to feel his lean, hard masculine body beside her, moving against her. A violent tremor heaved her body upward as Jai slipped his hand lower, touching the inside of her thighs.

An unbearable restlessness seized Julie. She gripped the hard muscles of his arms. Jai drew back, steadying himself, then swept her up against him, lowering his head to her full breast as he did so. His lips moved over the velvety skin, drawing the taut nipple into his mouth. His fine white teeth pressed against her, gentle but unyielding.

Julie's heart filled with light, opening fully to this man in her arms in a way never possible before. The love she felt for him poured forth to him through every pore of her slender, quivering body. Her wondrous, glorious love sought union with its source. . . .

"Jai!" Julie whispered, touching his dark head with her hand. "Jai! Love me! Love me now!" she begged.

As though he had been waiting to hear these words, he pushed her away. A cynical smile twisted his lips. He fought to control his breathing.

"But why now, Julie?" he asked with deceptive sweetness. He raised up on one elbow, his powerful body unbelievably handsome in the dim afternoon light that filled the room.

"Why now?" he asked again. "When it is obvious that I can have you anytime."

The waves of passion that had swept over Julie like thick crests of erotic pleasure began to disperse. She looked up at his beloved face inches away from hers. She struggled to understand.

"Don't...don't you want to make love to me, Jai?" She reached out and touched his dark chest with tentative fingers.

He moved away from her touch. "Oh, yes, I want to make love to you! Don't ever doubt that!" His voice was still husky—even the light contact with Julie's fingertips had been enough to fan his desire. He swung his feet off the bed and stood up.

"I still want you," he assured her. He stood beside the bed staring down at her, tracing the delicate lines of her body with his eyes. A fresh rush of passion extinguished the anger in his dark eyes for a moment. But then he was in control again, his face set in harsh, uncompromising lines and a mocking smile distorting his finely shaped mouth.

"But now that I'm certain I can have you whenever I want you," he continued, picking up his pants from the floor and pulling them on as he spoke, "I will take you at my leisure.

Today—'' He paused in buckling on his belt to glance down at her again. ''Today, Julie, I'm satisfied just with having heard you beg for love from the man you are betraying.''

''Jai! No!'' She had no recollection of getting from the bed to the center of the room, but suddenly she was beside him, clinging to his arm. ''Jai, no!'' her clear voice pleaded. ''You don't understand. There is more to all of this.''

''That I'm well aware of.'' His handsome face was impassive, but his eyes bespoke his loathing. He removed her hand from his arm and pulled his shirt on.

Julie clutched his arm again. ''Jai, you have to believe me. I love you!''

Two ruthless hands grasped her shoulders. Pain shot through her body. Julie sank to her knees, a low cry pried from her lips. Jai towered above her. His past anger was nothing compared to the fury that gripped him now. The tiger light flamed in the depths of his eyes, incinerating the final traces of his ardor.

''Damn you, Julie!'' he hissed between clenched teeth. ''Damn you! Don't you ever say those words to me again!'' He shoved her aside and strode from the room.

A deep silence filled the bedroom after he had gone. Julie remained where she fell, stunned and unbelieving, crumpled on the floor like a cast-off toy. So awash with passion only moments before, now she felt a numbness through her body. She stretched out one arm, closing her fist on a mound of soft fur. A cold void closed over her. Julie's only awareness was of a wide galaxy of nothingness stretching out before her into bleak, frozen, timeless, eternal space.

How long she lay naked on the sable rug she had no idea. At last she rose and gathered up her clothing. She dressed mechanically. A slow, horrible ache burned inside her chest but she ignored it.

As she fastened the buttons of her suit jacket she noted with detached interest a carved statue on the prince's bedside table. The intricate design of the glossy sandalwood figurine seemed vaguely familiar. Suddenly she placed it. Lord Shiva—one of the triad of major Hindu gods. Shiva, the four-armed. What did he stand for? Ah, yes. The Destroyer.

She cast a last glance around the bedroom. The ache in her chest was agonizing. She felt abandoned, humiliated, rejected . . . just when her heart had opened fully to a man for the first time. . . .

The pain was almost unbearable, making Julie want to cry out. She turned to leave the room. Jai. She would never forgive him. Not as long as she lived. Love him? How had she ever supposed that she loved him? A man who brought that much pain to another

human being—no matter what the reason—
for such a man she could only feel one emotion: cold, dispassionate hatred.

She left the door open behind her. The
faint fragrance of sandalwood drifted down
the hall lingering in the air long after she was
gone.

CHAPTER SEVENTEEN

JULIE LEANED BACK against the soft pillows of the love seat facing the French windows in her bedroom. She watched a distant night watchman cross the front lawn in the deepening twilight for his first security round of the evening. She shifted her position on the couch to keep him in sight, tucking her legs underneath her and pulling the edge of her robe out to cover her bare feet.

It was time to make plans. She pushed her heavy hair back off her face, massaging her scalp. It was difficult to think. Her mind felt as dull as her body. She continued to follow the watchman's progress, staring at the dark grove of trees at the corner of her line of vision long after he had disappeared.

Julie let her head fall back on the cushions. She wished she could fall asleep on the pretty love seat and not wake up for a hundred years. No, not even then. Never wake up. Just sleep and sleep. Dream and dream. Not have to think. Not have to make plans. Not have to face reality.

She would leave India tomorrow. That

much was certain. She could not go on after what had happened this afternoon.

Of course she would lose her job. It would be hard to face Wes Harding, tell him that she had failed. He was counting on her, trusting her to do the story. . . .

"But I just don't *care*!" she mused aloud. She turned over, pressing her face into the pillows. "I hate you, Jai!"

The cushions muffled her words. Immense fatigue quadrupled the weight of her limbs, making it difficult even to breathe. She wondered if she would be able to get a flight on such short notice. Sometimes Air India was booked to the United States a month in advance.

She knew she should be more rational. An inner voice warned her not to make any rash decisions. But a great tiredness overwhelmed her, dragging her down. She did not have the strength to make herself care enough to want to be reasonable. All she knew was that she would rather forget the story, lose her job, even lose her life than ever see Jai Mishra again. She must leave India.

A knock on the door startled her. Her heart leaped to her throat. A second later she was furious with herself. It was not Jai at the door. How could she think he might come? He would never come. Besides, she hated Jai, and she was not fooling herself to ease her suffering. She really did hate him. She would hate anyone who could do what he had done to her. To make her beg and then to—

The knock sounded again. Julie walked across the room and opened the door.

"Julie, dear," exclaimed the maharani. "Are you busy? Do you mind having a visitor? Priya has just left and that always makes me lonesome."

"Please come in." Julie opened the door wide. "I'm happy you've come. I . . . I need to talk to you." Here was one more problem: how to tell the maharani she was leaving. Julie searched for a suitable reason to explain her sudden departure.

"Let's go into the sitting room," Julie suggested. "Would you like me to ring for Sukundala to bring us some tea?"

"No, no tea, dear," the woman replied, seating herself gracefully in an armchair. "I usually don't drink it at night. Indian tea is so strong, you know, I find it keeps me awake. Were you ready for bed?" she asked, nodding to Julie's robe.

"Oh, no. It's just that . . . I'm done with my work for today." Feeling that this explanation sounded rather lame, Julie added, "I thought I would just eat dinner in here tonight."

The maharani searched Julie's face. "Are you feeling ill? You're very pale tonight." The kindness in her voice penetrated the numb cocoon Julie had been living in since leaving Jai's bedroom. It touched her on the raw.

"Fine, maharani," she faltered, turning her face aside. "I'm fine."

The Indian woman rose and went to Julie, who was sitting at the writing desk, arms wrapped around bent knees. She put her hand on her American guest's forehead, then clucked her concern.

"Perhaps you are worn out from your trip last night," she commented. "How unfortunate you got called away from Agra at such an hour!" She felt Julie's forehead again, then stroked the younger woman's hair with gentle, massaging fingers.

"Please don't worry about me, maharani. Truly, I'm just fine," Julie asserted. She felt the tension dissolving beneath the Indian woman's expert touch.

"You know, Julie," remarked the maharani, "I think maybe you're getting sick from the heat. With your fair skin and hair you must be extremely sensitive to it. A person must live here for a few years to become acclimatized. Usually your cheeks have such a pretty tint of rose in them—" She broke off, studying the white face of the young woman before her with a mother's eyes.

"It's very hot these days," Julie agreed. To her dismay her words ended on a sob. The maharani's gentle concern could not have been more ill-timed; Julie felt her emotions staggering under the day's stresses.

"My dear, I believe you are sick, whatever you say!" exclaimed the older woman. "Come, let me help you into your bed."

Julie obeyed. A few minutes later, tucked between fresh sheets, she closed her eyes in relief. The sickening ache of the afternoon still gripped her chest, but she felt more at peace. The maharani sat beside her on the bed massaging her neck.

"This is the hot season now, Julie," she was explaining, smoothing out the knots of tension from Julie's neck and shoulders. "The temperature reached 115 degrees today, I believe. Even at the first of the week it was as much as five degrees cooler. But now it will stay very hot until the rains come in mid-June."

She paused, then continued thoughtfully: "I think we should go to Jai's summer palace in Kashmir. It would be good for you to get away from Delhi. I was planning to move there for the rest of the summer a little later this month. Priya and I go every year about this time to get away from the heat, although Jai stays here. Delhi is more convenient for him to look after his businesses.

"Kashmir is in the hill country. It's much cooler there. The palace is on Lake Dal in Srinagar, right at the foot of the Himalayas. It's really very beautiful, Julie! You could do your work there just as well, don't you think? Although of course I don't really understand what your job involves. But there is a commuter flight to New Delhi every day if you needed to come back here sometimes.''

Julie propped up one elbow and turned over to face her hostess. ''Did you say Kashmir?'' she asked.

The maharani nodded, pleased by this sign of interest. ''Yes. Many upper-class Indians vacation there every summer to escape the heat of the plains. I'm afraid if you stay here now that the hot weather has come, you'll damage your health. I would never forgive myself for sending you back to Wes Harding sick,'' she added.

Despite the ache in her chest, Julie smiled. She had no doubt her boss would expect her to face illness and more to get a story. In fact, most foreign correspondents had an entire repertoire of ''sick stories'' to tell over drinks at the press club or during the endless hours of waiting for a newsbreak. It was impossible to travel all over the world, more often than not under adverse conditions, without succumbing to some variety of illness from time to time. The important thing was not to let it stand in the way of getting a story.

Now here was a lifetime opportunity for Julie. Should she take it? She had given up. She had quit. She had decided to leave India. But the story beckoned. The *dacoit* leader had said the terrorist conference would be held in Kashmir—probably in Srinagar—in five days' time. . . .

She had gone to Jai's office that afternoon to discuss their options, fully intending to be on a plane to Kashmir tonight. She still had four days left. She could find the terrorists without Jai's help, she felt sure of that. She could get her story, go home, let life go on. India—the wonderful country she had grown to love—would be only a lingering memory.

Her work, her boss, the respect of her colleagues, the companionship of her few close friends in the newsroom. It had been enough for her before. It could be enough again. Jai had destroyed the love she had felt for him. Why let him destroy the love she had always had for her work, as well?

"Did you say Jai doesn't go to Kashmir with you?" Julie asked, trying to make her voice casual. She propped herself up on the deep bed pillows.

"He seldom has time," the maharani explained, folding her hands on her lap. "And communication from the hill stations is often very poor—the phones and telexes are not reliable. Jai says it's impossible to run his business from there."

Julie did not think the prince would feel it necessary to go to Kashmir in person to organize the assault on the terrorist conference. He had sent one of his top intel-

ligence teams up there several weeks ago.
Besides, now it was a job for the Indian
police. No doubt Jai would simply relay the
bandit leader's information to the government authorities. His agents could advise the
military and police of how to trap the terrorists if any further involvement was necessary.

"Jai took Priya with him when he left this
afternoon," the maharani was saying. "She
has been so unhappy lately. I was glad that
she consented to go when he invited her—it
used to be that going somewhere with Jai was
her biggest treat," added the older woman
with a reminiscent smile.

"Where did they go?" Julie asked.

"Oh, on a business trip, I believe. Jai likes
to visit his factories often and meet his man-
agers in person. He said they would be gone
two or three days."

Well, Julie reflected, he certainly would
not have taken Priya along if he meant to involve himself with terrorists. Julie could
leave for Kashmir early tomorrow morning
so she would be gone before Jai returned to
New Delhi. With any luck at all, she would
be on the spot when the groups gathered.
She could finish this story and then return
to New York without having to see Jai
again.

The maharani, eager to get Julie up to the
cool hill country, agreed to leave the next

morning. She assured Julie that the summer palace would be ready for them since the servants had already been expecting her sometime this month. After the older woman left to make the necessary plane reservations, Julie placed a call to the paper.

She was sound asleep when the call finally came through. Jarred awake by the loud buzz beside her ear, she groped in the darkness for the old-fashioned black receiver.

"Julie! Can you hear me!" Harding's voice came over the murky lines, distorted by distance. She had not expected to talk with him, only to inform the news desk of her intention of leaving Delhi. She had the phone and telex number of the summer palace in case they needed to reach her.

"Where are you?"

"I'm still in Delhi." Julie filled in Wes on her encounter with the *dacoits*. She explained now she had to travel to Kashmir to follow up on the bandit leader's tip.

"Is Mishra going with you?" he asked.

"No, he's away on business," Julie replied, striving for nonchalance—a difficult impression to convey when shouting.

Harding's static-filled silence greeted her words. Julie reflected uneasily on the newsman's ability to sense something that was not quite as it was being presented.

"Don't take too many risks, Julie," he said at last. "I want a story, not a dead reporter on my hands. Remember that when the crisis comes,'' he admonished.

THE NOISE OF LANDING GEAR roused Julie as her plane approached Srinagar. She opened her eyes and turned toward the window. Huge mountains—the highest in the world— towered beside the small plane. Julie remembered the maharani telling her the base of the Himalayan mountain range was two hundred miles wide in some places; four of the world's six highest mountains formed a part of the chain.

Walking from the plane to the terminal later, Julie paused to stare at the surrounding peaks again. Sheer cliffs, deep in gleaming snow, lost themselves in the clouds. Julie had to tilt her head all the way back to see the tops of the peaks. At ground level, she could see green meadows strewed with tiny yellow flowers all around the small airport. The mountain air was the purest she had ever breathed. It made her feel life was full of promise—rare and precious, and filled with possibilities previously unseen. If only her heart did not hurt so much. . . .

"Already you look better, Julie," exclaimed the maharani, walking beside her. "I'm so glad we came!"

A car from the summer palace was waiting for them. On the ride from the airport, Julie gazed out the window. If New Delhi had seemed foreign to her, Srinagar was like being in another world altogether.

The people in the fields and houses along the roadside did not look like city dwellers, even though Srinagar was a good-sized metropolis. Their fresh, interested facial expressions, alert eyes and long-strided pace were typical of outdoorsmen. In the fields beside the rough road, farmers behind struggling teams of oxen waded thigh deep in mud through rice fields. Cars were few. The most common motor vehicle seemed to be a three-wheeled, box-shaped taxi. Julie later learned that one could travel all over town in one for a rupee or two.

"Are there a lot of farmers here?" she asked the maharani, who was leaning back against the seat, a contented look on her face.

"In this area, yes. This valley is part of the Vale of Kashmir," the older woman explained. "Srinagar is said to be the heart of the Vale. Because of the Himalayan and the Karakoram mountain ranges that cut across this province diagonally, only a small part of the land can be cultivated."

Julie could not help thinking how well the beautiful wildness would suit Jai. Regret that she would never see him in the glorious mountain setting filled her. The traits she had always admired so much in him—his high-mindedness, his resourcefulness, his courage—those qualities made him worthy to be associated in her mind with this lofty Himalayan fortress.

"Did Jai—did your husband's family rule this province before India's independence?" Julie asked.

"No," replied her hostess, "but they built the summer palace here long before my husband was born. The Maharaja of Kashmir allowed them to do so—he was also a Hindu. For Hindus Kashmir is a very holy place," she continued. "One of our oldest temples is right here on the hillside above Srinagar. Moreover, the Himalayas have always been the abode of many of our greatest saints and sages, both now and in times past. The religious fighting between Muslims and Hindus has been very bitter here," the Indian woman added. "It makes me sad to think of all this beauty despoiled by suffering and hatred."

Julie lapsed into silence. She knew Jai was not a devout Hindu in the same sense that the maharani was. Yet she felt sure he would appreciate the spiritual purity of these remote mountains. Again and again she had seen Jai use his influence in constructive, compassionate, life-preserving ways. To Julie his positive approach to life evinced a deep-rooted spirituality not dependent on religious convictions. She had never doubted that, in his own way, Jai Mishra was a deeply spiritual man. If only that compassion had extended to his relationship with her, she would have counted herself blessed. . . .

"Look!" The maharani's voice interrupted her thoughts. "Here we are at the palace."

The car had rolled to a stop at the edge of a stone quay. Julie's eyes followed the maharani's finger. She saw a marvelous structure of sunlit marble seemingly suspended in a sparkling blue lake.

"Am I seeing things?" Julie asked, turning to her hostess with a smile. "Or is it really floating?"

"It's built on a tiny island. Isn't it beautiful?" replied the maharani. "I always feel so content to return to Kashmir. I love to spend the summers here. Come, dear. Here is our *shikara* waiting for us."

Several men lingered nearby, casting admiring glances at the shiny limousine. As Julie stepped out of the car on to the quay the approving gazes shifted to her, but covertly. The men spoke among themselves, their eyes straying back to Julie from time to time. She caught Jai's name in their murmurs of appreciation—did they think she was his woman? It was clear they approved his choice. She forced back an agonizing sense of loss—of sadness.

"Hello, Abdul!" the maharani greeted one of the loungers. "How nice to see you again."

A man came forward from the group and

bowed to the maharani, a shy smile on his face. He pulled an ornate rowboat covered with a cloth canopy up against the stairs. Julie took his hand and stepped gingerly into the small boat. The maharani was already seated across from her. As soon as Julie sat down, Abdul shoved the boat away from the quay, leaped lightly into the stern and took up the oars. The small craft shot forward across the lake toward the palace.

"This is a *shikara*, Julie," the maharani told her. "You might say they are water taxis. Everyone who lives on the lake uses them to get from one place to another."

"Other people live on this lake besides you?"

In answer, the older woman pointed to the right. Julie saw a long line of flat-roofed boats drawn up one beside the other out in the wide neck of water that led to the lake.

"This is Dal Lake," explained her hostess. "People live on houseboats here. Some of the boats are like floating hotels. They are rented to tourists who come from all parts of the world to live on the lake for a few weeks."

With a flick of the paddle that seemed second nature to him, Abdul maneuvered their craft up alongside the dock to the summer palace. The dock was nothing more than a stairway leading down into the water from a wide veranda.

Julie debarked. She looked around, taking

in the fairy-tale appearance of her surroundings. An air of grandiose antiquity lingered about the floating palace she saw at the foot of the Himalayas. Julie could almost hear the bygone whispers of the courtiers, the swish and clang of swords, the sly, soft-footed stealth of almond-eyed rival wives.

Yet these shades from the past did not engender a feeling of gloom. Bright sunshine shimmered on the blue water, bursting into streams of silver light deflecting off the rapid oars of the many *shikaras* that scuttled back and forth across the lake on business or pleasure. Children played and swam in the water, or chased one another in their own tiny rowboats. Across the way, on the stone quay, an old man paused in his journey to kneel in prayer. Above it all the Himalayas—aloof, cold, pure; the home of saints. Yet it felt as if one could reach out and touch the snow-capped mountains reflected on the mirror of Dal Lake.

"Come inside, Julie." The maharani's pleasant voice broke in on Julie's reverie. "This is Abdul's wife. She will show you to your room."

Left alone, Julie explored the summer palace. She discovered secret gardens with jewel-inlaid gazebos. There, peacocks strolled at their royal leisure, dragging the weight of their heavy tail feathers with proud disdain. She came across hidden courtyards, resplen-

dent with golden statues of Indian gods, and
sparkling fountains that threw glittering
beads of moisture into the clear air. Lush,
hand-knotted, wool and silk carpets depicting
scenes of royal life, and a profusion of low
couches and pillows seemed to dispense with
the need for furniture. She rounded a corner
and came face to face with a stalking tiger—
stuffed, although somehow his glassy eyes
managed to convey a look of keen hunger.

Julie was enthralled by the subtle mysteries
of Asian life. So this was how Jai's ancestors
had whiled away the sweet summer hours,
when they weren't busy trying to save their
lands and necks from invading hordes or en-
vious neighbors. She had never seen anything
to equal the summer palace. She detested Jai
for his treatment of her, but she had to admit
that the palace was indeed the perfect setting
for him. She wandered out onto the wide, pil-
lared terrace and gazed across the lake at the
beckoning peaks. But in her mind's eye she
was seeing a man's smiling face, dark and
fine featured with burning tiger eyes.

"Hallo! Madam, hallo!"

The haunting vision of that once-beloved
face faded. The high-pitched call came again.
Julie leaned over the porch balcony. Floating
in a boat below, his young face lifted to her,
was the most handsome child she had ever
seen. He had the gorgeous almond eyes of the
Kashmiri people. Curling black hair framed

his round face. But more important than his boyish beauty was the undisguisable intelligence and the frankness of his eyes.

"Who are you?" Overcome by the legendary setting of the floating palace at the foot of the Himalayas, Julie could almost believe the remarkable youth to be the young Lord Krishna himself, so often depicted in Indian art as a child of about the boy's age.

"I am Gulzar!" replied her new friend, who obviously considered that a complete explanation. He gestured at the leather goods piled neatly in his small boat. "Would you like to buy something, madam?"

"These vests are beautiful, Gulzar!" Julie exclaimed, fingering one of soft suede lined with silky white fur that he held up to her. "Where do they come from?"

"My father is a hunter," he replied. "This animal he shot in the mountains last winter. My mother and sisters take the skins of the animals he kills and make them into coats and vests, and also fur hats."

Julie purchased the vest, noting that Gulzar was too good a salesman to betray his exuberance at getting what was undoubtedly a fine price. She sat back on her heels, pondering a new thought. She looked up to find Gulzar watching her, his eyes filled with an odd, mature seriousness.

"Gulzar, I need someone to show me around Srinagar. The places tourists go, and also other places where people like yourself live.'' When he grasped her meaning—that she wanted him to act as her guide and would pay him well—he nodded his head vigorously.

They arranged to meet at the same spot at eight o'clock the next morning. After Gulzar had gone Julie wondered if she had done the right thing. Perhaps she would have been wiser to ask the maharani to recommend a professional guide. Yet Gulzar inspired her with a strange confidence. He was alert and intelligent. His boyish curiosity and inexhaustible energy might suit her needs better than a professional guide who would wonder at her interest in anything unusual. Besides, Gulzar's command of English was excellent. Even the few Hindi words Julie had learned in Delhi did no good here, as the people of Kashmir spoke Urdu.

As far as Julie knew, she was the only journalist on the trail of the terrorist conference. Which was not to say that one of her colleagues might not stumble on it. If the *dacoit* leader was right, there were still three days left before the story broke. Once Jai informed the police of the highwayman's tip, the chances of other correspondents showing up increased dramatically—journalists always kept tabs on police activities. But the police would take great pains to keep the information from leaking out: all would be lost if the terrorists were warned off.

Julie had avoided fraternizing with the other foreign correspondents in Delhi, even though reporters tended to stick together, especially on foreign assignment. In this case, herd journalism would put the kiss of death on a story as delicate as this one was. Julie did not admit even to herself how vital to her self-esteem her own success had become. She and Jai had worked together closely on this project. Now that he was out of the picture, she had no intention of giving him the satisfaction of thinking that she had not been able to complete the story without his help. Her mouth formed a grim, straight line. She would get this story if it was the last thing she ever did.

Julie was seated in one of the enclosed miniature gardens an hour later studying a city map of Srinagar when a babble of voices in the corridor distracted her. A moment later Priya hastened through the open doorway and ran forward to embrace her American friend.

"Priya!" Julie exclaimed, standing up to return the young princess's hug. "When did you get here? I had no idea you were expected this soon."

"I wasn't!" the young girl replied with teasing laughter. "Mother is surprised, too! Oh, Julie!" she added in an impulsive rush of words, "everything is all right now! You will never believe how it all worked out!"

"Tell me."

"Well, you know that Jai invited me to accompany him on a short trip yesterday?"

Julie nodded. She dreaded any recital that included Jai, but she braced herself to listen.

"Julie, Jai is *wonderful*!" Priya's eyes glistened. "He was *so* kind to me, as though he knew I was in some kind of trouble—which he *did* know—and I ended up telling him everything!"

"You mean you told him about Lal?" Julie asked.

"Yes. Everything. Jai was so nice to me, Julie. Just like how things used to be between us. He seemed sympathetic—not so, well, so aloof. Suddenly it occurred to me that I should tell him the truth.

"My brother is very powerful in India. I thought maybe he could help me somehow. And when I told him, he wasn't even surprised. He knew all about Lal! Would you believe it, Lal is a *terrorist* just like those people you are writing your story about! He may even have tried to plant a bomb at our ball after I let him into the palace grounds that night—or at least he let someone else in to do it. I knew he must be horrible after he made me get those papers from Jai's office.

"You know, Julie, Jai doesn't... well, he doesn't make a fuss. But in his way he made certain that I was always safe. He said he *expected* some attempt to infiltrate his household or his companies, as soon as he heard the terrorists were organizing. They call themselves the Black Band, which I think is a stupid name,'' she added with youthful contempt.

"Did. . .did you tell Jai about the papers?''

"Yes. I told him everything. How I took them and how you stopped me and then put them back. Lal never would have gotten away with them even if I *had* given them to him, because my brother's men have followed him since he started meeting me. Jai says a lot of information that will be useful to the police has been gained from spying on Lal. He's so horrid! I wonder how I *ever* thought I was in love with him! I think my brother means to trap him,'' she added in a more thoughtful tone.

"Why do you say that?'' Julie asked. Her own voice sounded as though it came from a long way off. So Jai knew now that she had not stolen those papers. And yet he had not sent her any word. What had she expected? Forgiveness? An apology? She must have been mad.

Somewhere in Julie's heart a tiny thread of hope snapped. The bleak truth was that Jai had lied when he said he could have loved her. She was innocent, but it made no difference to him. Perhaps even his desire for her had not been real, only an instinct to conquer the enemy. Her heart burned with humil-

iation. He had conquered her once. He would
never do so again.

"He told me not to worry any more, and
that he is glad I like the fiancé he picked for
me," Priya was saying, her shy eyes downcast. "He said soon I will have a lot of children of my own and then I can worry all I
want!" she added with a giggle. "Jai likes
Prakash a lot. After he is my husband, Jai
will take him into the business as a partner.
He promised me that nothing will interfere
with my marriage, so I know it will not. My
brother always keeps his word.

"He forgave me *everything*, Julie!" exclaimed the Indian girl, overcome with humil-
ity. "And I was so very bad!" She rose to
leave. "But Jai said I had been manipulated
by experts and that it wasn't my fault. Now I
can marry Prakash. Even though I don't de-
serve to!"

"I'm happy for you, Priya," Julie managed to say. She even smiled.

CHAPTER EIGHTEEN

A COOL GUST of mountain air rolling down off the rugged Himalayan slopes brushed Julie's cheek as she stepped onto the terrace a few minutes before eight o'clock the next morning. Shivering, Julie returned to her room and pulled on tan slacks and a pair of sturdy walking shoes. A wide belt of glove-soft leather clasped a billowy white tunic top around her waist. In one hand she carried a rolled-up map of Srinagar.

Facing the day was a struggle. In the black hours between dusk and dawn, Julie had tossed and turned, trying not to think about Jai. Priya's revelation that he knew of Julie's innocence had destroyed the fragile hold she had on her emotions. That Jai had rejected her because he could not bring himself to believe in her innocence had been bad enough. That he did not want her now that he knew he could trust her was unbearable.

Julie felt utterly, hopelessly abandoned. Last night as she lay sleepless and numb, it had seemed to her that a cruel theme was woven into the tapestry of her life. Love for her always ended in terrible heartbreaking loss. Losing Jai brought back painful memories. Eddie, her mother, Jai—the three people in her life she had loved—and Jai more than anyone—were all gone now. It was hard to believe Jai would desert her now that he knew the truth—yet he had.

But she would go on. She must survive, if only to prove to Jai that she could. Julie refused to give up. She had loved without fear, without reason. Now she would use that same courage to face life without his love.

Gulzar was waiting for her in his small rowboat. Julie climbed aboard and seated herself on the wooden plank across the prow opposite her guide.

"How big is Dal Lake?" she asked. "How long would it take to row around it?"

Gulzar shrugged. "Two hours, maybe more. Do you want to go around the lake?"

"No, I guess that would take too long. Besides—" she glanced down at the bright-colored tourist map unrolled on her knees "—most of the lake looks open. Let's just go where the houseboats are."

Gulzar bent over the oars, dipping the streamlined paddles into the water with noiseless ease. Soon they were floating past row upon row of wooden houseboats decorated with hand-carved porch railings. Stairs led from the porches down into the water. Narrow wooden planks ran the length of the boats on either side just above water level to provide access to the exterior hull.

"Why aren't you in school today, Gulzar?" Julie asked, shading her eyes against the glint of the water.

"Today is a government holiday. Tomorrow, also. The next day I must go to school, so I cannot take you in my boat. But tomorrow I can."

"Good."

Gulzar maneuvered their craft among the houseboats without speaking, sensing Julie was absorbed in her own thoughts.

Which she was. She was trying to get a feel for life on Dal Lake, enough so that she would recognize something unusual. What better rendezvous for a terrorist conference than a houseboat in Kashmir? With the tourist season, the arrival of foreigners would excite no curiosity. A houseboat rented by one party would allow a certain degree of privacy not to be found in a hotel. Neighboring houseboats would be filled with tourists bent on sightseeing, rather than with natives who might sense something was amiss.

Julie had thought about the conference when she had been looking over maps of Kashmir the previous afternoon. Most of the tourist attractions were centered in the Vale of Kashmir. The other parts of the state were too rugged for anything other than climbing or trekking parties. Srinagar was the most important city in the Vale and would offer the greatest camouflage. Gone were the days of rebel meetings in lonely retreats. Nowadays it was safer in cities—hence the name urban guerrillas. Finally, the *dacoit* leader had favored Srinagar as the most likely meeting place. Considering the short time left, Julie felt forced to limit her efforts to Srinagar. It seemed both her best bet and her only hope.

She had visited the local police station yesterday afternoon, arriving with all the pomp and circumstance afforded by an open-air, three-wheeled taxi. The police officials had been polite. After learning she was an American journalist, they had done the best their limited English would allow to persuade her that they knew nothing about a gathering of international terrorists. Kashmir was for tourists, they assured her. She still had not decided whether the officers knew more than they were telling or not.

Her eyes strayed back to the houseboats. They were in a poorer section now, where the boats were smaller and unadorned. Two native women, dressed in pajamalike pants and tunics, gossiped across the few feet of water separating their respective boats.

"Tell me, Gulzar," Julie asked, "do you know most of the owners of the houseboats rented to tourists?"

"Oh, yes! I know everyone because I sell my furs to their guests."

"Are most of the people who come to stay on a houseboat married couples—man and wife?"

Gulzar paused in his rowing to consider. "Yes, I think so. Among the people from India, yes." Julie had noticed before that he spoke of India as though it were a foreign country separate from Kashmir. "Most of the others, also."

"Gulzar, I'm a reporter, a journalist. Do you understand that word? You know, newspapers?"

"Yes, I understand. We have one here."

"In English?"

"No, in Urdu."

"Oh, well. You could interpret for me. Do you know where the newspaper office is? I need your help, Gulzar. Let the boat just float for a few minutes and listen to what I have to say."

Julie explained her mission, working around the difficulties of language and Gulzar's youth as best as she could. The boy agreed to make discreet inquiries among his neighbors as to what kind of people were renting their houseboats just now. Besides knowing the houseboat owners, Gulzar's job as a rowboat "door-to-door salesman" made him a perfect accomplice for gathering information.

Julie told Gulzar to keep an eye out for a group made up of several nationalities, more men than women. She explained that the terrorists might stay inside their houseboat more than other tourists, although the risk of being recognized might be overlooked in a calculated decision to sightsee and shop so they would blend in with the real tourists. An unusual amount of coming and going in rowboats after dark was also suspect.

Julie told the boy she would pay well for information. She tried to set the figure high enough to merit Gulzar's wholehearted interest yet not so much as to encourage him to take chances.

After they finished their tour of Dal Lake, Julie carefully studied the layout of the rows of boats. The vessels suitable for tourists all seemed concentrated in the front row of boats on the wide neck of water leading from the Jhelum River into the lake. Of course it was possible the terrorists would meet in the home of a permanent contact in Kashmir. But Julie felt that was unlikely because the presence of foreign guests would not go unnoticed in such a tightly knit community. Another possibility was that the conference would be held in a public place under the cover of tourist crowds.

An hour later Julie was high above the lake, at the entrance to the Shankracharya Temple. She knew at a glance that no terrorist meeting would be held there. The temple, dramatically situated on a ragged pinnacle of stone overlooking all of Srinagar and Dal Lake, was too tiny. Its simple architecture would offer no concealment.

Julie climbed the high stone steps of the circular building and entered the one inner room. A pundit in saffron-colored robes sat motionless before a large metallic Shiva Linga, the traditional symbol of Lord Shiva, chanting the Vedic hymns. Julie had read that the temple had been founded by the great Hindu saint Shankara over two thousand years ago. A sense of timelessness flowed through Julie, washing her soul with wonder. She glanced once more at the priest in whose care the temple now resided. Did he feel, as she did, the lingering purity of the presence of that great teacher from the past?

The rest of the day was spent in less uplifting circumstances. Julie prowled the dirty streets of Srinagar's industrial section, glad of Gulzar's escort. She saw no other women on the street, except for one or two in purdah. Once she saw a tall man coming toward her—dark-haired with the gliding stride of a hunter—and her heart constricted in her chest. She could not say whether she was relieved or disappointed that he wasn't Jai.

Attempts to interview the shopkeepers and street loungers through Gulzar met with indifferent success. Julie's shopping bag filled with countless small souvenirs as she tried to engage reticent proprietors in conversation. Had they heard rumors of a terrorist conference? Had they seen anything unusual? Maybe the memory of guerrilla raiders from across the Pakistan border was still too vivid in their minds, because not even the inviting crinkle of crisp bills loosened their tongues. If indeed they knew anything at all.

A trip to the local newspaper proved equally fruitless. With Gulzar's help she conveyed her interest in terrorists to a journalist across a narrow desk in a windowless gray-walled room. The reporter's face remained bland as he listened to the boy's translation. Unable to scan his work because of the language barrier, Julie could only assume that he composed his articles from government press releases and that he probably knew nothing.

Next Julie visited the police station again. She spoke to one of the younger officers away from his superiors. She left him with an almost-new hundred-rupee note in the pocket of his uniform and the promise of double that amount if he could discover any useful information.

That evening Julie sat on the terrace of the floating palace, anxiously awaiting news from Gulzar. As usual, her thoughts turned to Jai. There had been no message from the prince on her return. Even though she hadn't really expected his help, it had occurred to her that information about the action the police meant to take against the terrorists might have served as an apology. Now Julie wondered why she had even supposed he would think one was necessary.

She tossed her hair back off her face with an impatient gesture. *How much more time did she mean to waste thinking about the whys and wherefores of her relationship with Jai? Whatever it had been, it was over now.* Julie wanted to put aside memories of his carefree laughter at Leon Calvert's party, of his kindness that night with the *dacoits*, of his muscular body as he lay naked beside her in the secret garden.... She clenched her fists in an effort to forget such useless daydreams of a foresaken love. She had more important things to think about. Such as the disagreeable fact that, according to the *dacoit*, the terrorist conference was scheduled for the day after tomorrow, and she still had no idea where it was to be held....

Julie had only to appear on the stairs to discover that other vendors besides Gulzar were hawking their wares tonight, as well. Evenings on Dal Lake were pleasant—a good time for merchants since the city offered little or no nightlife. A guest at the summer palace of Prince Jaiapradesh Mishra would be a promising customer.

Boats flocked to the foot of the stairway where Julie sat. She welcomed the distraction. She smiled and made a pretense of looking over the various cargos of chocolates, crackers, saris, shawls, even drugstore items including American-style toilet paper and Kleenex.

Making her questions casual, she asked the boatmen about their businesses. Did they sell to the houseboats? Really? Who bought the most from them? The women, of course. What about boats where there were no women? Then did the men buy from them? A few coarse laughs. They spoke among themselves, enjoying a joke. Always there were women, they assured her.

Hoping she wouldn't give them the wrong idea, Julie pressed on. The joke among the men intrigued her. Were there always women on every boat, then? A woman for each man? She saw a common glance pass between the men beneath downcast dark lashes. But when they looked at her again their eyes were still respectful. She felt the mantle of Jai's protection settle over her. No man insulted a woman visiting the home of the Tiger Prince, no matter how suggestive her questions might be.

The boatmen left Julie with the distinct impression that there *was* a houseboat known to them where the men outnumbered the women, an unusual circumstance in this romantic honeymoon-and-tourist spot.

When Gulzar appeared, however, he brought no news.

His serious young face—pinched in a bit

with tiredness now—reflected his disappointment so much that Julie hid her own. Business had been perversely good, and the boy
had not been able to visit all the houseboats in
one evening. Julie decided to tour the lake
again the next day in a hired *shikara* while
Gulzar continued his inquiries.

She paid Gulzar his wages for the day,
which cheered him miraculously, and
watched him row away toward the long line
of houseboats, aware suddenly of the aching
fatigue of her own body. Julie turned instinctively toward the rugged peaks across the
water. At night they were massive dark
shadows indistinct except for moonlit crowns
of snow. Their peace eluded her. Her hand
fluttered in a quick, hopeless gesture before
she turned away to seek the low couch that
served as her Kashmiri bed.

The following evening Julie felt even more
discouraged. Gulzar had been sent on an er-
rand to his uncle's rug factory, and three-
quarters of the day had been lost. Julie had
spent the day questioning whoever happened
to be sitting on the front porch of rented
houseboats. She could now eliminate a score
of boats, but dozens more remained. She had
also revisited the newspaper office and police
station, and had taken a taxi out to the
Moghul Gardens. Once the pride of a Muslim
conqueror, the beautifully laid-out gardens
complete with fountains and covered

ponds offered little potential as a terrorist meeting place.

She collapsed on her bed that night dead with fatigue. But the moment she closed her eyes the dread specter of failure loomed up in her mind. The conference would take place tomorrow, with or without her. She racked her brain for another way to uncover the terrorist hiding place. So little time left....

Gulzar's soft call burst through the thin veil of Julie's restless sleep with the force of an exploding shell. She was at the open bedroom window facing out to the front veranda before she was fully conscious of being awake. A blaze of red marked the right corner of the sky, reflected as a rich auburn in Dal Lake. Sunlight bathed the earth and water below in a bluish glow. The pine trees shading the mountainside opposite the palace freshened the early-morning air with their scent. Gulzar knelt in his rowboat at the foot of the stairs, looking up at the blank windows of the island palace anxiously.

"What is it, Gulzar?" Julie pushed back her blond hair from her forehead, running her open fingers through the waves. Her eyes felt as though she had not slept at all the night before.

"Madam Julie!" The handsome boy smiled with relief. "It's good I found you! Come quick! I think the police have come to Dal Lake to catch the men you seek!"

"Wait right there!"

Minutes later Julie joined Gulzar on the stairs to the water. She had dressed in black slacks and wore the white tunic blouse loose without a belt. A square bag filled with camera equipment complete with zoom lens hung from her shoulder. Julie clutched a small tape recorder in one hand and her reporter's notebook in the other. All traces of fatigue had vanished from her face.

"Tell me everything, Gulzar! Did you see the terrorists?"

"No, madam. I saw the police chief. I was going in my boat to the wide part of the lake. This time of the day is good for fishing. There are no—how do you say it—motorboats this early. They frighten the fish away. Then I saw a motorboat—but not for tourists. I know this boat. It belongs to the police chief. He is a friend of my uncle's."

"Was the chief of police in the boat?"

"Yes. With two other men. They looked to be fishing. But—" he gave an eloquent shrug "—I knew they were not. Why fish from a motorboat when a boat like mine is better? Besides, the motorboat was not where the fish eat this time of the day. Everyone knows it is on the other shore, not beside the road."

"Did you come get me then?" Julie asked, looking at her small accomplice with renewed respect.

"Yes. Right away. I rowed very fast," he

added with boyish pride. "I knew the police would not be on the lake to fish. Also, I have seen two other police boats now. There is one of them."

He pointed south toward where the mouth of the Jhelum River flowed into Dal Lake. Julie saw a sleek speedboat bobbing in front of Dal Gate, effectively blocking any exit at that end of the lake. From Gulzar's description, the chief of police's boat was between the houseboats and the main part of Dal Lake. It looked as though the police intended to close off the neck of the lake where the tourist houseboats were anchored, between the river and the main body of the lake.

"I think the police must be making a wide circle to surround the houseboats, Gulzar. The terrorists must be on one of the rented boats just as we suspected," Julie exclaimed. A pulse quickened in her neck.

"Here, Madam Julie. I will take you there."

"Wait. Let's take Abdul's boat, Gulzar. It's a real *shikara*. That way I can stay behind the curtains and I'll look like a tourist. We don't want to look unusual in any way." She recalled the night in New Delhi weeks ago when her stupid mistake had warned the terrorists away from Jai's guards. She must be more careful today. As much as she would like to be avenged, upsetting Jai's agents' plans was not the way to do it.

Julie stepped into the palace *shikara* that Abdul used to row the maharani and Priya back and forth to shore. "Can you row this?" she asked Gulzar, who had left his own much smaller boat tied to a brass ring beside the stairway.

"Yes, madam. I am very strong," he replied, flashing a wide smile. The boat moved forward at a leisurely pace.

Julie leaned back among the cushions. The lake was empty except for the police boat and clusters of empty *shikaras* tied to the wharf. It would be a good time for a raid, before the lake dwellers awoke to their daily business of tourism and selling. Julie pulled the ruffled curtains forward so that she could still see out but made it difficult for someone on the porch of a houseboat to see her face. The chance of one of the terrorists recognizing her was slight. Still, Lal Delal had known she was a journalist. It was just possible that he had described her to his colleagues, since she had the distinction of being Prince Mishra's houseguest.

Julie removed her camera from its carrying case and double-checked it for film, noticing with detachment that her palms were beginning to sweat. She hung the camera around her neck, much as any tourist would. The zoom lens could be attached to give her close-up shots from as far away as the shore. She accounted herself an adequate photographer;

few overseas assignments merited both a photographer and a correspondent.

Gulzar knelt in the stern of the *shikara*. Julie could tell from their slow progress that Abdul's longer oars were harder to use than Gulzar cared to admit. However, she had no need for speed. They had already reached the first of the houseboats. Julie scanned each vessel carefully as they passed. She needed a clue as to the boat the terrorists occupied. After that they would watch from a safe distance. Regardless of what else happened in the next few minutes, she must make sure that her young guide was not endangered.

"Madam, look! The other police boat!"

Julie twisted around to peer through the rear curtains. Gulzar jerked his head to the right as he applied his full energy to the heavy oars, his face flushed with excitement and exertion. The third police speedboat hovered opposite them against the shore.

"The houseboat we want is probably toward the other end of the row, then," Julie said. "The police boat would want to stay out of sight until the last minute. They undoubtedly have radios to keep in touch with each other if the terrorists make a break and try to run for it."

She continued to study each houseboat they passed. The boats were more elaborate at this end, bigger and therefore better suited for a large meeting. Besides, some key terrorist leaders were known to be wealthy by birth. They would enjoy a luxury boat. What possessed them to indulge in antiestablishment activities in the first place was anyone's guess.

A movement on the flat roof of one of the houseboats caught Julie's eye. A man, probably a houseboat owner, was piling up some thick logs beneath a huge cauldron to heat water for a guest's morning shower. A second man climbed the ladder from the main level of the houseboat to join the man on the roof. As he stepped over the low roof railing he glanced down at Julie's *shikara* and scowled. His mouth opened as though to speak, but he turned away instead. Puzzled, Julie was still leaning back on her couch trying to see where he had disappeared when Gulzar's short strokes carried them toward the next boat.

Shock and surprise knocked the air out of Julie's chest even as she heard Gulzar's soft gasp. No matter how prepared she was for this moment, the sudden realization that the terrorist raid was beginning left her weak. Her legs suddenly felt wobbly and the bitter taste of fear filled her dry mouth. Instinctively she flung her body forward in the *shikara* in an effort to shield her young guide. They were going to be too close to the action— much too close!

A man dressed in a gray brown woolen poncho leaped between the two boats, landing with a thud on the narrow planks that ran the length of the next houseboat a foot or two above the water level of the lake. Instantly a second man followed him, then a third and a fourth. They moved without a sound, except for their heavy ponchos brushing against the boat's sides. Each man carried a blunt-shaped Ingram Mac 10 automatic submachine gun.

Julie twisted around and motioned frantically to Gulzar to get down on the floor of the *shikara*. He obeyed her at once, dropping the oars and scrambling behind the minimal shelter her seat back offered, his lips parted and his slight body trembling with excitement. Already the last man had slipped into the rear window of the houseboat. The first three men glided toward the front of the boat, their crouching forms concealed from those inside by fluttering curtains drawn across the open windows.

A backward glance at the rooftop of the boat they had just passed revealed that the pretense of fire making had been abandoned. The "owner" and his friend were now poised at the rear corner of the roof, machine guns poised to cover the rear porch and the near side of the neighboring houseboat. Two more armed men emerged on the roof of the boat beyond the one under attack to cover the front porch and the far side. Julie recognized the diagonal deployment-attack formation used by police and military SWAT—Special

Weapons and Tactics—teams throughout the world, which allowed four men to cover the back, front and sides of a building, or in this case a houseboat, without running the risk of shooting each other in cross fire.

She fumbled for her camera, her fingers feeling stiff and strangely thick. She had no doubt that the conference was being held in the middle houseboat. She removed the camera strap from her neck and adjusted the focus. There was no need for a zoom lens at this short distance. The *shikara* drifted slowly forward across the gap between the two boats in the eerie, critical stillness that masked this deadly assault. Her heart pounding, Julie began snapping pictures in rapid succession.

The men had positioned themselves at the edge of the windows in the side of the houseboat. The first man nodded once. Pivoting their submachine guns through the open windows in front of them, they disappeared inside, moving with perfect precision.

An outburst of machine-gun fire shattered the morning quiet. Julie cringed, her throat so tight she could hardly swallow. A deep shout of surprise mingled with a brief spate of return shots sounded from the front room.

The low running form of a man emerged from the front door of the houseboat. He dodged quarterback style across the front porch, avoiding the immediate shower of bullets from the rooftop of the neighboring boat that greeted his appearance. He raised his head from between his hunched shoulders and looked out across the water. His eyes met Julie's.

A second later he was flying through the air toward the *shikara*, which had drifted forward to a position directly in front of the porch of the terrorists' houseboat. Julie half rose in horror, dropping her camera onto the cushioned seat. Wheeling around, she shouted to Gulzar to jump from the boat. Out of the corner of her eye she saw a second form appear on the porch, a man with black hair who moved with the grace of a panther. Then the escaping terrorist was crushing her down beneath him as he landed.

The small boat was in danger of capsizing as the man wrenched Julie from beneath him. He was rolling over, shoving her between himself and his assailants, when a second force rocked the *shikara*. Julie felt her attacker jerked into the air. She lifted herself onto one knee only to be knocked backward, one leg bent painfully beneath her body so that it felt like her hip was being dislocated. The terrorist's knee crushed into her chest.

A silver knife blade arced across the sky. Julie pressed back against the floor of the rocking boat, a hoarse cry breaking from her dry lips. Terrified, she struggled with desperate strength to free himself. But even as the cold dread of death clutched at her heart, her attacker gave a grunt of pain. The knife stopped inches from Julie's face. Unable to move, she twisted her head to see who was grappling with her assailant.

Jai! His powerful form, draped in a gray brown poncho, wrestled with the terrorist. One of his strong well-shaped hands grasped the guerrilla's knife arm; the other closed on his opponent's neck. The knife hovered above Julie's throat, held off only by the strength of Jai's grip on the other man's wrist.

"Release me or she dies," gasped the man, his close-set eyes strangely lifeless.

For answer, the muscles of Jai's forearm tightened. Julie watched helplessly as the long blade wavered above her. Then, slowly, the distance from her neck to the knife increased. She shifted her gaze to Jai's face. Every feature was locked in concentration. His eyes burned into his adversary's face with patient determination. She looked back at the knife. Its trembling point now faced the terrorist's own chest.

The man with the close-set eyes dropped the knife and lurched back in a lightening-quick motion, breaking away from Jai's hold. The terrorist grabbed at Julie with desperate hands, knowing his only hope of survival lay in taking her hostage. Jai lunged forward, his hands fastening on the terrorist's throat again as they all three plunged over the edge of the pitching boat into the lake.

CHAPTER NINETEEN

JULIE SURFACED FROM THE COLD WATER choking and coughing to find that everything was over as quickly as it had begun. A police speedboat whined to a reeling halt beside them. Jai handed the limp form of the terrorist up to the officers. Julie could see deep red marks on the man's neck. She wondered if he was dead, shocked to discover that she did not care if he was. A tremor stole through her body, making her shiver in the water. Now that the danger was past, her fear threatened to overcome her.

"Julie! Julie! Are you all right?" Gulzar's shrill voice above her broke into her numb brain. He was standing in the *shikara* holding one heavy oar gripped like a club. His anxious face relaxed with intense relief when she smiled up at him.

"I'm all right, Gulzar. Thank heavens you're safe! I'm sorry. I didn't realize we were right on top of them. I would never have forgiven myself if you'd been hurt! But is my camera okay? I think I dropped it on the seat."

"Do you always recover from danger so quickly?" asked an interested voice beside her.

Julie turned, treading water, to face Jai. His eyes were smiling at her—playful, teasing dark eyes. Water dripped off his black hair and trickled down the straight planes of his cheeks. He was very close to her; Julie felt her nipples harden beneath her clinging cotton tunic.

"Thanks for your help," she said, her voice even. She was thinking how much a look like that from him—tender and loving—would have meant to her a few weeks back. What a pity the warmer emotions were often so fleeting.... For now she felt nothing at all. She turned and swam the few strokes necessary to reach the porch railing.

"Wait a moment." A couple of quick strokes brought him to her side. He laid a hand on her arm.

She turned to glare at him as he gave a sharp command in Hindi. She wanted to get away from him. Her heart was beating too fast; she felt suffocated by his nearness, overwhelmed by his intense vitality. She had forgotten just what a powerful effect he could have on her—how, without trying to, he seemed to dominate his surroundings....

But a minute later she was glad to have waited. A man on the porch of the next houseboat tossed a heavy parcel across to Jai. The prince climbed out of the water onto the terrorist boat. He unfolded a heavy woolen poncho like the one he was wearing.

"Here, put this on." He held the poncho over her head as she climbed up the porch stairs from the water. He dropped the heavy, concealing cloth around her shoulders without touching her.

"Thank you," she said again through tight lips. She had not paused to think how the sheer white cotton of her tunic would cling to her wet skin like a transparent glove. She turned toward Gulzar who had brought the rowboat over by the stairs. The boy's eyes, alight with hero worship, were fixed on Jai.

"Could you please hand me my camera and equipment bag, Gulzar? I can stand here on the porch and be out of the way, I think." She grasped the camera he passed up to her. A quick glance reassured her that it had survived the commotion in the rowboat. Julie adjusted the focus for a closer distance just as the first terrorists were led out, handcuffed and surrounded by machine-gun-armed police.

For the next hour she was too absorbed in her work to think about her reunion with Jai. Several of those captured were indeed major international figures. At least one man was wanted in several nations. A grim satisfaction flooded through Julie as, standing wet and bedraggled on the porch, she clicked pictures of a stoop-shouldered man with a distinctive full mustache being led away, prodded lightly in the back by the persuasive nose of an In-gram Mac 10. He was Sergio Orcagna, the Red Brigades leader credited with the planning and execution of the attack on the Rome train station. Two of the prisoners were women.

After the terrorists had been loaded onto the police speedboats and taken away, two bodies were carried out. The first one, handled with careless disregard by its two native bearers, was riddled with bullets beyond recognition. Julie turned away quickly, making a note to check with the police later on the corpse's identity.

The only mark on the second body was a thin red line of blood encircling the neck. The swollen face looked vaguely familiar despite its distorted features. She looked again. Lal Delal! A vision flashed into her mind of the beginning of the raid, when the last policeman to board the terrorist boat had slipped onto the back porch and disappeared. He must have met Delal there, standing a half-hearted guard over a meeting too important to include himself. So this was the final outcome of all Delal's schemes. . . .

At that moment the head of the Kashmir police force strode out of the houseboat, accompanied by the military officer in charge of the raid. Julie stepped forward and presented her press credentials, secure in the knowledge that most officials tended to be receptive to interviews that would be to their credit. Both men graciously agreed to answer any questions she might have. Jai reappeared on the porch, also, and accompanied the small group back inside the houseboat.

"Are you acquainted with Prince Mishra, Miss—ah Connell?" asked the chief of police when they were seated. "We are greatly in his debt in this affair."

Julie acknowledged Jai's presence with a brief nod and began her questions, asking how Prince Mishra had aided the police.

It seemed that one of Jai's agents in Kashmir had succeeded in infiltrating the fringes of the terrorist organization sometime back. About two weeks ago he had been contacted to rent a houseboat suitable to accommodate several people.

Julie paused in her note taking, her eyes involuntarily on Jai. So he had had that lead even before she had left for Kashmir and hadn't told her! He met her fuming look with a bland smile. Julie turned back to her notes, her face flushed with irritation.

She asked the military officer to describe what had happened inside the houseboat during the raid. He did so in a voice devoid of emotion. The guard—Delal—at the back of the boat had been killed. The terrorist leaders were gathered in the main room at the front of the boat, having arrived at staggered times throughout the night. Jai's man had insured that the windows would be open with the curtains drawn. Faced with two machine guns at the front windows and two more at the inner door leading to the back of the houseboat, all but two of the terrorists had surrendered on the spot. One—a German whose name Julie recognized—had been shot to death. The other was the man who had leaped onto Julie's boat.

After a few minutes more of questions, the chief of police brought the interview to a close. Julie thanked both men for the interview and got the correct spelling of their names from one of their aides. Tomorrow she could fill in any details in a wrap-up from the official police records. Now she needed to transmit this story to Wes Harding. With luck he could have it in time for this morning's edition, since due to the time difference she was several hours ahead of the New York newsroom.

If she got this into the morning paper before anyone else smelled it out, there would be rockets going out from every major news desk in the world demanding a story from harried journalists all over Asia. Any significant triumph of good over evil always had news value. A major blow to the heart of the international network of terrorists would bring sighs of relief and contentment to Western democracies. Maybe her story would get picked up by the syndicates. . . .

Julie slipped out onto the front porch, leaving the men still discussing the incident. Out of the corner of her eye she saw Jai rise as if to follow her. But the military officer intercepted him, much to her relief. She had no desire to discuss her work with Jai Mishra. She had no desire to see him ever again once this story was filed. She would leave his home forever and never think of him again if she could help it.

Gulzar had had to leave for school, so Julie hitched a ride in one of the police boats back to the palace. The maharani, whose husband had been an avid amateur photographer, had already offered her the use of the palace darkroom as well as the telex machine there. Julie had brought a portable transmitter with her, which would allow her to send pictures of the raid as soon as her prints were developed.

An hour and a half later she pushed her chair back from the telex machine, her copy filed. She sat still, her hands lingering on the keyboard, her mind floating free. All at once the weeks of waiting, frustration and painstaking research seemed worthwhile. The conference was halted; the world had the story.

It had come out easily, she reflected—a story she had been wanting to tell for a long time. She had started with an account of the morning's dramatic events and then filled in all the supplementary background information her months of research had uncovered, much of it written ahead of time. She made a special point to underscore the subversive nature of terrorism, which created a feeling of chaos where no breakdown in the structure of society actually existed. The international network manipulated the vast population of the world just as Lal Delal had manipulated Priya. Forewarned was forearmed. Julie wrote it all down. She was satisfied.

Julie shut off the telex and rose from the desk, feeling suddenly let down. The purpose that had been sustaining her these past days no longer existed. Without her work to distract her, her future loomed before her with bleak clarity—a future that could never include the man with whom she had once wished to share it. . . .

Back in her own room, Julie rang for Abdul's wife and asked for a hot meal to be sent up. She used the delay before the food was brought to take a quick bath and wash the mud and sewage of Dal Lake out of her hair. She dressed in a fresh lavender sundress. After she had eaten she collected her notebooks and wandered down the corridor outside her bedroom until she came to a small enclosed courtyard.

Intending to start on tomorrow's wrap-up, she sat down on a bench beneath a broad-leafed tree. The beauty of the courtyard soon distracted her from her work, however. She let the notebook drop to the ground. She leaned back against the tree trunk, listening to the gurgle of the carved-stone fountain. Nearby a peacock pecked at his plumage, ruffling his wing feathers with his beak.

The tensions of the morning slowly drained out of her. Julie let her thoughts meander. She speculated on what her next big assignment might be—maybe those talks in Geneva Harding had told her to prepare for next month. She viewed the prospect with a marked lack of enthusiasm.

"Am I interrupting?"

Her effort not to think about Jai had been so great that it took Julie a full five seconds to realize that he had actually spoken to her. She picked up her notebook and set it on the bench before she turned toward him, managing a half smile. She preferred to keep her last meeting with Jai neutral. After having made a complete fool of herself over him, the least she owed herself now was a dignified, I'm-a-busy-woman-and-have-to-get-on-with-my-next-assignment exit out of his life.

"You're angry with me." Jai moved across the tiny courtyard to an ornamental railing. He leaned against it, one elbow draped over the top, watching her. He had changed into dry clothing—blue jeans and a denim shirt open at the neck. His thick hair still looked damp. Julie noticed three small cuts on his left cheek.

"Yes. I am angry. Don't let it worry you, however." Julie felt her throat constrict. In spite of her resolve not to confront him, her fury got the better of her. "Why, after Priya told you that I had not stolen those papers from your office, didn't you send me word about the houseboat? I'd been sharing my leads with you. I don't like being double-crossed."

"To be truthful, I didn't want you to find it," he replied, his dark eyes boring into her angry blue ones. Jai moved toward her.

Julie stared at him as though she had never seen him before. Regardless of what had passed between them, she would never have guessed that he would resent her success. She felt surprise, and oddly enough, betrayal. Whatever his doubts had been about her character, Julie had believed she had won Jai's respect as a researcher and journalist.

"Don't look at me like that, Julie. You don't understand. I think it's time we talked."

"No. We have nothing to talk about, Jai." She stood up. "I'm leaving India tomorrow."

His hands dropped onto her shouders. "Hear me out, Julie."

Whether it was the gentle warmth of his touch or some unspoken, pleading note in his voice, the rigid control that had governed Julie's actions since arriving in Kashmir deserted her all at once. While her attention had been on getting her story, she had been able to suppress her own agony. But now the desolate hurt of rejection overwhelmed her, beating down her defenses. Her eyes burned with sudden tears. The anguished grief she had tired to fight against since that last day in Jai's bedroom in New Delhi wrenched through her now, crushing her beneath it. She looked up at him, teardrops spilling down her cheeks.

"How could you, Jai?" she whispered. "How could you leave me that way? When you knew I loved you so much...."

A spasm of pain distorted the planes of his handsome face.

"I'm sorry, Julie." His hands tightened their grip on her shoulders. "I'm so terribly sorry."

Through a blur of unleashed emotion Julie felt Jai's arm around her waist. He half led, half carried her out of the courtyard. She felt the rhythm of his long strides against her hip, heard the soft click of his footfalls on tile. Racking sobs tore through her. She hunched her shoulders, struggling against the distress that filled her heart.

They entered a room. In the dreamlike reflection of a brass urn by the door Julie caught the impression of unrestrained opulence. Overlapping carpets of incredible richness and design layered the floor. In-

tricate silk tapestries hung on the walls—
hand-stitched murals commemorating the
lives of Mishra princes, folk heroes and blue-
skinned gods. Life-size statues gleaming with
the purity of India's sunlike twenty-two-karat
gold posed in various corners of the chamber;
one waved four arms, another had a golden
cobra entwined around its neck. A stuffed
tiger, larger even than the one Julie had seen
in the hallway, stood raised on its hind legs
clawing at the air. The pelt of a snow leopard
draped onto the floor beside the bed, brilliantly white. The ceiling resembled a tent
canopy of bright patches of fabric.

Then Jai was pulling her down beside him
on a low couch strewed with dozens of soft
pillows. Julie clung to him, burying her face
against his shoulder, lost in the torment of
her weeping. He held her in his arms, silently
and without passion, in the way one friend
comforts another. Only when the last temor
of her sobs passed away did he begin kneading the knotted muscles of her neck with his
powerful fingers, his dark eyes steady on her
face.

"Do you feel better? You've been under a
lot of pressure. This room always relaxes
me."

He shifted her shoulder so that he could
massage her back. His hands traced light,
soothing designs upon her body. A slumber-
ous ease crept into Julie's limbs; she realized

for the first time how tension filled these past few days had been. Her eyes met his, only inches away.

"This is your room, isn't it?"

"Uh-huh. I spent my summers here as a child."

"It looks like something out of the *Arabian Nights*," she murmured. She drew a little away from him. "Why did you bring me here?"

"In the old days," he replied, "the people of my family's province would come before the Mishra princes to have their disputes judged and settled." He paused, glancing sideways at her. "Now, Julie, a Mishra prince comes before you."

"I don't want—" She started up on one elbow, anger flooding into her face. She could feel his influence stealing over her, chipping away at her protective shell...tingling in her body. She did not want to hear what he had to say. She did not want him to stir her heart one more time, to dislodge the cool dislike she was glad to be able to feel for him. She did not want to be deserted again... hurt again.

"Wait." His fingers covered her lips. A self-mocking smile twisted one corner of his mouth. "You must listen before you judge." The unsure, questioning look in his eyes was so out of character for him that Julie's resolve gave way.

"All right," she replied, her voice flat. "Talk."

He relaxed back onto the couch, his eyes leaving her face. He glanced over at the woven murals on the wall. "My royal legacy," he said, with a wave of his hand at the tapestries. "Along with fear, distrust, suspicion. Even in these days, Julie, the political climate of Asia is remarkable for its vicissitudes. One never really feels safe. And you know the old saying: the higher you are, the farther you have to fall.

"Your coming to New Delhi coincided too closely with the beginning of terrorist operations in that city. Of course, journalists often get accused of spying, to the point where being a foreign correspondent would be a poor cover for a real spy. Nevertheless, I wondered how it was that you seemed to be the only one covering this story. It was only later that I became acquainted with the nature of your newspaper, learning that the *Courier* specializes in just this sort of thing.

"But I didn't know this when you arrived as my mother's guest. Even my mother's and sister's reaction to you increased my suspicions, by the way. You became a member of our family circle too easily—it worried me."

"Like how Lal Delal wormed his way into Priya's affections, you mean?" asked Julie. "You thought I was capable of that!"

He glanced over at her, his eyes glowing

with sudden intensity. "I *thought* you could be capable of that—after all, only the very best would be sent to infiltrate a household such as mine. But when I began to *feel* in my heart that it could not be true.... Well, that's when my agony started. I began to doubt myself, to doubt my judgment."

"You wondered if I was getting to you, too, you mean?" Julie sat up on the couch, looking down at him. She could appreciate the torment of a nature as strong as his being in conflict.

"I knew you were getting to me," he replied with a sudden smile. "I just wanted to keep it within certain boundaries...." He watched the slow flush spread over her face and neck. He reached out and touched her hand. "I wasn't using you, Julie. I was just afraid you were intending to use me."

When she did not reply he continued.

"Anyway, I fought against trusting you. Unfortunately, there were a lot of convenient arguments to use against you. The night the terrorists saw you in the window. The fact that the man I had following Priya to guard her in case Delal tried to abduct her for ransom reported that you met with my sister and her boyfriend in Chandni Chowk the day after the ball."

"I'd forgotten that!" Julie exclaimed. "Once you told me in Agra that you had guards for your mother and sister—"

"And you, my love—"

"And me," she mused. "Then I should have known you knew all about Lal. I protected Priya that day in your office for nothing."

"Oh, yes. That day in the office. . . . The exact papers I knew the terrorists would require. Can you see, Julie, how damaging the case looked against you? Yet even then, believing what I did about you, I knew I was willing to sell my soul to the devil to have you for my own."

He looked up at her, his face grim with the memory of his fear. "After that, I knew I must destroy our relationship once and for all. I couldn't trust myself any longer to resist the feelings I had for you. I did the only thing I could think of to alienate you so completely from me that no hope of happiness could remain for me to cling to. . . ." He flipped his palm up in a quick, fatalistic gesture.

Julie sat still, watching him. Slowly the whole picture fell into place. Things she hadn't understood before. . . like Jai's abrupt change of heart the day after he made love to her in the secret garden. The man she saw coming out of his office the next afternoon must have reported seeing her in Chandni Chowk with Delal.

She remembered other things, as well, about how Jai's father had raised him to distrust the motives of others. She hadn't realized how deeply that training had penetrated. Jai hadn't been able to see her own deep feeling for him for what it was.... This fantastic room, the remote and legendary setting of the floating palace—all made her conscious of the uniqueness of his life and upbringing. She realized how real a threat she must have seemed to him, especially when he found himself in danger of falling in love with her....

"So you rejected me that day to drive me away from you," she said finally.

"I did." He had been observing her changing expressions as she reflected on the past. She saw the relief her words brought in his eyes. Julie reached out spontaneously and touched his face, tracing the straight line of his jaw with her fingertip.

"But why didn't you tell me about the houseboat?" she asked. "You knew by then that I could be trusted." Her eyes lingered on his freshly shaven cheek, then moved upward to meet his gaze. She drew in a long breath. The naked force of his desire held her fast.

He rose up on one elbow. A look of satisfaction flitted across his fine features, as though he suddenly realized his power to communicate his ardor to her.

"I didn't want you involved in the capture," he told her, his dark eyes locked with hers. "I was afraid there would be danger. I wanted you kept safe...for afterward. For now."

"But I'm a journalist, Jai," Julie protested. "I needed to be there on that houseboat. It's my work."

"I know that now," he replied. "I faced that fact this morning, watching you conduct your interview so coolly minutes after a terrorist had tried to take you hostage." His smile flashed. "I was surprised to discover how proud I felt of you."

Jai took hold of her bare shoulders and pulled her gently down beside him. "You know, Julie, you could stay here and keep writing. India has a lot of stories to tell. Or we could travel. I have several homes around the world. We could spend part of our time in the United States—I've been wanting to expand my business in that direction anyway." His deep voice ended on a questioning note.

A feeling of certainty filled Julie's heart and soul. A wonderful simplicity settled over her mind, as though she could know the answer to anything merely for the asking. She understood with sudden clarity that the bitter dislike she had tried to feel for Jai had not been real. It had been her form of self-preservation just as distrust had been his.

She loved him. She had never stopped loving him. He loved her. He had never really stopped loving her. It was a moment before she realizel he had spoken the words out loud.

"I love you, Julie. Do you hear me?"

"Yes. I hear." A warm radiance filled her, blossoming out like golden rays of bliss from her heart.

"Will you marry me?" he asked, his dark eyes watching her face with burning intensity.

"Yes," she answered, a soft smile creeping into the corners of her mouth. "I will."

He pulled her closer on the pillow-strewed couch, his hand stroking her golden hair with fierce pleasure. He brushed her eyelids with his lips. "How long I've waited to ask you that!" he murmured. "And now it all seems so simple."

She wrapped her arms around his neck in reply, seeking his lips with a longing born of the deepest love she had ever known. Awe filled her heart, and gratitude: to love and be loved by such a man! Every atom of her being opened to him as he lay beside her. Radiant light infused every cell of her body, the light of pure love.

"No more doubts?" she whispered, when he at last freed her mouth from beneath his.

He kissed her again. "You teach me faith, Julie. You give me back my life."

She closed her eyes, her body trembling as his hands slid over her, removing her clothes with great gentleness. She knew what he meant. She felt that way, too. That lost, empty feeling of abandonment, the flat despair of bereavement—somehow his love for her had eased away the sorrow that had shadowed her for so many years. He, too, had given her her life back again. A new life, rich with love, rich with joy.. . .

His mouth moved over her body leaving a fiery yearning in its wake. He had discarded his own clothing now, also. Julie thrilled to feel the naked length of his body pressing against hers. She locked her fingers in his black hair as his kisses trailed down her throat to her breast. He took her nipple into his mouth, caressing it lightly with his tongue. His left hand stroked her flat stomach. A blazing flame of desire rushed through her, awakening a burning, aching need.

"Make love to me, Jai," she whispered, her lips touching his ear.

"Mmm. Yes." He traced the cruve of her breast with the palm of his hand. "But first I will make you love me."

"I already do."

The words hung in the air between them like the sweetest incense. Then, gently, he lowered his body onto hers. Rejoicing in their love for one another, they freed the desires so long held in check. Their hearts were joined together for eternity. Now they united their souls, as well, rising together to experience the unbounded joy of love's glory.

"I feel very wanted," she murmured a long time later.

"You are," he replied, touching his lips to

her neck. "You are, Julie, you are. To have lost you would have killed me. . . ." He pulled her to him again, this time with an almost desperate passion.

ABOUT THE AUTHOR

Raised in Colorado, Cynthia Parker left home after university graduation to travel and further her studies in Europe. She returned to the States in 1978 and in 1980 began her writing career with a western, *Gunfire at Timberline*. A year later she spent seven months in India studying ancient Vedic literature and its relationship to modern science. While there, she got the inspiration to write *Tiger Eyes*, her first Superromance.

Writing about love has made Cynthia aware of "how really important it is to be careful of people's feelings and to treat the delicate impulses of the heart with great tenderness in all our relationships—not just romantic ones."